The Sutra of Spring

SOLSTICE SHIELD BOOK 1

KACEY LEE

BECKY TAMA

Dear Reader,
This series is NSFW... or the bus... or a plane.
;)

Chapter One

"I'm home!" I used my heel to kick the door shut. Apparently a little too hard, because my mom rounded the corner, mouth half open, ready to fuss until she saw me hefting my multiple brown bags.

Her eyes widened. "I just said milk!"

"I was there; this was more efficient," I replied. "Also, you're welcome."

"Did you get my cookies?" Chris hollered from the other room.

I rolled my eyes, hefting the three grocery bags I managed to balance in my arms. He'd have to get off his lazy ass to come and see for himself. I shuffled down the dark hall—I really needed to remember to replace the light—into the small kitchen of our apartment with outdated wooden cabinets and yellow, floral wallpaper I'm pretty sure was from the seventies.

"I only said milk," Mom grumbled under her breath again as she followed me.

I ignored her comment, assisting with unpacking the very much needed food into the empty cupboards. I'd stocked up on lots of frozen and nonperishables so it'd last us a while. I paused, frowning at a can of green beans. My mom was a great cook from working in restaurants all her life and could make canned items bought from the dollar store taste like a professional meal. If she had dreams of owning a restaurant she never said anything, putting everything aside to raise Chris and me. Sadly, down payments weren't an easy thing to save for when we lived paycheck to paycheck.

One day. One day Chris would be a college graduate, my mom could be her own boss, and I could finally travel the world. But today was not that day, and it seemed like tomorrow was never getting any closer, no matter how many days I worked through. I looked up at the world map hanging in the corridor, with not a single pin placed to show where I had been. I'd hardly left Stowe, Vermont, even in the military.

I shoved the last box of spaghetti into a much more filled pantry. At least this would last us a couple weeks. Chris still got his free and reduced lunches from his private school, even if we paid the main tuition, so that helped a ton.

My mom frowned at the cookies before her eyes raked over my form. Instantly, I felt like I was thirteen and it took every adult thought in my body to stand there unfazed instead of crossing my arms over the areas that were extra curvy.

"They're for Chris." The excuse tumbled out before I could stop it.

"I see. Well, I'll be sure to take them to him." She paused beside me, reaching over to tame a stray, brown curl on the side of my face. "You have such a lovely face. I only wish all your physical training helped a little more."

"Mom," I groaned.

She raised her hands in a placating gesture, already apologetic for the snide comment. "I know, I know. Health comes in many shapes and sizes."

Yeah, it did, and it took me a good decade of repeating that before she started saying it back, but it was clear her prejudices were still there. Although, being left by her husband for a younger woman, and with society's beauty standards, could I really blame her?

When my mom took her next step, I noticed her favoring her right side. "Mom!" I grabbed the cookies from her arm. "What happened?"

She waved me off. "Nothing, don't worry about it."

"Are your feet acting up again?" I stared at her feet like I had x-ray vision and could see through her black tennis shoes with dried bits of food on them.

Her mouth pinched together instead of answering, or rather as her answer.

"How many times do I have to tell you to go to the doctor?" *I work my ass off to make sure we have health insurance after all!* Not that I said the last part out loud.

"I can't take the time off, you know that. Plus, what can they really do? Tell me to take it easy?" Her eyes sparkled at me. "Ha! We both live to work, you and me."

Reaching under my mother's elbow, I helped her over to the chair at the two person dining table, because that's all that could fit in here, and lowered her into the seat. "I can take some extra shifts—"

"No." She cut me off. "You already do too much. I'll be fine. I'll pop some aspirin and be good as new."

We stared at one another for one long minute, waiting for the other to back down. Recently I'd caught her wincing more and more as she walked around, and of course Googling it led to some nasty twists and turns. The last doctor we'd saved up for had referred her to a neurologist, thinking it was something to do with her nerves. It sounded expensive. Every month it came down to Chris's school fees or the doctor, and Mom always insisted it go to his fees. He was smart, too smart for his own good at times, and the main reason we'd put him into a private high school despite the cost. We both wanted him to go places and live a better life.

With a sigh I dropped my gaze. "If it gets worse promise me you'll take some time off, even just half a shift, and go to the doctor?"

"Fine," she conceded, but I knew it was as empty as all the times before when we had this conversation.

With a shake of my head, I started walking to my brother's room. "I'll be back, gonna drop off his cookies."

"I'll be here," my mother answered.

"Resting!" I retorted as I rounded the corner then peered back around to see her. She rubbed her arms slowly, a soft touch, as if feeling they were still there. My gut clenched. This month, I'd do double shifts and reduce spending to get her to the neurologist. Talking of reducing spending, Mr. Expensive Tastes was going to have to savor these cookies. They'd be his last for the year at this rate.

My brother's door was open a crack, so I barged in. He huddled over books splayed out across his desk, furiously scribbling answers to what looked like a math problem spanning many pages.

Crap, now I felt bad. He'd been studying, not lounging, which was exactly what he should be doing. Ever since he lost his scholarship, he really did step it up. I think he believed he could earn it back, but after lots of discussions with the principal, I knew it wasn't possible. I had yet to tell him that because, well, he was doing his work. Why fix it when it wasn't broken? Keeping things from him—such as how close we were that one time to eviction, saved only by the landlord's whim—wasn't new.

I tossed the cookies toward him, which landed with perfect aim right beside his scratching pencil.

He startled. "Hey!" Quickly shoving a hand under the desk so it was out of view.

Odd. I leaned my hip against the door jam, folded my arms over my chest, and smiled. "I think you mispronounced 'thanks'."

His narrowed eyes broke off into a small genuine smile, a rare sight from him at his age these days. "Thanks."

"So," I took a step inside, "whatcha got there?" I nodded to where his hand was still hidden under the desk.

I swear his eyes widened for a split second before he schooled his features. "Nothing."

"Uh huh," I said, my big sister senses tingling. "Give it here!" I jested, launching myself with outreached hands like I was going to tickle him.

"Mari, stop! It's not funny. I'm busy! Stop or get out of my room!"

I pulled up short, shocked at the literal outrage in his voice. As my baby brother, his being annoyed with me I had gotten used to, but I rarely heard him legit *pissed.* Guess that was what happened when they grew up. "Okay, okay. Sorry," I mumbled before rubbing the back of my neck.

Grumbling to himself, he settled further into his chair, shoving whatever it was into his pocket. I took a moment to properly look at him. Mussed hair and wired eyes despite the dark circles under them. Worry curled inside my stomach like a snake ready to strike. Shit, when was the last time he slept?

I nodded toward the papers at his desk. "How's school going?"

He gave a one shoulder shrug as he tore open the bag of cookies, shoveling one into his mouth. "Got an A on my English paper." Bits of cookie flew onto his homework, which he brushed off to land on the floor.

My hands itched. Teenage boys had a different level of hygiene that grossed me out before, but after the strict spit-and-polish of the military, his habits seemed a whole new level of disgusting. However, that was not a battle I wanted to fight right now. If he got ants I'd be sure as hell making him scrub this room from floor to ceiling, which it probably needed in the first place.

"Don't you have to go to work?" He lifted his head, matching brown eyes meeting mine.

I pulled my phone from my pocket to check the time. *Fuck!*

I didn't even say goodbye as I rushed out. I had ten minutes to change and get to work. I unbuttoned my pants as I raced to my bedroom, my shirt already half off as I nudged the door open. I didn't even turn on the light as I grabbed clothes from my bartender pile. I sniff-checked them and tugged on my work shirt with a pair of tight jeans that made my ass look great, judging by the tips they always raked in. I snagged my makeup bag off my desk because there was no way in hell I was leaving that. I'd have to do it at stoplights on the way there, but it made me feel better. I'd prefer people be drawn to my eyes, what I was told was my best feature, instead of other parts of my body.

"Bye!" I yelled at them as I sprinted out of the house, unable to wait for a response back.

I PULLED down Mystique's signature sleeveless vest to hide my midriff. I had barely made it in time, Benny, the bouncer, checking his watch as I raced in through the back. I shot him a smile; the last thing I needed was to be docked half an hour pay.

I stumbled into a stiff back.

"Hey, Mari, watch it!" my boss, Ryan, barked.

I jumped back, grimacing from the beer on his breath. He was half tanked already, as per usual.

He scowled at me. "Get out front. They're relying on you, and you're day-dreaming here in the back!"

"Yessir." I snapped off a salute, a hangover from my stint in the army. I tried to shake off the leftover adrenaline and get into my bartending mindset, fixing a sultry smile in place while I mentally totaled up the tips I needed to make to get Mom that neurologist appointment. This job sucked, but it could pay well, and I'd been relieved when this second gig dropped into my lap. Convenient and what I wanted.

Really.

A wave of sound washed over me as I moved from the staff corridors to the bar. It was hot, heaving with people, and loud. Techno mingled with people shouting over one another to be heard, especially at the bar, as customers rattled off drink orders the two current bartenders rushed to fill.

"Hey, Mari!" Anthony was sweating through his shirt already, running up and down behind the bar. He seemed like a good person, quick with a joke and a smile for everyone, and was always willing to trade shifts when needed. But other than that, I didn't know much about him. Not a lot of time for talking when you were one of the few places for nightlife in our small town.

"Hey, Anthony. Where can I get started?" I smiled, shifting further into my bartending persona, ready to make sociable small talk while I poured drinks. Sometimes it was hard to tell who the real Mari was anymore.

He pointed to a knot of people gathered to the far end of the bar. "Bachelorette party over there! They've just come in." He lowered his voice before adding, "They tend to tip decently."

Anthony was a sweetheart. "Thanks, I owe you one."

He hustled to serve his customers, and I made my way over to the gaggle of girls at the other end. They looked to be about my age, taller than me of course, especially in heels, and comfortable in the tight little dresses they wore. The bachelorette was easily identifiable by the long white veil decorated with little penises all over the hem.

I nodded to it. "Lovely outfit! So, we're looking to celebrate?"

"Yes!" An overenthusiastic friend howled.

"Oh my gosh, I love your hair! Isn't her hair great?" A blonde complimented me, using the bar to help hold up her teetering self

"Yes, and that rack!" Another pouted as she stared at her flat chest. "I wish I had boobs like that." She tried to grab what she had, but it was mostly fabric.

It was only six, and it was clear we were not their first stop. I had a bad feeling I would have quite a bit of cleaning up to do at the end of their night. Seemed blondie didn't know how to hold her liquor. On the other hand, if they were already locked and loaded, they may be a bit freer with the tips.

"Oh, hush." I waved at them playfully, acting coy. "Y'all are beautiful. Every size big or small is beautiful in its own way." And I meant that. Yeah, I may have the boobs, but I had more cushion for the pushin' all over my body, and with her petite frame, I bet she didn't have nearly as much trouble finding cute clothes that fit.

"Ohm' gsh, yorso niiiiice," Blondie's slurred words made it difficult to pick up with the music blasting.

Impatient, the rest of them spouted out their very large order, and I mentally tallied up their tab as I went. People having fun were often flashy with money. I couldn't afford to do the same, and the toe-curling total made me feel ill.

I pasted on my smile. "There we are, ladies. Can I take a

card for behind the bar?"

"Here." The penis-draped bride smiled at her friends then passed me a card.

"That's very generous of you, especially as it's your day!" I said with a smile.

For some reason, that made her laugh, cheeks reddening. I was pretty good at telling whether someone was lying, and she was hiding something.

Whatever it was, it wasn't my business. I put the card in the safety box and gave her the matching token. "Enjoy your night."

She said nothing, scooting away from the bar, but the overenthusiastic friend shouted at me, "Thanks for the drinks!"

"You're welcome."

That made them all laugh for some reason. Despite the sweet remarks from earlier, a prickle of self-doubt coiled under my skin, making me tug my sleeveless shirt lower. Were they laughing at me? I probably didn't look my best. I sighed. You'd think the fear of the 'mean girls' vibe would eventually wear off. I've heard it does in your 30s. That you don't give a fuck anymore. Damn, I sure hope that was true.

I snorted to myself. I was definitely projecting my insecurities. The bride was wearing a penis veil. Hardly haute couture, unless I was *really* out of the loop.

I took a few more orders. This was a craft beer place, so complicated cocktails were few and far between thank goodness, and it was so much quicker to pour and serve. However, a few patrons looked funny at the foam top. "Give that a few more pulls, love," one of the customers advised me.

I didn't have time to over pour. It was wasteful, and if they just let it settle, it would taste the same. "It'll be fine. Is that all?"

"Mari," Ryan breathed behind me, hot with anger.

Chapter Two

I hitched up my smile and turned. "Hey, Ryan."

His red eyes narrowed at me. He swayed a little. "I've told you eight times how to pour. That's half foam in that guy's order."

"It'll settle."

His nostrils flared. "Don't talk back to me."

Great. I mentally hunkered down, prepared. I'd had to endure the sergeant at arms-style shouting; Ryan had nothing on them.

Still, I hated getting a dressing down, particularly as I was trying to save him money. "Yes, sir."

"I'll watch the next batch," he said, folding his arms and leaning against the counter. A real bump on the log since everyone had to squeeze past him in the small space behind the bar.

My eyes prickled, but I forced them wide. No way would this asshole be making me nearly cry if I wasn't so stressed and sleep deprived recently. No, this was just the late nights and early mornings getting to me. Maybe I should take a few shifts off bartending. Give myself a chance to relax for once, and I knew Anthony would happily cover them. I released a deep breath. *Yeah, right.* Nothing but a pipe dream. Relax? Enjoy life? More like sitting at home and being reminded why I needed to work, then probably just deep cleaning the house out of guilt.

I forced a smile, holding it in place with supreme effort, and turned to come face to face with my coworkers from my other job—Bishop, Lillian, Julian, and a few others who had different shifts than me. My stomach dropped. What the hell were they doing here? Wiping the shock off my face, I plastered on a brighter smile. Based on the way they eyed one another, it wasn't a look they were used to from me.

Bishop ogled my chest, and I thought he was about to make a comment about my tits when instead he said, "Wow, Mari, your arms are huge."

"Thanks." I resisted the urge to rub them. Was that huge in a good way? I could probably break him over my bicep. The look he gave me suggested that he might just like it if I did.

Lillian was pink-cheeked between Bishop and Julian and looked rather stunned as she stared at me. She blinked slowly. "Mari, I don't think I've ever actually seen you in civilian clothes before." A crack of a smile formed before she burst into giggles. Bishop soon joined her, while Julian stayed straight-faced, never taking his eyes off me.

I picked at my sleeveless vest. "Hardly what I'd choose to wear on the daily."

Julian flashed a smile, dragging my attention to him. "Hey, Mari. Uh. You look . . ." He looked me up and down. "Healthy."

I slowly set my teeth together. On our one and only date, he had complimented me on my recent weight loss. I could tell he thought I could stand to lose a bit more.

Still, customers were customers, and out came my tip

smile again. I'd have to wipe it off tonight with how oily it felt. "What can I get everyone?"

The others in the back spouted off some of our local beers, which I began filling immediately, but Bishop leaned onto the counter. "You know my usual," he said with a wink.

Vodka and coke. The bile in my throat was a fun little extra. "Sure. And you?" I looked between Lillian and Julian, the two of them eyeing one another's outfits just a little too much. Oh, bloody hell, those two were definitely hooking up.

"Uh, a Bud?" Julian asked, as though he were offering.

"I . . . don't have that here, but I have some bottles of guest ales."

Julian looked thoroughly relieved and requested the lightest of the bunch. That left only Lillian.

"I'll try the heff—hei—"

"Hefeweizen. Sure." I pulled it for her, trying not to feel my arms flex with Bishop's eyes trained on them. This was the easy part of any job, the physical aspect. Mom said I had to be descended from farm stock, ready to push a plough all day.

I spared a quick glance at my boss, but Ryan was frowning at something near the door. I put the rest of the drinks on the bar top. "There. Beautifully poured."

Bishop nudged Lillian with a stupid smile on his face. "Hey, uh, this wasn't what I asked for."

Ryan's frown snapped from the door to him. "What did you say?"

I pushed my fingernails into my palms. "He's joking—"

"I'm talking to the customer," Ryan snapped at me.

Bishop seemed to realize what he'd done, but now he was tongue-tied in the face of Ryan's abrupt fury. "Uh . . . Never mind!"

"No, it does mind. Matter." Ryan swung around to face me. "That's coming out of your pay."

My stomach pitched. "He was joking around!"

Bishop opened and closed his mouth, then scurried off with his drink in hand. Lillian shot me a sympathetic look, and Julian snuck off like he was avoiding eye contact with the Shield supervisor. The others followed without even a thank you in my direction.

Assholes.

I squared my shoulders and faced Ryan. "They know me, from my other job—"

Ryan frowned. "You have another job? Which bar? That's against your contract! You can't work for one of my competitors!"

I resisted the urge to wave his breath away. "It's not a bar. It's security." You'd think after I had been working here for years he'd know this, but I guess it's not something I openly talked about since it was semi-confidential.

He glared at me. "We'll see about that."

Although I was trained in confrontation and could keep my head in dire situations, this hit too close. My shoulders tightened. "What do you mean?"

He probably saw the reaction in my eyes, the jerk. A sneer marred his lips. "Just that. If I find out you're working for another bar, Mari, you're out of here."

I should retort. I wanted to. *Good luck replacing me. I'm a good worker*, I wanted to say. I always turned up. I never phoned in sick even when I was. Hell, I rarely drank on the job, and when I did it was at the insistence of the customer and I always made them pay for my drink. I know for a fact the other bartenders, aside from Anthony, frequently enjoyed a shot here or there to help get through the night. No one else would stand for this kind of treatment, his blatant lack of trust so evident.

Another part of me held back. If I burned this bridge, what could he do? If I lost this job it would rattle my house of cards, but it wouldn't topple. If I lost the CSON gig? That would send everything scattering to the floor.

I couldn't do that to Mom and Chris. I couldn't. I could take this for now.

I tried a smile. I probably looked like a wide mouthed frog trying to swallow a huge, gross fly. He had no leverage on CSON, and he couldn't influence my main job. "Do what you need to do," I told him, pleased my voice was low and calm. "I haven't done anything wrong."

He snorted. "As if that matters. If I want you gone, you're gone."

Do it, then, asshole. Pull the trigger. Don't stand there torturing me for the fun of it. Small dicked man on a power trip.

"Well?" he said.

I nodded. "Sure. We understand one another." It was past time to look for another side job. I needed the money, but as long as I kept him satisfied for now, I had breathing room to find something else.

Although the idea of looking while working two jobs didn't exactly fill me with excitement. It was something else for me to add to my never ending task list, where the reward for hard work was more hard work.

I turned back to the bar after taking a breath. "What can I get you?" I asked a clean shaven blonde man whose button up shirt had one too many unbuttoned.

He blinked at me as though in surprise. "Uh, I'll take a whiskey mule."

"Coming right up." I gave him my best smile as I dove for the ingredients, mashing the lime in front of him.

He made eye contact with me several times and butterflies fluttered in my stomach. Hell yeah, this was exactly why make up was a complete necessity, especially for me.

"You know," he said leaning onto the counter so I could more easily hear him.

Anticipation swam through me, heating my blood, and I did my best to act casual as I poured a little extra whiskey. "What do I know?" I threw in my best flirty tone with a soft smile.

"You're actually quite pretty. You have a lovely face," he finished with a wink. And it was like a sucker punch. I went from hoping I was going to get asked out to wanting to throw the drink I was making this fucker right in his face. I was *actually* pretty, and another fucking comment about my face. Why were people so damn surprised when an overweight woman was pretty, and why was it always her face and nothing else? Couldn't I just be beautiful, *period*, end of fucking story?

I had no words, or rather I didn't trust the words that would come out of my mouth if I tried to speak, so I just smiled.

"I think pretty face is a bit of an understatement," a new voice broke in. "I'd wager she's the beauty of the bar."

Mr. Blondie let out a small snort that he probably thought I didn't catch, and I shoved the drink at him, a bit spilling over the lip of the glass. "That'll be eleven bucks," I grouched.

"Eleven?" He gaped. "It was only ten last week!"

"Oh, sorry! Did I say eleven?" I widened my eyes before deadpanning my features. "I meant twelve."

The customer cursed as he pulled out cash and threw it on the bar, sans tip. "I'll be talking to your manager about this."

"Feel free." I beamed at him like everything was fine and that was the real price of the drink, when I definitely planned to pocket the extra two bucks. Blondie snagged his drink and more spilled over and onto his shirt. His head whipped toward me, ready to blame me, but I was there holding out a napkin to him with the same shit-eating grin. "Careful," I said.

He swiped it from my hand and marched away.

"Bastard," I whispered to myself, then I turned to the asshole that felt the need to come in and make what I would consider an even more condescending remark. My claws were out and I was ready to kill the jerk with kindness . . . until I looked at him.

It was like the floor flew from underneath me. He was tall, easily 6'3", with broad shoulders and solid biceps that stretched out what should be a loose, black t-shirt. His glossy black hair fell across his forehead, and his deep brown eyes were alight with intelligence, taking me in. And then he smiled at me.

Fuck, that smile. A quirk of his lips spoke of a mischievous personality, his lips soft and pliable in the low light of the bar. It was like it was meant just for me, illuminating the space around me and only me. It was so sexy all thoughts fled my brain.

"That dick deserved the entire drink thrown on him." The man who could've been near the top on the world's hottest list nodded toward where the other guy disappeared.

I chuckled, breathing through the butterflies gathering in my stomach. *Be cool!* "Trust me, the temptation was there."

"Tell me . . ." He smiled again, and my calm nearly slipped. That smile needed to be patented, stat. He leaned forward to whisper so no one else heard like it was our little secret, his breath tickling my ear. "Was the drink actually twelve dollars?"

"No," I admitted with a shrug.

He pulled back, erupting into laughter. His joy was deep, filled with so much light and happiness, I couldn't stop a genuine smile from crossing my face.

Wiping his eyes, he sat forward and lifted his drink in salute. "He was wrong, you know. You don't just have a pretty face. You are absolutely breathtaking." His face was serious, tone even, and there was nothing that indicated he was messing with me. Still, I searched the room behind him as though waiting for a bunch of his hot friends to be snickering in the corner like they dared him to do this.

He turned, trying to follow my gaze, but there was no one there. He cocked his head at me. "Looking for someone else?" His voice was light, but there was a tightness to his face, like he was steeling himself to be let down. Like me.

"I—nothing." I shook my head once before looking at him again. "What can I get you?"

"Your number." Another charming smile, this one on the edge of hesitant, and I was ice melting into a puddle beneath him. His cheeks flushed a soft shade of pink as I just stood there, and he ruefully rubbed the back of his neck. "Sorry, too forward? I didn't mean to be. You must get guys hitting on you all the time, and you're working." He dropped his hand and glanced away. "Forget I said anything."

"You're serious." I couldn't hide the shock in my voice. *He* wanted *my* number?

"Yes, absolutely." His smile faded into a completely serious face as he looked back at me. "I may like to play games, but this isn't one of those times."

"Uh, yeah, sure." I grabbed another napkin, scribbling my number onto it. *This was real and actually happening to me!* I leaned across the bar to hand it to him.

He took it with both hands, his fingers grazing mine and leaving warmth in their wake. A shiver ran all the way up my arm, hairs prickling on end, and words evaded me once more.

He studied it carefully, holding it in front of his face like I'd handed him a gold plated award or something. His smile was back again, smaller but no less filled with delight. "Thanks. I'll definitely call you." He gave me a wink, still holding it as he slid off the bar stool. "Hope to see you soon," he said, before turning and sauntering off into the crowd.

I stood there dumbfounded until I couldn't see him anymore. Never in my wildest dreams did I expect a GQ model to compliment me, ask me for my number, and mean it. I didn't even get his name, and he didn't ask mine! Damn. But the prospect of the flirty game I could play with him, maybe give him a hard time when he called, flitted through me before I frowned.

If he called.

Gah! I needed to work, not fawn over Mr. Sexy No Name.

Once I refocused, I got back into the swing of things for the rest of the night. Every drink served chipped away at the time in my shift before I could go home. Tips came in slowly, as I wasn't quite up to my usual level of banter, and I had to hide a yawn behind my hand once or twice. Ryan chilled out to my immense relief and went to drink his profits in his office.

The shining light was the bachelorette party, happily drinking their way to a huge tab and hopefully a great tip. I jumped to serve them whenever I saw a penis decoration waving its way toward me.

Edging toward one a.m., things started to slow. I was nearly swaying on my feet now. How long had I been standing today? I didn't like to count the hours, but I liked totaling up my pay. Shifting columns of money around in my head was like paying some kind of mental game of candy crush, especially when it all lined up and financial burdens vanished for a little while.

"Mari!" Anthony's voice was panicked.

A surge of adrenaline sharpened my vision, flooding my limbs with a tingling awareness. Was there an altercation? "What's the matter?"

"The bachelorette party, they're gone." He pointed frantically to the booth they had been camped in. The glasses were all left, empty, two ice buckets dribbling condensation onto the table.

"I'll clear up. There's probably a discarded penis or two—"

"Did they pay their tab?"

The adrenaline turned red hot now, my temples pounding. "I don't know. They left the card. We'll have to charge it."

He snagged it from the shelf and handed it to me. His hands were shaking, but mine were steady. Of course they were. Everything would be fine.

We ran the card.

Declined.

"Shiiiiit," he said, voice low.

"I probably put it through too fast. Let me try again." I ran it through again, a little slower, with a flourish at the end as if I were acting in a movie. But this was real life. I could hear everything clearly. The music thumped in my chest, sweat trickled down between my breasts, a strand of hair clung to my neck, and pain radiated across my forehead.

Declined.

"Fuck." Anthony stared at me. "I'm so sorry, Mari."

I put the reader and the card down. "It's not your fault."

"What a bitch!" He loosed more colorful phrases, but I tuned him out.

Think. Think! What was I going to do? "I followed policy. I—"

Ryan's hot breath washed over me. "What is it?"

Exactly what I didn't need. "I have a problem. I'm sorting it out."

"What kind of problem?"

I opened my mouth to ask him to give me time to sort it when Anthony chipped in, "A customer defrauded her."

"Defrauded *her?* Or defrauded me?" Ryan glowered at Anthony, then at me.

I screwed my fingernails into my palms, the pain grounding me. I had to keep calm. "It was a fake credit card, used to hold a tab. We need to call the police."

Ryan's face went pale. "How much of a tab?"

Anthony looked at the receipt and he too went a strange color. "Five hundred."

Five hundred dollars. I closed my eyes.

"That's on you," Ryan growled.

My eyes flew open. "Excuse me? The business was stolen from."

"You didn't run the card. You didn't check before opening the tab."

"That's not our policy!" I argued, trying not to shout.

"It is now." Ryan wouldn't look me in the eye. *Coward.*

"I've got it." The deep voice intruding on the conversation made me jump.

It wasn't often I could be snuck up on, which was a huge let down for Chris when he was small and was always trying to scare me. Turning and still flush from my fight with Ryan, I faced a man in a suit and tie who held a credit card in my direction. Square glasses, so clean the bar light reflected off of them, obscured his eyes. His dark brown hair was brushed off to the side, completing his pristine look.

I shook my head. The bill was outrageous. "No, we couldn't possibly—"

Ryan shoved me aside. "Thanks." He swiped the card and handed it to me with a quick, "Run it."

I stared at the shiny black American Express, but didn't reach for it. This didn't seem right.

Ryan leaned down, his distillery-breath wafting across my face. "Run it or you're fired."

My heart pounded in my chest. I needed this job, but it was my mistake and I should pay for the screw up. My gaze fell on the man over Ryan's shoulder.

He gave a stiff nod. It felt like an order, and I don't know if it was because I was so goddamn tired—from working, of fighting, of life—or if my military training kicked in to follow a command, but I squared my shoulders, reached out, and snagged the card.

I spun around to the credit machine, typed in a number, and swiped.

Accepted.

The tension left my muscles in a rush, and I doubled over. I thrust my arm against the counter, lightheaded with relief. "Would you like a receipt?" I asked over my shoulder.

"Yes, please," the stranger replied, taking a sip of his beer.

I'd cover his drinks later somehow. Whatever he drank was undoubtedly cheaper than this bill. I tore the receipt off and cringed at the number printed on it as I turned around.

Ryan smirked at me, a slimy smile filled with arrogance as if he'd won something just now. It made my stomach twist. Without another word, he walked away, not even acknowledging or thanking the customer that just saved the day.

The guy didn't seem to care, his gaze on me. I guess he hadn't saved Ryan but me.

I passed the credit card and receipt over to him. "Thanks, that was really too kind of you."

He gave a stiff shrug, plucking a pen from a cup. "Consider it a good faith gesture."

Good faith? In what? That not all people were douchebags?

He left the signed paper with the pen on top and returned his card to a black, sleek wallet. "I paid my tab with the other bartender earlier."

A prickle of discomfort tugged at my belly. He covered my mess up and I had no way of paying him back, even a little, and the only reason I still had my second job was because of this man.

I gave him my bartender smile, pushing away all the tumultuous stormy energy that still raged inside of me from being stiffed and my interaction with Ryan. This man didn't deserve my annoyance after what he just did. "Thanks again, and have a wonderful night!"

He paused, and even though I still couldn't see his eyes, I knew he watched me. "I'm sure I'll see you around. Good night."

Okaaaay. Unsure if that was an "I'm going to be a regular" or "I'm going to stalk you." Either way, it was kind of creepy, and it took every ounce of willpower to keep my faltering smile plastered on my face.

The man gave me another nod before turning and striding out the front door.

Shaking my head to clear it, I picked up the receipt to put it in the register with the rest and paused, doing a double take at the little paper.

I had expected a signature, but this guy has also tipped me 30%. *What the actual hell?* Was the good faith he mentioned that he planned on trying to be my sugar daddy or something? I mean . . . I could use the money, but I wasn't the kind of woman most men would seek out for something like that. I was money oriented, sure, but purely from a survival point of view. Luxury was a word I was aware of, but it only meant a good night's sleep to me.

The rest of the night was quiet, filled with drunk people who decided to close down the bar, including my coworkers tonight, and they were always rowdy. But no more incidents came up, minus Bishop being overly flirty with any woman who would give him the time of day. Even me as I tried to do my job. My biggest relief was I didn't see Ryan for the rest of the night. At one point Lillian and Julian slipped out, thinking no one saw them, but leaving one minute apart made it pretty damn obvious they were going home together. I mostly focused on filling orders and minding my own business. I was still mopping up, thankful for the quiet of the closed bar, as the first rays of dawn lightened the sky.

"You good?" Anthony called from the front door.

"I'm good. I'll close up the back." I worked the mop harder on a spot where the syrup of a fruity drink had dried a little too well.

"'Kay. Have a good one." Anthony shut the door before I could thank him, probably as ready to go home as I was, and the lock *snicked* shut from the outside, followed by the faint jangle of keys and his footsteps getting further away.

Wiping my forehead, I stood and surveyed the room. The bar was restocked for tonight. Chairs were up on tables, the floors were shiny from being recently mopped, and the lights were off except for the back. I continued my mental closing checklist, completing some extra stuff for the opening shift, which would be me tonight. Future me would be really fucking happy with present me because if I thought I was tired now . . .

I checked my watch and scowled. Yup, there wouldn't be enough time for any sleep before I had to be out guarding the house. At least I had time for a shower. I sniffed my armpit and my nose scrunched. I desperately needed one.

On dead feet, my mind already turning into hibernation mode, I made my way to the back, grabbed my purse, and locked up. If only I could be like a dolphin, sleeping with half my brain at a time, or something.

"Ms. Marigold Stewart."

My training kicked into high gear. I swirled around, keys between my knuckles and fist pummeling toward my unexpected visitor. By the time I'd registered it was the man in the suit, it was too late. To my relief, he dodged as if expecting it, pushing my fist aside with the palm of his hand.

"I'm so sorry!" Taking a step back, I rebalanced and quickly scanned the area. He was alone. Even though I was glad I didn't hit him, warning bells went off in my mind. I was in an alley and alone with a stranger who clearly had some kind of combat training.

"When you said 'See you soon,' I didn't realize it would be this soon." My tone didn't match the joke.

"My apologies." He looked exactly as he did earlier, and with a quick once over I didn't see any weapons. He also didn't look very apologetic. "Of all the Shield agents here tonight, I've determined you would be perfect for the covert op we have planned."

I blinked several times. What the hell was happening? Was this a dream? Had I passed out from exhaustion and hit my head?

Undeterred by my lack of response, he reached inside his coat pocket and pulled out a piece of paper. I didn't reach out for it, studying him carefully. He didn't move, but he seemed completely confident, hanging out here in a back alley just as dawn shot pink streaks across the horizon.

Covert operation? That sounded more like my day job. "Who are you?"

"I work for CSON."

I jolted. My main income was for Central Security of Nations, or what we—Bishop, Lilian, Julian, and I—called CSON. They were associated with the government, I guess. From what I understood they were like the United Nations, but for the military. It was like another branch I had never heard of until they poached me from the Army. That was about all I understood. I was in my early twenties and didn't care enough to listen. I had joined to see the world, potentially get school paid for . . . Not that either of those panned out. But mom needed me. And since the position was government and military related, it wasn't exactly Googleable. All I knew was I was now paid to spend my time staring at an empty street. Boring, but it kept me local for my family, and I would still be able to get college paid for one day. It hadn't included the traveling I was excited for with the Army, but it was a hell of a lot safer.

With the sky continuing to lighten, and no more bright lights reflecting off his glasses, I could easily make out his hawk-like brown eyes surveying me as much as I was him.

I widened my stance, ready to fight or flee. "Prove it."

Without hesitation, he pulled out a badge, a shield surrounded by a plant, or four plants, really, one in bud, one in full flower, one wilting, and one cracked and bare. It was our badge and legit.

"Fine," I said, holding out my hand for the envelope. Honestly, this was such a dramatic way to get a message. Couldn't they have emailed or texted? At the same time, my curiosity was winning out. I hadn't heard from the company once I got my job. As long as I showed up to work, a direct deposit made its way into my account monthly. He must have heard the others were coming here for a night out and wanted to assess us off duty, as if we weren't being watched all the time already.

The trouble was, had I impressed him somehow, resulting in this mission? My gut churned. Maybe now he had leverage over me. *What was this job?*

I tore open the manila envelope. The missive was short. Only a few sentences, really. *'You are hereby requested to enter the house you are assigned to guard. Inside by the front door you will find four boxes. In the fourth box, you will locate a key labeled 207. Door 207 is on the second floor, and you are ordered to slip the key underneath at ten hundred hours sharp. This assignment is of the utmost importance and must be kept top secret. Compensation of $100,000 will follow.'*

The amount made my breath catch in my lungs. I was normally able to cope with shocks, but this . . . this was something else. It was the answer to all my prayers—Hail Marys and otherwise. The knot in my stomach loosened so quickly it felt like I'd been dropped off the training tower.

I squeezed my eyes shut, then opened them again. The letter was still in my hand, the words were still there, and my heart was still racing. My boss's signature was scrawled along the bottom, written with fresh ink instead of printed like the rest.

Um. What?

I checked the other side.

"There's nothing there," the man said.

How often had I dreamt of suddenly receiving a windfall of money? My daydreams revolved around the IRS giving me some kind of refund, or the school taking Chris back on full scholarship, or even perhaps some kind of money from my dad trying to make amends for ditching us when Chris was born and leaving us with all his gambling debts we were still paying off to this day. I clung to the letter as if it was the only tether to reality. *A life line. A real lifeline.*

So why did I feel like I had just been thrown out to sea?

Shit. This was some kind of test, wasn't it? A test of loyalty, or whether I could be bought, or something. It was a legit request from Karen, my boss. Maybe I should ask her. I did have her number for emergencies. Again, why a physical copy though? Why not call me herself?

"Do you have the necessary information to complete the assignment?" The agent cut through my inner monologue.

I scanned the paper again, noting all key information, my eyes snagging on the whopping compensation one more time. "Yes," I said.

He pulled the paper from my grip, and flame burst from his other hand lighting it on fire.

My jaw hung as I watched the piece of paper incinerate in his hand. Okay, well, maybe I wouldn't be calling my boss. They were taking this top secret thing seriously, and if they didn't want a paper trail then clearly they didn't want an electronic one either.

"Understood," I breathed as I stared into the flames, as though my commanding officer was before me.

What had I just signed up for?

Chapter Three

"Ugh, my head," Bishop groaned from his position a few feet away.

"I told you not to take those vodka shots," Lillian sighed and rolled her eyes.

I opened my eyes slowly. My extremely tired eyes, as I was running on pure adrenaline from lack of sleep and anticipation of my new assignment. "Would you please stop doing that?" I said before being taken over by a yawn as I faced Bishop, who kept clicking the damn false snap on his holster.

"What, Marigold, didn't get enough sleep last night?" He smirked down at me.

I massaged my temples. "No, in fact, I didn't." Being around a new hire who was easily distracted by his new shiny gun wasn't helping my raging headache. "And my name is Mari." I put enough of the sergeant voice into it to show I meant business. No one called me Marigold, and I mean no one. Not even my own family. Nothing made me feel more like a ninety-five year old grandma with dentures rather than a stocky twenty-five year old who knew how to knock someone out in seventeen different ways.

Bishop, whose first name I had yet to learn, leaned forward until he was further in my view. "Why work at Mystique anyways? This job pays well enough."

"Leave her alone, Mark," Lillian chastised with another roll of her eyes.

Ah, so that was his name. I think I would stick with Bishop. Didn't want the pretty boy fresh out of fraternity life getting the wrong idea. Despite him being a recent graduate, he still partied like all he had to worry about was getting passing grades, and not a paycheck to take care of the bills. He didn't understand that this job didn't pay well enough for all of us, especially when they had a family to take care of.

Family always came first, something I did *not* learn from my dad.

I blew into my hands, hoping to warm them up. Today was the first day of spring, but it sure didn't feel that way up here. Everywhere else in Vermont was thawing out, but there had to be a weird microclimate in this little valley that kept it much cooler.

What's the weather like at Lake Como right now? I shook my head to try to focus. I gave up the only way I'd ever be able to travel, the Army, to be close to home and for good reason. The bills were piling up, and there was no way I would leave Mom and Chris with those. I would do anything for them, and that included working this boring ass job simply because it paid well enough.

This was my life, in all its glory. Work, eat, sleep, and repeat. I meant, work, work, eat, and sometimes sleep.

Pushing away from my perch, I walked along the road, further away from where Lillian and Bishop reminisced about their antics the night before. My combat boots thudded along the pavement until I stood at the wrought-iron gate. It was closed, as always. I had never seen a car enter or exit through here. I peered between the bars, following the gravel driveway winding up to the mansion at the top of the small hill.

Long on the one side with two wings facing into the courtyard in the middle, the building was three stories tall, judging by the doors at the bottom floor, then a set of windows all regulation straight above them, and then smaller, square windows right at the top. The roof was gray wherever I could see it behind the intricate detailing on the edge, a repeating vine pattern scrawling along the top. Built of creamy stone with an occasional marble-looking column detail to outline the grand entrance in the middle of the house and the smaller entrances to the east and west wings, it struck me as quite a European-looking building. Like it would have tall ceilings held up by cathedral columns inside. It was probably some pop star's McMansion. I had no idea. I was literally just the schmuck on door duty.

"It is of the utmost importance."

I was tasked with protecting this place, from what, I don't know, and now I was supposed to commit a crime by breaking and entering? It didn't feel right. Sure, it came from my boss, but they wanted me to move something inside to a different room number, and for a hefty sum. Numbering rooms was odd for a home. Maybe it was some kind of top secret hotel. Whatever the case, they clearly didn't mean for me to go up to the front door and knock. We weren't allowed on the property; we just patrolled the perimeter.

"Slip the key under at ten hundred hours sharp."

I glanced down at my watch. We used military time, so I knew it meant 10 a.m., and right now it was 9:15. I didn't know how hard it would be to get inside, find the key, and then slip it under the right door. There hadn't been much instruction aside from a general place to find both the key and door. I didn't want to miss the deadline, nor did I want to be stuck inside the house with too much extra time.

Fuck me.

I didn't know if I wanted to do this at all. Even if this order came from my supervisor, it was a legitimate crime, right? We guarded the house, but we didn't need to step foot on their property. I know because I asked when I first got this job. And now not only did they expect me to go past this gate, but they wanted me to sneak inside and . . . and what? Slip a key under a door?

I mean, did that count as stealing? It was more like moving an object in their house from one place or another. So, I guess I could plead "Not guilty" to the judge for theft.

One hundred thousand dollars. One hundred fucking thousand dollars! That was life changing money there. And I really was only just locating an object and moving it? What harm could that do?

Okay, it was now or never.

Rubbing my sweaty palms together, I inspected the house again, studying the windows and looking for movement of any kind. I had spent so many hours staring at the front exterior of this house I could probably draw it from memory. I could do this. In and out.

"Hey, I'm gonna go use the bathroom." The words slipped out. Was my voice pitch too high? Too late now.

Bishop and Lillian's conversation broke off as they turned to me. "You're what?" Lillian's brows rose to her hairline.

"The bathroom," I repeated.

Bishop snorted. "That's a first."

He was right. I had a bladder of steel with all the training I had undergone. "Long night," I retorted. "When duty calls, you have to answer." I tried to end it with a laugh, but that only concerned them more because I don't think they'd ever heard that sound come out of me either.

"Right." Lillian frowned. "Well, there are some good bushes around the bend. Although I suggest staying on the right because the guys use the left and I'm sure they get it everywhere, including their shoes."

"I do not!" Bishop hollered. "I was able to pee standing up when I was only—"

Feeling no need to learn any more TMI about Bishop, I tuned them out as I walked away to the designated "rest area." Gross. But that was what happened when we were given a piece of road to secure and nothing else, not even an outhouse.

My nose scrunched, waiting for an assault on the senses like a Port-a-Potty, but it never came. I guess that was one plus. Once I was safely out of sight, I veered into the small grove of trees and bushes. Pushing my way through the budding branches, it wasn't long until I came across the fence. Black iron topped with spikes lined the whole property, and there were no weak spots. If there were, I would know, because I took pride in doing my job well. Minus the fact that I was about to enter the territory I was sworn to protect on a secret mission.

No, it was an order from my boss. "I'm sure it's fine," I muttered to myself.

With a running jump, I grabbed the top of the fence, the metal cold and edges biting into my palms. I hauled myself up and over the spikes. *Ha! All muscles, baby! Hell yeah.*

I landed on the other side with a soft thump. Staying in a crouched position, I slunk between the trees, keeping an eye on my surroundings. Parts of the mansion peeked out between the trees, the windows dark, nothing flickering within.

When I got to the woods' edge, I slowed, peering from behind a thick tree trunk and breathing deeply and evenly. The excitement was getting to me. My heart beat wildly with the mixed emotions of right and wrong from breaking in while following orders. There were multiple windows in the east wing partially open, light flashing off of them from this angle. Seemed the owner wanted to enjoy the spring day too, and that made it my lucky day. Most of the windows that were open were on the upper floors, but at the corner near the front of the house was one pane of glass cracked a few inches open on the bottom floor.

Bingo.

Careful of anything underfoot, I ensured each footstep was light and soundless. I side eyed the front gate to see that Lillian's and Bishop's backs were to me. Now I just had to hope whoever was in the house wasn't looking right at me as I stealth side-stepped across their lawn.

I'd expected manicured gardens with those regulation-straight mow lines etched up and down, but closer to the house I slipped through long grasses and thin reeds whispered against my calves, heavy with seed heads and bobbing as I passed.

The window slid open with ease, sucking in cool air which pulled a strand of hair free from my bun. Hauling myself inside was easier than the fence, and I returned the window to the original position in case anyone passed.

Damn, I should've gotten more intel. Was it an old man who lived here? Would I come across a hoard of children, or was it a person who had no time on their hands except to listen in case someone slipped inside? I had no idea what to expect and cursed myself as an idiot for not having asked more questions.

Too late now.

I was in a corridor, brightly lit from natural daylight streaming in from the big windows to my left, the courtyard outside empty. Doors lined the wall to my right hand side, all closed, but the variety of handles made me pause. Some were bronzed filigreed things of beauty, while others were utilitarian brushed steel bars.

The corridor opened out into an entranceway. I say one, because there was bound to be another in the west wing, although this was big enough. A balcony lined the upper floor, a glass ceiling with scrollwork arching above, and columns with some kind of swirly design on them marching along the sides. Four sofa sets fit in here—four!—two facing each other. Only one seat looked sat in from a divot worked into the extreme left hand side next to the fire, and a pile of books beside it was topped with an empty wine glass. Plush carpets with a Turkish pattern spanned the entirety of the room over the perfectly polished brown hardwood peeking out at the ends.

I paced along the edge of the hall a little further, holding my breath. *Strange.* I expected many rooms to radiate from this one, but it looked like the walls were . . . blocked off? Blank walls faced me, looking for all the world like there should have been doors, trims in doorway shapes and sizes, but all looked like pretty solid walls otherwise.

Weird. At least it smelled nice; fresh and clean, like jasmine and cardamom and honeysuckle. I loved honeysuckle, but I wasn't here to sample the air.

I glanced up at the ceiling, my steps halting. What I'd taken for intricate metal scrollwork was actually a series of intertwining plants. Shit, there were thick tree climbing vines in here, thrusting out from the hardwood floor and twisting around the columns, throttling the balcony above and crawling everywhere to blot out the sun above. No wonder the owner had blocked this place off. The vines were as thick as my arm.

Once on the other side of the hall, I pressed my back against the wall to the side of the cased doorway opening. It kept me hidden, but in sight of the front door of the east wing. And there, to the right of it, sat a wooden table with four boxes set upon it.

Ha! This was easier than I thought.

I listened for a minute but heard nothing, and chancing a

glance into the courtyard proved no one was in sight. I made my move. Dashing into the foyer, I raced to the table.

The four boxes atop were beautifully ornate, hand carved wooden chests. The furthest on the left was carved with cherry blossoms and in a happy pink, the carved calligraphy proclaimed "Spring" atop it. The next read "Summer" in a deep forest green, thick and vibrant. The third was "Autumn" in a golden hue with spindly branches that intertwined like lovers in the night. Finally, the fourth—my mark—had stark silver-blue edges and silver writing that read "Winter." My fingers reached out of their own accord to trace the wintry snow storm delicately gracing its surface.

Gently, I flicked the clasp and raised the lid. Inside were keys . . . so many keys. Basic ones you could get from a department store, while others were brass and as big as my fist. Others seemed old; old and so brittle they could break at the slightest touch. Amongst them were key cards too, just like a hotel, and on every single one, no matter the style, was a number.

"207, 207, 207," I muttered to myself, skimming through. It was in numerical order at least. *180, 190, 200...*

Aha! My hand closed around a white plastic keycard. Modern and boring compared to what it was housed in, and very easy to slip under a door.

I shut the lid, replacing the fastener, and spun around to the double staircase leading to the second floor.

"Woah," I breathed. I had been so focused on reconnaissance, I hadn't fully realized the opulence of this place. Maybe this was a residence for a diplomat of the U.S., like a king or queen of another country. A summer home, if you will. Which meant that no one would be here.

I checked my watch. 9:56.

Shit. I needed to hurry.

On tiptoes, I hurried up the stairs, trying not to scuff up

the clean marble with my boots. Even if no one was here, I didn't want to make anyone aware someone had been inside the mansion. Thinner vines wove their way up here too, but not as thoroughly as the ones strangling the east wing entrance hall, the leaves shivering as I passed.

At the top, I was faced with two hallways, one to my left and one to my right. The doors were all different too, some warm woods, dark oaks and light beech, and others corporate-looking, cold metal and crisp lines. How would I know which way to go? Another failure in my preparation, I should have asked for the layout of this house. Patrolling it from the outside had made me too confident.

Peering above the doors, I saw small numbers, and they all started with '2', as if this was a hotel. Inspecting them closely, I realized my left was all even numbers. I padded to the right and was rewarded with 201. Odd numbers down here.

It was only four doors down for Room 207. I approached the door. It too was different, but nothing to mark it as really special from all the other array of doors. A white, laminate door, like in a modest house.

I checked my watch again. 9:59.

I waited for that digital dial to flip over, staring at my watch with rapt attention, slowing my breathing to listen hard for any sounds. It was utterly silent, the air close and undisturbed. A little dust swirled in the air, as if waiting, like me.

10:00.

Without hesitating, I bent over and slipped the card right under the door. Like some kind of idiot, I stared at the thin little crack as though I expected to hear a thank you. Of course none came. Apparently my little mission was slowly making me insane.

Pressing against my knees, I rose from my crouch. Alright, done and done. Dollar bill signs bounced around in my head, and I was already daydreaming about how I'd spend the money. I'd pay off all outstanding bills and get Mom to that neurologist. Relief loosened my lungs as my mind raced.

"Who the fuck are you?" A deep voice said from behind.

I froze, my mind disbelieving and turning sluggish.

"Who are you?" The shout rumbled through every bone in my body, and when I turned I came face to chest with a wall of man. Broad chested in a wife beater, and pale skinned with tattoos as intricate as the boxes downstairs. I craned my neck upward. Holy hell, he looked like a modern-day Viking; all muscle and intensity.

I took a step back, my back hitting the door. "I—I—"

Muscles bulged beneath the thin fabric, his biceps as big as my head. Icy blue eyes pierced through me, and an intense chill swept through me. Shock? No. The air was suddenly bitingly cold, and dust motes sparkled like ice and clouded my vision. I did the one thing I could think of, especially since neither my mouth nor brain seemed to be working.

I ran.

"Fuck!" he hollered, his bellow echoing down the corridor. "We got an intruder!"

I ran like my life fucking depended on it, and from my quick glance and the murderous gaze barreling down on me, I'm pretty fucking sure it did. He was shouting to someone else, and the last thing I needed was his backup arriving.

I tried a door handle as I raced past. It was locked, but behind me the chill was getting worse. The carpet crackled under my boots, my breath steaming in the air. *What the hell?* How had the temperature dropped so quickly?

I pumped my legs harder and took a stairway, leaping up two at a time. The cold wrapped around my chest, restricting my breathing. I ran harder and rounded another hallway, twisting down another endless corridor. Where was I now? A quick glance outside showed me the north side of the courtyard with the view down to the perimeter fence, where I should be right now. *Shit.* I was running deeper into the house.

"Whoa, she's fast." Someone said from behind. A voice that didn't match Mr. Viking.

Fuck, there were more. Shit! Fuck! Mother fucker! How the hell was I going to get out of this?

I took another corner and a door down the hall caught my eye. One with a bolt. Which meant I could unlock it without a key.

I barely slowed as I slammed it open, wincing as the metal banged into my hand. Footsteps thudded closer. I twisted the handle with success and rushed through the door, slamming the door behind me and twisting the lock.

I was in an even tinier hallway, this one warm and steamy, and it smelled of . . . ramen?

The dark hallway was narrow but short, lined with some kind of paper. The air clung to me, now too hot to breathe. What was with the temperature in this place? Noise beyond sounded like a radio, a light chatter I couldn't quite catch. I bolted to the end but stopped dead in my tracks.

A row of people turned and looked up from a bar in surprise. Some had noodles hanging from chopsticks halfway to their mouths, while others slowly lowered their bowls back down. Three Japanese chefs paused behind the counter, faces contorting with confusion.

"あなたは誰か," one of them said, raising his voice at the end like it was a question.

What the hell just happened?

Chapter Four

It was dead silent in the ramen shop except for a warbling song coming from a tinny speaker while muted conversation filtered from outside the red flaps separating the shop from the street.

"あなたは誰か," he said again, this time more urgently, coming toward me with a tiny colander on the end of a hefty handle of wood. It wasn't much of a weapon, but I had no desire to find out how much it might hurt if he whacked me with it.

Behind me, boots clattered in the hallway on the other side of the locked door. "Where'd they go? How many?" A raspy voice with a Spanish accent boomed.

"One," the Viking rumbled. "In there."

"Really?" A tenor. "Oh boy. This is a mess." The door handle jiggled.

"Hand me the key," the Spanish accent said. "Why was *la puerta* even open? Nevermind, we'll talk later. Haru!"

I watched behind me in horror as the lock turned and the door swung open. A man, nearly as giant as the Viking but with a more menacing glare, stepped through the door, filling the corridor with his broad shoulders. He had tousled dark hair cropped close and an earring glinting from one earlobe. Yet I was mainly locked in place by the sight of his torso. Chiseled muscles on his chest tapered to a tight six pack, his white shirt unbuttoned. Perhaps he threw it on hastily before the chase.

"Stop right there," he said, but he didn't move toward me. He leaned forward instead, lips twisting with anger, and exposing three more silhouettes behind him.

Fuck.

"I can explain, I'm following orders—" Wait, it was a top secret assignment and I'd signed the official secrets act when I took this job. If I spilled my mission, I could expect jail time, a huge fine, or—an even more likely scenario—I'd be fired. Or this was some top secret military shit, and people disappeared when they encountered that.

My lips clamped together as I searched for something to say. "Just let me out and I'll go. I didn't take anything or do any damage."

The bronzed man's eyes narrowed, but the Viking shoved through from behind him, pale skin nearly white in the dim light, and those ice blue eyes shards of biting anger. "There she is!" he roared.

No way could I handle these angry men in this tiny corridor. I turned and bolted through the red flaps onto a dark street.

"Winter! *Mierda!* Haru, get in there!"

I ran as hard as I could, skirting between tables filled with men in suits whose shocked expressions gave rise to a flurry of Japanese I didn't understand. I wheeled out between the flaps, expecting . . . I didn't know, but it wasn't this.

I ran under the night sky. *Night,* when it was 10am? My legs shook. This was stupidly realistic. Men and women, all of who appeared to be Japanese, frowned at me. The cobblestones under my feet, the stalls tightly packed shoulder to shoulder and jutting out into the street, thick broth in steamy clouds, frying noises, laughter, flashing neon signs, a man stumbling ahead of me with a briefcase . . . It was all so real.

I tried to dodge but he was too close, and I knocked into his shoulder. He spun, briefcase hitting the sidewalk and papers flying.

"Sorry!" I grabbed his shoulders to stop him falling.

"ごめんなさい," he muttered, blinking at me. "外国人ですか." The rising note at the end sounded like another question.

My chest was overly tight as my mind struggled. A street? How come there was a street in this house, on an upper floor, and all done so realistically?

"I don't know what this is," I offered, less than helpful, before running feet behind me sent a spike of fear straight through my heart.

I scrambled away, ducking down between colored flaps into what I hoped was a side alley, and smashed straight into a steel box. An air con, attached to the building. My hips twisted into a roll as I landed, but man, that hurt. It knocked the air out of me like a squashed balloon. I sucked in a breath between my lips, forcing my ribs out to inflate them. I could not fall or afford to lose any momentum. I ducked, feeling a swipe above my head just where my shoulders would have been, and launched forward, running again.

This was some kind of trick, right? The details of this street was incredible. I forced myself to focus on my pursuers. The guys I'd seen were huge, and I wasn't as tall or wide as them, an advantage in this closed in place. I turned sideways as the alleyway closed in, risking a look back.

A tall but slight man followed me, keeping pace and so close I could almost see what color his eyes were. He had black hair and a serious expression on his face. A face that I recognized.

"You!" His jaw dropped with shock and he stumbled for a moment.

It was the sexy guy from the bar, the one I gave my number to. What was he doing here? "I just wanna talk!" he called out, and I stumbled myself when he broke into a wide grin, my stomach swooping.

Yeah, fuck that. I quickened my pace. No one expected a big girl to know how to run, and at one point I hated it, but it was something I learned to love after joining the Army. Sidling past doorways, I knocked on them, trying the door handles, anything. What if this was a dead end? I spilled out into a more open area containing a red building, its roof hung with bright little lanterns, before running down a wider alleyway.

"I'm Haru, by the way," he panted behind me. A little too damn close behind me.

I accelerated, but the wider street meant he could possibly try to overtake or intercept me.

I pumped my arms and snatched gasps of air. It tasted different, thick with city smoke and heat. I slipped past more air conditioners blasting out warmth, sweating in my dark uniform.

The man snatched at my arm, fingers yanking my shirt backward. "Stop, please!"

My training kicked in and with a twist of my arm, I broke the contact. Running was my priority, even as my knees ached. I had to keep going and lose this guy. The consequences of my actions were unclear and therefore to be avoided.

Where were the exits? This had to be an elaborate set, right? How was all this here in the house? Surely it wasn't this big.

The alley opened up onto another street. An actual street,

with cars passing by, and tires hissing in the puddles. Cars. Puddles. My stomach soured by the second.

What was going on?

"Hey!" Two hands landed on my shoulders.

Twisting around, I swirled my arms in an outward circle, smacking his forearms with the side of my hands and thrusting his arms wide and off my shoulders. I could hold my own in a confrontation. I'd trained extensively with guys twice my size, but that was a last resort.

He gaped, eyes wide, and I bolted, sidestepping around a group of teenagers dressed in otaku-style outfits in the night-time streets. I chanced a glance behind me as I passed. They blocked the guy at the perfect moment, slowing his steps. He towered over them, which caught their fascination as they surrounded him and excited Japanese flew from their mouths.

He smiled at them, "すみません." He tried to push past them, but they took out their cell phones, holding them up with pleading gestures as I got further away. He cursed as he whipped out a cell phone, pressing it to the side of his head. "Otto, I need you," he yelled. "She's scrappy."

Scrappy? I think he meant 'trained professional.' My pace slowed to a brisk walk as I held out my arms to the traffic in request for them to stop. Cars slowed, horns sounded, and I jogged on.

"Otto, I know! We have to risk it." His voice reached me once more, the only proof I needed to know he was on my tail again. He wove around the cars, lifting his hands in placation and shouting, "あんなことして、すみませんでした." At home, drivers would have stepped out for a punch up, but while the drivers stared, they didn't act with overt anger.

"Stop, stop!" he called after me, but once I stepped up onto the sidewalk on the other side, I bolted again, getting into my second wind. "Otto, door . . . Six nineteen! No, wait, eight fourteen!"

I hastened along the street, neon signs flashing by, when a very handsome man wearing tweed stepped into the path ahead of me. Tall and broad with a carved jawline and short dark brown curls, he raised his hands as I raced toward him.

"That's her!" the man chasing me said. "Don't let her escape you!"

That didn't sound ominous at all. The man lunged, arms swiping, and I spun into the alleyway behind him, careful of the air con this time. A door stood propped open a few paces in and I darted inside, slamming it shut behind me.

Panting, I backed away slowly. Had they seen me go in? Should I run?

I turned to do so and smacked into a wall of muscle.

I looked up, up, and up some more, my head tipped so far back it ached, and stared straight into the eyes of Angry Viking.

"Wha—How?" How was he here, when I'd run half a mile at least? I stood in a corridor, plain wood floors and beige wallpaper, one side bright with morning sunlight streaming through the windows. I was back in the house, and it was daytime again.

Oh, shit, this was deep top secret stuff.

"Winter, back away," the lyrical deep voice of the huge Spanish man said. My gaze landed on him behind the blonde giant's shoulder. He was dressed a bit more at least, white collar askew at his throat but his shirt buttoned over his wide bronze chest.

Bronze god laid a hand on Viking's arm. "Winter. Back away."

The Viking's simmering glare stayed brutally cold as he took a pace backward. It didn't help me feel less hemmed in, the pair of them still filling the corridor.

I blinked the sweat out of my eyes, sucking in breath after breath. "I—This is a film set, right? A really exclusive and expensive set. That's the story I'll tell, I swear." I licked my dry lips, heart beating too fast.

I had been running on a street. There were cars. I had tasted the air and smog had filled my lungs.

That was a city. A city, when we were twenty minutes from anywhere, and a foreign one at that. At least it didn't resemble any city I'd been to in Vermont. This was big, deep secret stuff. No wonder I'd been set to guard this.

The faces of the men swam in my vision, silver and gold, as I put one hand to the lurching wall. *No!* I couldn't faint, even though this was incredible and terrifying, because of course no one could know about this.

The Viking darted toward me as if to catch me, but Bronze god said, "No," in a harsh tone, shouldering past him and grabbed my arm as if to hold me from sagging. His hand was hot, and not by a little. It was like this man ran at 120 degrees. "Who are you?" he hissed.

I stared up into their faces, shaking my head mutely. I was in so much trouble.

The door behind me burst open. "You pulled me into Japan, Haru!" a cultured accent with a British twang protested.

"There was nothing else for it!" The man who had chased me came up behind me, closely followed by the man in tweed.

The latter picked pink petals off his jacket. "That'll mess up sakura season," he complained.

"Who—who are you?" I asked. I might as well. I was already in deep shit.

"That's funny, I have the same question for you," the bronze god said, his voice a dangerous growl. His hand tightened on my arm.

"I'm Haru," the Japanese model-man bounded up to me with a smile. "Like I said earlier, although you might not have heard me, given that we were running at the time." He lowered into a small bow, the smile on his face broad and genuine as he straightened.

I narrowed my eyes at him. I wasn't falling for his tricks again. "Yeah, I guess we didn't have a chance to exchange names at the bar, just a number."

The others looked at him in surprise, the bronze god quirking an eyebrow.

Haru shrugged. "Can you blame me? I had to try!"

The other three took that as an opportunity to inspect me. Three pairs of eyes, browns and blues caressing every curve of my body. I was easily the shortest. I always was, but next to the Viking I was positively miniscule. He would be able to pick me up under his arm no problem. The Latin god was not too far behind, his shirt straining as he flexed his iron grasp on my arm. The man in tweed peered at me as he absently plucked petals from his clothes, and, closest, was Haru with the lovely smile and warm brown eyes. The Viking glared, the tweed guy kept his lips pursed, and the guy holding me had anger seeping from the tight hold on my arm. Having all their attentions made it hard to breathe. None of them objected to Haru's obvious attraction to me, but they didn't seem to agree either.

Haru leaned so close to me his honeysuckle scent filled my nose, and that little bit of friendly familiarity eased the tension in my stomach. "And you are?"

I tried to smile back, my cheeks aching. "Where am I? What's happening?" I asked him instead, voice shaking. I couldn't fall apart. I wouldn't. I forced the tears back.

Concern knotted his brows, and leaning in so close his breath wisped across my ear, he whispered, "It'll be alright. We'll explain everything."

My heart thundered in my chest at how close he was. He eased back, concern still knitting his eyebrows, and those dark brown eyes looked between mine.

"No we bloody well won't," the man in tweed snapped.

"We need to talk about this, and she needs a moment to recover." He stretched out his hand toward me. "This won't hurt a bit," he told me.

That was exactly what someone said when it was going to hurt a lot. I flinched back, but the bronze god tightened his grip. The corridor grew colder still, the edge biting into the air in my lungs.

"Winter!" the man holding me snapped.

Was that his name?

The Viking tore his gaze away from me, bunching and relaxing his fists with effort. I heard every crack of his knuckles.

"You'll be alright," the British man said, laying his palm flat on my cheek.

"We'll see about that," one of them said. Who, I didn't know, because a split second later, everything went black.

Chapter Five

First there was sound. Nothing but muffled voices like the adults on *Peanuts* at first, then they became louder and clearer. My consciousness slowly came back to me, a familiar feeling from having been knocked out plenty of times. It had been part of my training, but not since I was a fresh greenie several years ago. I hated it though. It was like drifting through a black nothingness as I slowly settled back into a body. When my weight sunk in, bound to my limbs once more, I still felt heavy and unable to move.

Now fully present and aware of my body, I kept my breathing even and my body still like I was still asleep.

"I told you there would be issues, Haru." The British voice was easy to make out.

"Yeah, but it's not *that* bad." The soft lilt, taking everything with an easy demeanor. His charming smile popped into my head and damn it all to hell if there wasn't a mild swoop in my stomach at it.

Wow, Mari, one extremely hot guy gives you notice and even though he chased you, you're still all butterflies around him?

Pretty sure I officially watched *Beauty and the Beast* too much as a kid.

"Except your beloved cherry blossoms are falling off the trees as they go back into hibernation. I knew I shouldn't have gone." The British man huffed. "It's already all over the news."

"Fine. Next time, I'll be sure to let her get away," Haru retorted, an edge of annoyance lacing his voice.

"Otto, Haru, *basta*. Fighting isn't going to solve anything. Otto, how are you feeling?" The Spanish accent of the bronze god washed over my senses like the balm to a sunburn.

"I'll live," the Brit said, whose name I could only assume was Otto. "The real question is, why was the door unlocked for her to go through?"

There was a heartbeat of silence before Haru answered. "It was dead bolted on our side. I was more focused on people coming in rather than going out."

"You'll need to spend some extra time in Osaka over the next week or so in order to rid the area of my influence," Otto sighed.

"*¡Maldito sea!* Which is a mistake you'll have to make up for later."

"Summer, calm down or you'll warm the place up." The soft growl off to my right could be none other than the Viking.

Shit, they had me surrounded.

"Right, because I'm the one who needs to worry about controlling my powers, Winter," Summer retorted irritably.

The big man let out a grunt that sounded more like a growl. So his name was . . . Winter? And the other was Summer?

Silence fell in the room. With no words to concentrate on, I turned my attention to what I could feel. I was warm with something soft beneath me like a comforter, and my head was definitely being supported by the fluff of a pillow. Actually, this felt like a Tempur-Pedic mattress with how it supported my wide hips. I half expected to wake up in a jail cell, not a luxury bed. Jail was where I belonged after all. Had they called my superior? How long had I been out for? Clearly not long if no one from CSON had arrived to apologize and discard me. Damnit, I was totally screwed.

A thudding footstep moved closer to the side of the bed, stuttering my pulse and my breathing.

"*La mujer* is awake." Summer's accent made itself known with the roll of the 'r' on the tip of his tongue.

There was no use faking it anymore. Using up all my stored courage, I opened my eyes.

I was in a room bigger than my own at home. There didn't seem to be any windows, but there were two closed doors as well as one that was open, leading to a hallway. The bed I laid on was covered in white sheets and a cream comforter, but the room looked oddly bare aside from the gigantic bed, almost like a hotel room.

Four paintings hung on the wall in a square, all in the same place, a bridge over a small creek with trees lining the banks, but each depiction was during a different season. The winter picture had snow covering everything including the tree limbs, and ice had locked the water. Beside it, green and blooming buds filled the spring painting, the bank muddy from the melted snow. Summer was vibrant with greens, deep and luscious to where some of the trees were obscured compared to the autumn painting beside it. That one had leaves falling, drawn so beautifully I could almost hear the crunch, the colors burning oranges, yellows, and browns.

Pulling my gaze away from the framed artwork, I finally inspected the living artwork of the four men surrounding me.

Summer, in the same white shirt from earlier but now buttoned up fully—his toned muscles still on display—stood to my left, half leaning over the king sized bed. His thick eyebrows drew together above his light brown eyes, and I couldn't tell if the look was out of concern or distrust.

Moving clockwise, my eyes landed on Otto, who sat in a chair at the foot of the bed. Dark circles tugged his eyes down like he had been awake for days. There was no way I had been out for that long, had I? Worry tugged in my gut. His dark brown eyes studied me through a pair of black framed glasses, his hands holding an open book in his lap. The way his long finger rubbed the spine as he inspected me made me half wonder what else he could do with his—

Ah! No! Bad, Mari! Sure, they were the epitome of hotness and even though I was pretty certain I would never be surrounded by such beauty ever again, I needed to concentrate.

The Viking, who I understood to be Winter, shifted his weight in the corner of the room, drawing my attention. He leaned against the wall with his arms folded, making his biceps bulge out of his shirt sleeves. The shaved sides of his head swirled with intricate designs reminiscent of his tattoos, and the long blonde hair atop his head was tied off in a messy bun. His piercing gaze stole my breath away, wracking a shiver through my body.

Finally, to my right, was Haru. His smooth skin made him look young, but the way his eyes inspected me made me feel he was much older than he looked.

Eyes crinkling, a soft smile broke across his face. "How are you feeling?"

I bolted upright, so quickly that it actually made Summer and Haru take a step back. "Stay back!" I threatened. I could take one of them, maybe two if I was really on my game, but there was no way in hell I could take down all four of these men who looked more like gods than humans. Usually it would be a woman's wildest dreams to end up in a room with possibly the four sexiest men to have ever lived, but I didn't feel so lucky right now.

"We don't want to hurt you." Haru held up his hands in a placating gesture as if to prove his point.

My gaze swept to the murderous one in the corner. "Tell that to Winter over there."

Haru's eyebrow raised before looking toward Summer with amusement sparkling in his gaze.

"A perceptive little one, aren't you, *chica*?" Summer's serious expression turned into one of surprise.

"You better back the fuck up, Summer." That's right. I knew his name, and I wanted him to know. I wanted them all to know. My narrowed eyes turned. "Otto," I noted, "and of course, Haru." My attention settled on the guy from the bar, who seemed ready to burst into laughter at any second.

"I don't mind feisty, but I'm not one who likes being told what to do." Summer stepped forward, his broad frame so imposing I couldn't look away. He was calling my bluff, but the joke was on him if he thought I'd go down without a fight.

I bunched the bedsheet in my hand, catching his intrigued attention. "If you hadn't knocked me out, we wouldn't have a problem."

"Don't break into our house." His brown eyes bored into me.

I couldn't look away. Sweat beaded on my temple. Was it getting hot in here?

"How about we try playing nice?" Haru offered lightly from behind me.

Summer's gaze lifted over my shoulder. After a split second, his demeanor shifted, and it was like a cool breeze blew through the room. "By all means, feel free to clean up your mess."

Haru's jaw dropped. "This isn't my mess! Winter was the one that found her."

Winter pushed away from the wall, taking a thumping stride toward Haru, and I swear the room dropped by several degrees. "I wasn't the one who left a door unlocked!"

"It technically wasn't unlocked. I dead bolted it," Haru shot back.

Otto shook his head. "It doesn't matter who's to blame, the real questions are: who is she, how did she get in, and what is she doing here?"

Four sets of eyes turned to me expectantly.

Oh, hell no.

"Well?" Summer growled, his voice a command.

Naturally, the authoritative way he spoke pressed the button that took me straight into obedient soldier mode. I wouldn't answer all of them, but maybe if I offered something, they would answer one of mine. Plus they were going to find out eventually once they got ahold of my boss.

"Ex-Army, current CSON operative, Marigold Stewart." I chattered off my title and name like I would for any commanding officer. Perhaps these were my ultimate employers, so maybe I could get lucky. And despite being surrounded by four drool-worthy men, I was sad to say by 'lucky,' I meant a warning instead of a bullet to the head. Or worse, being fired.

"Marigold?" Haru's stunned voice was a whisper, matching the three other sets of widened eyes like they'd be bowled over with a feather. "And you work for CSON?"

"Yes." I dragged out the word with some hesitation as I tried to gauge the odd reaction. Damn, maybe they knew I was in command during my shift. Could I use that to my advantage? "When I was guarding the gate, I noticed some windows open. Since that is a potential threat to security, I took it upon myself to inspect the premises."

"Surveying and security, eh?" Haru's eyes widened with realization. "You're one of the Shields from out front!"

I sat up straight, but that just pushed my rack forward, drawing their attention even if only for a short moment. *Damn it.*

Otto cleared his throat, eyes meeting mine. "Just to get this clear. Despite the contract clearly stating to not trespass directly onto our lawn, you decided for *safety* reasons to make sure no one had broken into our home, by breaking and entering yourself?"

"I wouldn't say I did any breaking . . ." My voice trailed off.

"Just entering," Otto finished for me.

I didn't correct him, staring over his head at the four paintings on the walls.

"We really need to start being proactive with learning about the Shields that guard the compound." Summer shook his head and pulled a cellphone from his back pocket. "I'll call CSO—"

"No!" I cried out, twisting toward him with my hand outstretched. "Please don't!"

I don't know if it was my sudden movement or the desperate plea in my voice, but Summer's finger paused above his lock screen.

"Summer," Winter warned from behind, "she's seen too much."

My mouth bobbed. *Shit.* "No, I—I . . . honestly, I'll just tell someone it's a film set. I'm sorry. I shouldn't have entered your private property. I'm so sorry. But I—" I hung my head, a flush creeping up my neck. "I need this job." The words were strained, a last ditch effort and laying more of myself bare than I ever liked to in front of others.

My heart thudded in my chest, making the extended silence scrape against my nerves with every second that passed. Fear wrapped around my limbs, making it so I didn't dare lift my head. I was so screwed. I bit my lip to stop it from trembling. I'd lose my job and would be branded as bad news for any other security gig or any role in general, really.

Haru finally spoke, his voice soft like he was pleading with them. "If we call CSON, what will they do? She's seen too much, even if she doesn't understand, and can we really trust them to take care of this?"

Actually, that was a great question. Could these guys trust CSON at all? It was orders from the higher ups that had me here in the first place. I didn't dare expose that, because I didn't need to get myself in any more trouble. Whichever way the coin dropped, I needed to make sure it favored me, and the less they knew, the better.

"I hate to be the first to admit this, but he has a point," Otto added after a moment.

Finally, I lifted my head, finding honey-brown eyes inspecting me.

"Please," I begged Summer, my desperation meeting his flinty stare. Not my finest moment, but I would be totally screwed if he called CSON. There was no way I'd get my 100k pay out, and I'd probably lose this job, right after probably losing my bartending job. This had really turned into a shit couple of days.

His hard eyes softened, warming to gold and sending an echoing thrill of heat deep into my chest.

"Fine," he said, pocketing his cell phone as he leaned over me.

I shifted back until my back was pressed against the headboard, my hands balled at my hips and ready to attack if needed. Towering over me, he leaned further, putting his hands on either side of my head. The scent of a desert breeze, ripe with hot sand and blooming cacti, washed over me. My breath came in short spurts, but the heat from his closeness was dizzying.

"Don't make me regret it." Summer's warm breath wafted

across my face, stirring the loose hairs that had broken free from my bun. The growl in his voice spiked through me, bringing his heat all the way to my center.

I squeezed my legs together and nodded, unable to speak.

He pulled back, crossing his arms. That one warning was all he needed to give, and the openness of the threat of what he would do . . .

Relief swept through me as he headed for the door, the air seeming crisper and cooling the further they walked away from me.

Winter was right on his heels, like he couldn't stand being in this room with me for a second longer. Haru stepped around the bed and helped Otto to his feet.

I scooted to the edge of the bed, readying to follow them as Summer loomed in the doorway, the others filtering past him. His eyes were back to burning when he glared at me. "You've seen too much. You're staying right here until we can figure out what to do with you."

Over Otto's arm slung around his shoulders, Haru gave me an apologetic look before Summer pulled the door shut.

The door shutting in my face was something I could handle, but my body froze when I heard the lock click into place.

I was trapped.

Chapter Six

The old tumbler style lock sure looked impressive, but it only needed a few pieces moved inside to unlock. They were stiff though, requiring a lot of force applied as carefully as I could. All of this would be pointless if it gave suddenly and I smacked into the door with a bang, alerting them all. I didn't hear anyone posted outside, but they could be using a camera to keep an eye on the door remotely. There was little I could do about that inside the room though.

I moved another tumbler, pushing it back slowly with a hairpin from my bun. Sweat trickled down my neck. Okay, so I had entered the property, but locking me up was absolutely inappropriate.

Who were they? And despite having worked here for years, why had I never seen them enter or leave the house? The answer was wild, impossible, but it had to be some kind of amazing, top secret travel technology. Speaking of tech, the bastards had taken my phone and my badge. I hadn't realized it at the time, and I had rummaged through the room to try to find my things. I had the clothes on my back and that was about all. I had never been more thrilled I had completed extra training in hand to hand combat while everyone else focused on firearms.

With a clunk, the lock finally gave. *Time to go.* Mom and Chris would be really worried by now, and I had to get out of here.

I had turned off the lights ages ago to give my eyes time to adjust to darkness. Easing the door open to dim light and straining to listen to the hallway outside, I stood slowly, silently begging my knees not to click at this crucial moment. I'd have to book it out of here just in case they did have an alarm system set up.

This area of the house had wooden floors and sconces on the walls, of all things. The doors were all wooden, but the locks ranged from filigree detailed door handles and colorful knobs, to stainless steel swipe cards. It was bizarre. Why did they put all these different types of locks in? Wouldn't it both look nicer and be easier to have one kind of key for everything?

I came to a grand staircase in an atrium. Craning my neck up to see three more floors, I nearly gasped at the ceiling. Glass revealed the night sky, the whole Milky Way with stars close enough to touch. I'd never seen the naked night sky without light polluting the view. There were just so many stars.

I wrenched my attention down to the floors below. Only two floors. I put each foot on a step slowly, mindful of every creak, my hands gripping the well-worn wooden banister. How old was this place? It felt like a manor house from a period drama or a French palace, except there were few soft furnishings. I'd expected a red and gold carpet on the stairs at least if this was some kind of mansion made to look like it had been dropped from a period drama set. The way this place mixed old and new, and with such variations of taste, intrigued me in a way that made me wish I could explore more.

The stairs were bare until the next floor where someone had painted two black lines on the wall, one near the ceiling and one near the floor. I frowned. What were they for? I dragged my hand on the smooth wall, feeling the natural bumps and flow of the plaster. The lines were joined by a u shape, turned to the side and building into a pattern as I descended to the next floor. *Scales?*

On the ground floor, the walls burst with glorious color, predominantly blue from peacock and royal through to lighter shades. It was some kind of snake, perhaps, meant to circle with the stairs as they spiraled up the floors. The finished parts down here were beautiful, bright royal blues and iridescent glacier, with hints of gold along the scales.

Rubbing my sweaty hands on my pants, I turned, walking down yet another hall away from this room as quickly as I could while still being silent. Being on edge was exhausting. I would sleep well after this. That is, after I filed a report to my boss. Employers or no, they shouldn't have shut me away, and who knows what they would have done to me if I hadn't escaped before they returned.

Cold crept across my skin, prickling my arms and stealing my breath. Perhaps it was midnight air from an open door somewhere. I felt my way toward it, like some backward game of hot and cold, seeking out the frost instead.

The chill led me down an unlit corridor. The doors here seemed older, more weathered, but as I moved further the frames were cracked and splinters lay on the floor. My left foot slipped slightly when I put it down. Halting, I bent down to brush the slippery surface. Ice so cold it burned, my fingertips stuck with the lightest pressure. I pulled them off, panting, as blue light flared ahead of me.

This corridor was filled with ice, stalactites looming from the ceiling like jagged teeth. I backed away, my breath clouding the air. How was it utterly frozen in here? Ice had covered the walls and doors further down the corridor, finding its way into cracks and pushing them open. The floor was impassable with ice and broken pieces of wood frozen in despair. At the far end of the corridor sat a final door, so covered over I could hardly see the dark oak underneath.

I narrowed my eyes at it. *What could cause something like this? What was behind that door?*

No, no time for questions because it just made me want answers. All I needed to know was that it was a dead end.

I hurried to the first corridor and hustled down it. It opened up into an expansive space like an indoor garden. Actually, just like an indoor garden, with sweet-smelling vines dangling from the ceiling, pink blossoms spiraling to the floor, lush peace lilies lining the walls like guards, and bright orange plants blooming wide. Water trickled somewhere, and that amazing night sky lined the far glass wall. This had to be an indoor-outdoor greenhouse or sunroom, and someone had filled it to bursting with life.

Weaving around the plants carefully, I touched a leaf here or a petal there, soft as silk and pulsing with vibrant life. About halfway into the room sat a snarl of brambles, the thick briars wrapping and encasing something. I peered through, seeing the edge of another doorway. This one's frame collapsed around the door, jamming it from ever opening again. Threading my way around the edges and picking off the thorns that pricked at me, I had to contain my exasperation. Someone had really let this get out of control and needed to tackle a bit of weeding.

Still, it was beautiful in a wild way, like an untouched piece of land left to nature, savage and mysterious. I walked away from it but couldn't help the feeling that prickled up my spine, as if the plants were alert and watching.

Stop it. I forced myself to walk slowly and quietly. It was just my mind playing tricks.

"Hi."

I whirled around, fists up, as Haru approached from the

side. He walked confidently, each step carefully placed, and he didn't trip or stumble on any plants. I backed away, scanning for an exit as my heart thumped. There at the back of this indoor forest was a window big enough for me to fit through, and mercifully open with a big branch of cherry blossoms thrusting through it.

He lifted his hands, empty and palms up. "Hey, you got out at last. I had a feeling you would."

I shifted my weight, ready to lunge forward and kick if I needed to. "How could you know that?"

He winked. *Winked at me.* My stomach fluttered. "You're a Shield, but the way you evaded me was super impressive. You have some fantastic skills! Do you do free running? Maybe capoeira?" He backed up further, putting distance between us, but I also fancied he was luring me away from the door. He looked me up and down. "You look . . . incredible. Fit."

I almost laughed. Almost. He was one of the first people whose initial response to my form was 'fit', and the irony it was from someone who could be a literal model wasn't lost on me.

He spun in place gracefully, then flopped backward onto the long, low couch covered in moss. It gave a little crunch, like he'd landed on hay. "I'm tired. It's been a rough day. Did you get any rest at all?"

"Tell me where the exits are," I ordered, my voice low to stop it from wobbling. How had he snuck up on me?

As if he hadn't heard, he pointed to another door across the hallway, shadowed in darkness. "I just came back from Venice. It was early there and really quiet."

Wow. More evidence of this super-secret travel technology. "Actual Venice? Like Venice, Italy? What was it like—" I cut off. I couldn't get all travel happy right now!

He was non-threatening where he was, lying sprawled on the couch with his legs wide and planted on the floor, bouncing as if with nervous energy. Quietly confident. "I'd tell you about it, but, uh, we haven't had the best start, have we?" He patted the space next to him in invitation, his smile wide and warm.

I stayed standing, weight balanced evenly and nerves singing, and his lips twisted with sorrow. "I apologize for locking you up earlier. You tied Summer in knots, and he doesn't like it when that happens. But I can promise we won't hurt you."

As much as I wanted to trust his earnest smile, I couldn't. I eyed the window again, only a few steps away. He was only one guy. I'd taken out three at a time in training. It would be a cinch. But . . . I found I didn't want to hurt him, even though I would if he came any closer. Not because he looked delicious, but because of the way he smiled at me. Warmth flooded me each time, like I was the center of someone's world for once.

"Look, I—I know we started off a bit shaky," he tried.

A bit? Kidnapping someone was a bit? I opened my mouth to give him a verbal lashing, but I hesitated. He wasn't immediately trying to grab me, and he seemed to want to talk. If I could keep him distracted long enough, I could get closer to the window before I turned tail and peaced out of here.

He took my silence for interest and continued, "Our choices are: we keep running from or imprisoning each other, which will probably end in one of us getting the shit kicked out of us and Summer will never let us forget it," he paused, smiling ruefully, "or we can maybe start over." He held out his hand, as if I could shake it half a room apart. "Hi, I'm Haru. Why'd you break into our house?"

That floored me, because, heck, I had to admit it was funny. "Well," I said, trying to lighten my voice and make it seem like I was coming around, "you got my phone number, but you didn't give me yours. How else was a girl meant to get in contact with you?"

An eyebrow raised slightly, along with his spreading smile. I could tell he didn't really believe me but he would listen to see where I was going with this.

"I just couldn't wait any longer," I said, raising a hand to my forehead dramatically.

This time he broke into laughter, the sound warming me like spring sunshine. He tried to stifle it. "Oh dear, you are a handful." He finally composed himself, and once again the heat in his eyes spoke right to my core. "Can I tell you something?"

"Uh . . . sure." I took another side step, one pace closer to the window. Good, my tactic of playing nice was working.

He leaned back, hands behind his head. "You got them all shaken up, It was amazing." He inclined his head toward the rest of the house. "The guys, I mean. I've been telling them we needed something new, something different, but I never imagined it would take a break-in to stir them from their stumps. And I can definitely say their stumps are stirred." He grinned, and the vines shivered gently. Was there a breeze in here? Must be from the window.

"Glad to hear I've made an impression," I returned with a shrug.

"Yes, you have. And I want to know more. Much more." This time the interest in his eyes was undeniable. His body angled toward mine, muscles flexing under his tight shirt, and my eyes wandered from my goal and over his shoulders. I did like shoulders in a guy . . .

No, Mari, focus! I took another step, pretending to examine the plants and turning my back to him. I knew his eyes went straight to my ass, and I gave it a little shimmy as if stepping over a root. His jaw nearly dropped as I glanced over my shoulder, swallowing hard as he wrenched his eyes from my backside to my gaze.

Darkness must have skewed my vision because I tripped over a root, ivy tangling on my arm. I yanked, but somehow I only got myself more wrapped up.

"Oops, sorry," Haru said, rocketing up and pacing toward me. "Hang on, I'll help pull the plants off you." His arm brushed mine, and I swear his breath caught. The flowers swelled in my vision as their aroma intensified, intoxicating honeysuckle mixed with pure man scent. He tugged at the rope of ivy, and I was jerked with it, straight against his chest. He steadied me, hands flexing on my shoulders.

My breath hitched as he loomed over me. I glanced at the window again. I didn't want to hurt him, but if I could squeeze through there, he definitely could, so it didn't leave me much of a choice.

It was now or never.

I spun out of his grip before he could think better of it and using the momentum, I flexed my hand and brought the heel of my palm to his nose.

A crack echoed through the space.

"Ow! Fuck!" His hands flew to his face, which was already dripping red.

I kicked my foot around, swiping his feet out from under him. He crashed into a bush, looking rather surprised, but I didn't stop to see if there was added damage.

"Sorry, not sorry," I said then squeezed out of the window, breathing in the night air in a relieved gasp.

I ignored the guilt clogging my chest and ran like hell.

I HUSTLED BACK over the fence to the compound for my car but those guys had taken my keys. I'd have to jog home. Fortunately it was only a few miles back to Stowe, even if it was all uphill. Perhaps I should ask the night shift for help?

No. I broke into the place I was supposed to be guarding, and the guy outside the bar had made me burn the orders so there was no proof now. I probably shouldn't file a police report either, even though they'd kidnapped me.

Damn, damn, damn.

Still, I'd be lucky to keep both of my jobs at this rate. My phone was probably blowing up with calls from Ryan asking me where the fuck I was; not out of any concern for my well-being, of course.

As I started the jog, my anger melted to a softer, more triumphant feeling. I'd done what was asked of me *and* trumped those guys, whoever they were. The familiar streets opened up in front of me, and I ran faster. I was only a couple blocks away from home. My phone was probably on to the triple digits with missed calls from Mom. I tried not to think too much about that. I was headed toward her now, getting closer every step.

Finally, I walked the stairs up to our apartment, not wanting to wake anyone and legs shaking. What time was it? I slowed my gasping breaths and knocked on the door.

"Mari? Christopher?" A bang and some thuds sounded as Mom leapt to the door, and I winced for her sore legs. She must be panicking. She slid the bolt and flung the door open, eyes awash with tears and cheeks blotched red. "Where were you? What happened?" She hiccupped.

"I had to do a special assignment, and they took my phone. I've lost my keys." Technically all true statements. "I had to run home. I'm sorry."

She wiped her face, movement jerky with anger. "They couldn't let you call, or they couldn't call me? Or—or—" She huffed, and my anger flamed. Those guys had scared my Mom, cutting us off from one another. *Assholes.*

"It'll be okay, come on. I'm alright, Mom." I guided her in, but she grabbed my forearm.

"Christopher," She sobbed, "he hasn't come home either."

I snapped to full awareness, adrenaline pumping and making all exhaustion flee. "What do you mean?"

"He said he was going for a walk to clear his head. You know how he works so hard." She could barely speak through the tears as I walked her to our sagging sofa. It was the first time I'd ever heard he went for walks. He was always locked in his room studying. But then again, I was always out working.

"Where would he usually walk?"

"He mentions the Lamoille River a lot." Mom shook as she sat down. "But I didn't ask him. I didn't check with him! Why didn't I check where he was going?"

There wasn't time for what-ifs and regrets. "I'm going to get him," I promised Mom, storming back into the early morning. This was way too late for Chris, and on a school night too. Maybe something happened, but I'd rather be fuming at him than paralyzed with terror as Mom was.

I thumped down the street headed for the riverside, keeping my anger in check but using it to fuel my unrelenting pace. I could run forever, silencing the doubts swirling in my head at any time, but now my mind was overrun with what could have kept Chris so long. I made it in mere minutes and scanned the scrubby banks along the smooth, flowing river. Cars parked in a circle alerted me to people a quarter of a mile downriver. Maybe they had seen Chris? I approached, wiping my clammy hands on my clothes, until a shout snapped me into combat mode.

"You hear me, asslicker? Or do I need to kick some sense

into you?"

I knew a threat when I heard one. The silhouette in the center of the unwavering glare of the headlights slowly extended its arms up in surrender and recognition turned my blood cold. *Oh shit.* I ran as quickly and silently as I could.

"Look, I don't want any trouble," Chris said, his voice clear but trembling, as anyone's would be. "I quit. I'm not ferrying this stuff around for you."

"This stuff? It's important medicine!" The guy speaking was sitting on the hood of a car, the humming of the engine a low purr under his words. He shook a small white bottle at Chris. Pills? *What the fuck?* What was Chris doing with drug dealers?

"I'm done, Darren," Chris replied firmly.

Darren slid off the car. He was a head taller than my little brother—way taller than me. "You're not done until I say you're done. You owe me, Brainiac."

"I'm not—don't call me that." Chris' hands rolled into fists.

Oh, shit, Chris, don't fight them! I hadn't taught him anything about combat. He tried judo for a few months before we had to pull him out to use the fees for something else.

Darren laughed, tipping his head back and exposing the thick, ugly tattoos on his throat. His buddies laughed along, probably at least one per car but the blinding light from the car headlights hid how many there were. Chris had balls, I'd give him that. But he'd lose all street kudos when his big sister swung in to save him.

"Enough!" I bellowed in my Army Sergeant voice. Darren jolted and Chris flinched, shoulders leaping, then spun around to face me.

The relief in his face made it worth it. "Mari? Mari!"

"Your girlfriend?" Darren shaded his eyes to sneer at me as I stomped into the circle.

"None of your business." I jerked my chin at Chris. "We are going now." I turned to lead the way out, but three guys slid in my path.

"Mmm, nope," Darren said with a snort.

"She has nothing to do with this!" Chris shouted, outraged.

Aw, he expected them to play fair. Bless his innocent self. I shifted my weight and tensed my muscles. Maybe not so innocent, depending on what was going on here. I raised an eyebrow at Chris.

He seemed to realize how deep the shit we were in was and hurried to say, "Adderall. That's all, I promise."

"Adderall? But . . . why?" Of course I knew why. I hadn't shielded him from feeling the pressure, the weight of all our hopes and dreams resting on him. I had sacrificed so much for him and he'd seen that, transmuting what I thought was opportunity for him to grow into pressure to perform. "Chris," I said softly, tears clogging my throat.

He hung his head. "They want me to start running it into other students, but you can get expelled for that. I—I won't."

"Good, but let's talk later," I told him under my breath. I couldn't afford to be distracted even as my world tumbled to pieces at my feet. I quickly assessed the exits from the circle of cars. There were five cars, but three to four guys in each opening between them. *Damnit.* I couldn't take this many.

Swallowing hard to steady my nerves, I said with more confidence than I felt, "Move out of the way."

"No 'please'? That's not very nice," Darren said with a leer. He took a baseball bat from the bed of a truck. *Double shit.* "I need to break his arm at least, for being a chicken motherfucker."

"We will press charges," I warned. "I'm wearing a button cam. I work security and it's recording." I hoped they would at least hesitate in the face of my lie.

"Cool, I've always wanted to be on camera." He shook his head with a grin, greasy locks flying. "That just means I gotta strip you down and burn your stuff, idiot." He reached for me.

I blocked his arm and punched him in the stomach, and he staggered back from the force. I coupled that with a kick to the side, where my senses told me some guy was coming up fast. I caught one of Darren's friends in the balls, and he crumpled like an empty chip packet.

"Wow, Mari." Chris gaped at me.

I couldn't help my answering grin, but then I had to duck as Darren's baseball bat whistled over my head.

"Bitch!" Darren screamed. "Cut them up!" he ordered his goons, and my heart lurched as steel glinted wickedly in the headlights. Many of the gang pulled knives from their waistbands. *Fuck.* Now I had no choice but to hit hard and not stop.

I kicked, aiming for their hands so they'd drop the knives, but there were way too many. My back bumped up against Chris and he grabbed my arm tight, fear shining in his face. I leaned back in a side kick, breathing like a freight train. I couldn't slow, couldn't stop. I couldn't fail Chris.

Someone slashed and caught my boot, but I sent his knife clanging to the ground. A hand grabbed my throat, causing me to choke. Rolling my head back, I saw Chris struggling with a knife to his cheek, Darren's grin getting wider with triumph.

No. No! I grabbed hold of my attacker's arm but darkness swarmed across my vision. My heart beat banged against his hard fingers and a scream lodged in my throat, unable to erupt.

The guy suddenly dropped me.

I hit the ground, coughing and spluttering. Long thin shapes flickered like a mirage in front of me, outlined by the garish lights of the cars. Were those whips? I curled my hand into the grass underneath me, which throbbed in time with my thundering heart.

And then a man stood above me. My fist arced but he snatched my wrist, bending down low.

"Are you alright?" Haru panted. His eyes searched mine, then swept down over my body, free hand patting for a wound. "Are you hurt?"

Despite the circumstances, or maybe because of them—dancing close to danger being just as heart pumping—my chest swelled with delight, tears filling with joyous relief. I swept them away before he could see and tried to get to my feet, wavering only once. "I'm fine."

He threaded his arm underneath mine and helped me stand, holding me in a firm support. "I've got you. You're lucky I found you when I did."

I pressed away from him when I was steady and blinked slowly at the devastation around me as my mind focused. The cars were covered in a blanket of shrubbery like they'd been abandoned for years despite the light filtering between the leaves. There was no sign of the gang except for dropped knives, tangled in vines, and snatches of clothes hanging off wicked thorns.

"What the . . ." I stumbled against Haru, but he didn't falter.

Instead he wrapped one arm around my waist, the other running through his mop of hair. "Uh... I can explain."

"Explain *this?*" I fixed him with a glare, but a new fear gripped my stomach, as prickly as the thorns that surrounded us. What had Haru done, and who or what were the guys I had guarded in that house? No wonder they kidnapped me because of what I might know. Now I'd seen even more.

Haru looked resigned, sad even. "I'm glad I got to you in time."

"Where's my brother?" I rasped. "Chris? Where are you?"

Haru gestured to a limp form nearby.

I fell to my knees next to my brother, a sob forming as I desperately looked for a knife wound to staunch. He had a nasty cut on his forehead, but fortunately it was shallow.

Haru touched my shoulder, a wave of warmth flooding my side as he hunkered down next to him. "He's okay. I could see he was in too much to handle on his own, just like you. Although you have some mad skills, especially when you took me by surprise at the house." He scrubbed his face. "Argh, I'm babbling. He fainted when he saw you in trouble, and I didn't let any plants attack him, is what I mean to say, because you seemed to be working together."

I pulled my bandages from my pants' pocket, ripping off a stretch with my teeth. "Didn't let plants do what?" I asked as I patched Chris up, half distracted with my brother.

The plants around us shivered and then spiraled up, growing taller. I sucked in a breath, scrambling away, as Haru lifted his hands. The grass headed toward him, twisting and seeking, and he ran a hand through it.

"I can accelerate growth," Haru explained quietly. "Among other things. It's why I could heal my broken nose so quickly."

My pounding heart took on a new timbre, one that sang of the danger of the unknown, but also excitement. "You can?"

"Mmhmm." He sat back on his heels, sweat rolling down his forehead as he settled his hands back in his lap, long fingers twisting with nervous tension. "Look, you've seen too much, okay? But I've never seen a Shield like you before, with actual proper skills. Mostly they seem to hire career nobodies."

Ouch. I gritted my teeth and tried not to glare at him.

"You could be really useful! I'll point that out to Summer. It can be the proper explanation why you're no longer allowed to go out on patrol anymore, and why you'll have to stay in the house with us until we get to know each other and our motivations better." He cast his hand over Chris's peacefully sleeping form. "You've got your hands full, I can see that. But we can help with your family too." He stayed hunkered beside me, leaning forward eagerly, hands clasped between his knees.

Help? What kind of help? "Look, I don't know what tech you've got, or who the fuck you are." I leaned over Chris, protecting him with my body. "But my family is not a part of this, understand?"

His eyes sparkled with hurt. He was captivating, I'd give him that much. Even tired he held himself easily, confidence and enthusiasm dampened but not extinguished, until I'd said that to him.

He steeled himself, as if a mask came down over his face. "Fine. I'm sorry, but it's too late. You've seen too much. I've offered olive branches multiple times, and all I can tell you is we . . . *I* would want to help you. I'm not saying we give each other all the answers right away, but we build that first little seed of trust. The foundation to everything else." He nodded to Chris. "We will make sure they are comfortable, okay?"

My heart drummed, trying to think hard. *Shit.* He had his hand around my family's throat and knew just what to say, and there were more of them. I wouldn't be able to defend against them all.

Why had I taken those orders? My life was in tatters now, and I might even take my family down with me. From a hundred thousand dollars to buried underneath feral plants. I glanced back at the covered cars and shivered until the hair on the nape of my neck stood on end.

What choice did I have?

"Fine," I ground out. "But just me. You leave them alone. They haven't seen anything and I haven't told them anything."

"Right. I believe you," Haru said, standing up. That smile was gone, and in its place was a wary, colder look. "Let's get back to the house."

Chapter Seven

Haru picked Chris up, slung over his shoulder like a bag of dog food.

"I can take him," I insisted as I led Haru back to our apartment.

He looked me up and down, brown eyes searing with anger, need, or something else I wasn't sure of. "I know you can, but I got it."

I pressed my lips into a hard line. "I know I'm short and stocky, but I can break a man's neck with my thighs."

Haru's lips quirked up. "I have no doubt about that." His gaze landed on my thighs and slowly moved to the curve of my ass before flitting back up to my face.

Strangely, I didn't mind him looking. "I'm serious," I said even as warmth spread in a wave up my body.

"I know." His face was the most serious I'd seen it.

"Including yours," I threatened, even though I knew it didn't hold much merit. I frowned at his nose. It now had a small groove on the bridge from where it had been reset. He must have done it himself with how quickly he got here. I had to give him credit for that.

"It'll heal quick enough," he noted with a shrug.

Flustered, I quickly turned my head. "I—I'm not worried about that." I didn't want him to see the guilt on my face. He and his behemoth friends needed to know I wasn't someone to mess with, and showing all my cards would mess that up. Hell, he already had figured out my family was my weakness. I didn't need to give them any other pieces of myself.

"Does this mean you plan to put up a fight after we drop your brother off?" Haru watched my face, like he was memorizing it—or something. Either way, having his full attention on me had my stomach twisting.

Swallowing, I said, "Are you going to do as you said and leave my family alone if I come willingly?"

"Actually, I said we'd do one better and make sure they were taken care of." He smiled, but I didn't reciprocate the gesture and soon it fell away. "Yes, you have my word," he said, solemn.

"Fine." I quickened my steps to walk a few paces ahead. We were almost home and I needed to clear my head before seeing mom.

Once back home, my hand shook on the door knob. How was I going to explain what happened? It would kill mom to know what Chris was caught up in, but I needed her to look over him too.

Haru, either sensing or noticing my hesitation, leaned over my shoulder, his breath tickling the shell of my ear. "We will take care of them. That includes making sure Chris stays away from poor decisions."

I scrunched my shoulders from his closeness, trying to ignore the way it made my heart patter, and pulled away, throwing a glare over my shoulder. "I got it. This is *my* family. I'll take care of it," I snapped.

Haru's face darkened, his eyes losing their twinkle, as he shuttered himself away. "Right."

My chest ached as guilt planted itself there. Just because they would help my family didn't mean we were friends. He wasn't giving me much choice but to go with them, and that didn't mean I would be a nice house guest.

Taking a steadying breath, I opened the door. My mom was there in an instant, her swollen eyes widening when she took in Haru and then Chris on his shoulder.

"Oh my! What happened?" She ushered us inside. "Come, come. Lay him down on the couch."

Haru followed the instructions silently, moving away immediately after he'd let Chris slide down. Mom immediately went into action, checking his vitals and looking underneath the bandages. "He seems to be alright." She released a relieved breath and my shoulders dropped as well.

I put my hand on her shoulder. "He'll be fine, but make sure you keep an extra eye on him for a while. Maybe don't let him go anywhere except school for a couple weeks."

She looked up at me, jaw going slack. "You mean ground him?"

I grimaced because, yes, that was exactly what I meant.

"But why? What happened? Where was he?" Her attention turned to Haru, quickly taking in his broken nose. "Did he do this?"

Haru opened his mouth but I cut in, giving him a glare in hopes he'd pick up on the 'shut the fuck up' face. "No, no, he didn't. And you don't need to worry about what happened. Chris is fine and that's all that matters." I hated that I was downplaying this. That I was hiding things from my mom. But was I really supposed to just reveal my brother's association with drugs and then dip? I couldn't do that to her.

"I don't understand." Tears welled in her eyes, different seeds of guilt turning into trees that threatened to burst from my chest.

I pulled my mom into a hug. "It'll be fine. Promise. And

keep an eye out for a check," I looked over at Haru who nodded. "It'll tide you over for a while."

My mom pulled back. "Wait what's happening?"

I brushed my hair out of my face. "I'm, uh, gonna be gone for a while. Work thing." A good lie was built on a half-truth. "So, like I said, keep an extra eye on Chris and I'll contact you when I can."

And who the hell knew when that would be with my newfound situation. But as long as they were okay, as long as they were taken care of, that was what mattered. Standing, I left my mom beside Chris with her pale face aghast as I walked away, her expression seared into my brain forever as I shut the door.

"I fucking hate you," I murmured to Haru, swiping at my stinging eyes, but vines could come ripping through the house or something at any moment. And what tech or powers or whatever did the others have? I hated I was leaving my family at a time like this. I hated that I was being given little to no choice. And I hated the reason this was all happening. *I should have never gone into that damn house.*

Haru jolted like I'd struck him, and I swear the pain I saw on his face was even more than when I had broken his nose.

I SAT bolt upright in bed. Shit, had I missed my alarm? I scrambled for my phone, fingers swiping against soft silk. That wasn't right. My sheets could be considered cotton knock-offs with how scratchy they were.

My surroundings caught up with me. I was back in the big room with the paintings of the brook during different seasons. My heart dropped immediately.

Damn it. I bet Ryan was having a cow since I didn't show up for my shift last night, and apparently wouldn't be any time soon, so I was as good as fired. Perhaps when this was all over and with the right amount of begging, I could get it back. I thought of my grade A a-hole boss. On second thought, I doubted it.

I flopped back down to regroup and prepare myself mentally because, boy, was I going to need it. I skittered away from the memory of breaking Haru's nose, escaping, getting home, tracking down Chris only to get overwhelmed, and then Haru doing whatever weird science miracle magic he did. Then my mother's face as I left. Pressing the heels of my hands against my temples, I breathed deeply and evenly. It was some kind of trick. It had to be.

Right?

My gut said something else was going on. Something I didn't yet understand. As I relaxed, a lovely, refreshing scent filled my nostrils. *Coffee?*

Removing my hands from my face I noticed a golden tray sitting on the sideboard, a silver French press and a ceramic mug in the center.

Yes! Laying across the bed was a thick cotton bathrobe wrapped with a red ribbon. Was this for me? I touched the edges of the soft fabric, then pulled my hand away. Probably not, right?

Balanced against the side of the French press was a letter, with the letter M scrawled along the side. Now this *had* to be for me. I opened the thick white envelope. The paper was weighty like a court summons, with looping handwriting weaving all over the page.

Mari,

I brought you some coffee, but sleep as long as you need. It doesn't look like you get very much.

Yeah, because I looked like shit.

The letter continued:

Not that you look bad in any way. Anyway, breakfast is downstairs when you're ready. Take your time. There's toiletries in the bathroom for you to use and warm towels on the rail. We will need to sort something for you to wear, so the bathrobe will have to work. Best I can do for now.

It was signed "H." with a daisy as the period. It certainly sounded like Haru. All stream of consciousness but thoughtful all the same. This was . . . well, it was almost sweet, if I discounted the fact that they were holding me against my will. And they had some kind of super tech. And I was still pissed.

I fucking hate you. I winced at the words and at the way Haru had reacted. They were bitter, angry words, and even though I meant them at the moment, some of my anger had died away since. Was this ideal? No. But I would get through this and get back to my family. I just needed to keep reminding myself of that.

The coffee was still warm, just the right temperature to wrap my hands around the mug when I poured it. Inhaling the sharp bitter steam, I took that first, all-restoring sip, trying to ease the tightness in my stomach.

I suppose they could have thrown me in a dungeon somewhere—no doubt this house had one of those—but Haru must have come in here while I was sleeping to deliver the coffee, robe, and note. *How out was I?*

It was clear Haru didn't know what to do with me, but I guess I preferred his attempts to talk over, say, Winter and his methods. Maybe I should have taken the chance to get Haru on my side instead of slapping him down over and over again. Another wave of regret slammed through me at what I had said to him.

Sighing, I decided to take a shower to clear my head. The power of the water sluiced over my skin and flattening my hair to my face.

Right. Four guys lived here, and I had never seen them before even though I guarded this place. And believe me, I would have noticed these guys. I had to keep them unsuspecting, believing me to be cowed. I would work on Haru first. He seemed eagerly open. A twinge sliced through me at the thought of using him, at his warm smile and easy way of making conversation, but I pushed it down.

I picked up the soft robe. Would wearing this give me an advantage?

Not at your size.

Fears bubbled up inside me that they would be repulsed if I wore a bathrobe around the house. But my only other option were the clothes that I'd been yesterday, sweaty from my multiple fights and flights. Feeling super self-conscious, I put it on and, before I could second-guess myself, pulled the door handle. It was unlocked.

Chapter Eight

I shouldn't have been surprised with Haru's invite, but I still stuck my head out first to make sure it wasn't some trick. Creeping out of my room, I shut my door as quietly as I did last night, still feeling out of place in this house.

I was essentially a captive who had been invited to breakfast. What kind of Beauty and the Beast shit was this? How the hell was I supposed to find breakfast in the mansion anyway? It's not like my escape last night helped me make any sense of this maze—I blinked at the floor, my mind blanking.

Grass and clover blanketed the carpet, making a clear path screaming "this way." That had to be ruining the floorboards. I followed it curiously, dandelions and daisies appearing further on, and then a whole slew of buttercups down the stairs. Had Haru done this? By accident or to lead me to breakfast? Seemed a bit extreme when he could have left a map.

Once I got to the lower level past the half-finished dragon painting, I recognized the wide hallway leading to what seemed to be the living areas, including the sun room. A little further on came sounds of sizzling food, smells of doughy bread, and a hiss of water being poured.

I paused outside the threshold, not daring to take another step as I listened closer.

"You are definitely not yourself." Otto's accent stood out, but so did the rasp in his voice, like he'd been coughing all night. My heart twinged for him.

Haru's voice was even worse "Neither are you."

"I have an excuse. I had to use a large amount of power."

A clatter by a plate on the counter was followed by Winter's gruff order, "Eat."

"Not first thing, Winter," Otto demurred gently.

"No excuses," Winter barked. "Eat. And you, Haru."

"I'm not hungry." Haru's voice sounded muffled.

I poked my head around the corner where the voices came from, steeling myself to face the guys again. What room would they all be sitting in? A torture chamber?

The sight of a massive kitchen, easily as large as the apartment I shared with Mom and Chris, stole my breath. The ceiling had a massive sunroof, the white and silver appliances gleaming like a show home.

Winter held court in the middle, moving from the stovetop to the guys at the breakfast bar and back like a mother hen. Otto slumped like a drunk trying to get to the last dregs of his drink before bar closing time, a blanket wrapped around his shoulders. I couldn't see Haru's expression as his back was to me, but he held his head in his hands in front of an array of breakfast goods set out on the counter top. Winter slid a sausage onto a plate and placed it next to his elbow. Haru nudged it away, shaking his head and Winter glowered at him.

"Eat!"

"I don't feel like it," Haru replied, and a fuzz of dandelions sprung up on the counter. He spouted a rapid-fire tirade of Japanese, what I presumed to be swearwords from his tone.

Otto reached out a hand toward the greenery, but Winter seized his wrist, shaking his head. Winter glared at the plants like the intruders they were—so, exactly like he looked at me—and they withered into frost-blackened stems. Shit, whatever Winter did killed those plants like it was nothing, and I didn't see any tech on any of them.

Was that my fate? I drew my robe tighter around myself, as if that flimsy thing could protect me. *We're definitely not in Kansas anymore, Toto.* The world I thought I understood opened wider like crocodile jaws.

Haru's hands curled into fists. "Thanks, I guess."

Otto winced as he shifted in his seat. Was he in pain? "Haru, your emotions are bleeding everywhere. Can you please try to find an even keel, just while I'm nearby?"

What did that mean?

"Can you blame me?" Haru cried. "Look, we have a damn captive upstairs. What are we going to do?"

Winter scowled, glancing at Otto. Otto wrapped his long fingers around his mug, peering in as if that held the future. "I don't know," Otto replied honestly, "but we still have our roles to fulfill."

Roles? What? Like taking hostages?

My teeth clenched.

Haru lifted his head to glare at him. His face and eyes were puffy, as if he'd had hardly any sleep. He did look much reduced rather than his energized self yesterday. "Aren't you going to take some of your own advice and skedaddle off to the southern hemisphere?"

"When I can manage it."

"That'll put you behind schedule," Winter pointed out to him.

"It can't be helped," Otto replied, rather exasperated.

Winter ran a hand over his tied back hair, making his bicep flex and the tattoos there expand. He also seemed stressed, eyeing both Otto and Haru. He only relaxed when Otto slid a bite of oatmeal into his mouth. Putting both hands on the counter, he ducked lower to catch Haru's eye. There was a softness in Frosty's gaze. "Eat, Haru."

Haru shook his head. "I don't take that kind of order from you."

"Haru, eat *ahora*," a voice behind me intoned. The way he rolled his 'r''s half made me wonder what else could be done with that tongue.

I spun, fighting stance at the ready and launching a punch, but his fist deflected mine, a strong hand gripping my wrist.

I looked up into Summer's grimace, close enough to see the dusting of a five o'clock shadow on his jawline. His attention fixed on the bathrobe I was wearing, now straining against its ties.

His hot gaze trailed up to my face. "Good morning at last, Ms. Intruder," he rumbled. "I was beginning to wonder if you'd ever wake up."

The low threat in his voice made the skin on the back of my neck shiver. "Room service is a bit lacking," I said, the best I could come up with on short notice.

His gaze traveled down my lips to my neck, lingering over my cleavage. "Room service, eh?" He leaned in, his heat washing over my skin. My nipples pebbled instantly, rubbing against the robe with every breath sending shooting sparks deep in my core. My back was against the wall, and if he took my wrists and raised them—*Shit, I couldn't be thinking like this!*

The dark desire in his eyes flickered, a mirror to mine, before I turned my head away. Haru and Otto had come to the threshold of the kitchen, both of them staring at me and my arm in Summer's grasp.

Summer eased back from pressing me against the wall,

loosening his grip on me. "Seems our intruder got out again," he said, voice low and dangerous but directed at Haru.

"I didn't exactly lock the door," Haru grumbled with an eyeroll.

"You should, before she breaks something else." Summer put the tip of his index finger on the end of Haru's button nose, then flicked it up to flip Haru's messy fringe. "You look like shit."

"Good morning to you too." Haru stepped back, letting Summer breeze on past, and watched me warily, thumbs hooked into his low slung jeans. "And you, unless you're going to bite my head off for that."

"Only when I haven't had my coffee," I returned. I shifted my weight, uncertain. He seemed as worried and confused as me, but I couldn't have any pity for him. He was one of the perpetrators.

He raised an arm to gesture me into the kitchen. "Come in. Grab some breakfast." As I passed him, he definitely took a quick breath in, his gaze darting down to the bottom of the robe.

Flustered by Summer and trying not to show it, I pulled up to the breakfast bar next to Otto, who settled slowly on a stool, and Summer in the space on my other side. I scanned the food on offer, especially surrounding Haru—French toasts to crumpets, bacon and eggs to what looked like a salad.

Winter grunted at me as he put a plate of toasted bread in front of Otto. "Eat."

"Go on," Summer said. He rolled his eyes as he took in my stony expression. "We aren't going to starve or poison you. At least, not until we work out what to do with you."

Again, that should have jangled all my threat-alarms, but my gut told me his bark was worse than his actual bite. I slid off the stool and stepped closer to him, toe to toe, and relished in how his eyebrows shot up under the artful flop of his hair. "Still not decided?" I asked, giving him a sweet smile.

He couldn't back away. I knew guys like him refuse to in case it damaged their ego. To my surprise, the smile he gave me was respectful with a hint of amusement mixed with something deeper. "Go on. Eat," he said, folding his arms across his massive chest and daring me with a crook of his lips.

I sank slowly into a bar stool.

"Good girl." The rumble of words was under his breath, causing surprise to course through me and heat prickle my skin, and I shifted in my seat trying not to tug at my bathrobe, just in case I accidentally undid it. I didn't feel completely safe sitting right opposite a guy who could be a literal wolf-wrestling Viking, judging from the muscles, tats, and long hair in braids, but I also remembered Haru's promise from yesterday. I glanced at the others, trying to gauge whether they were on board with not hurting me. Summer's face was smooth, eyes smoldering as he watched me. Winter was so still he could've been an ice sculpture, giving nothing away.

Meanwhile, Otto looked positively green, giving the toast a glum look. "Are you feeling alright?" I asked him. Was he getting sick? Is that why they stayed in the house? Why he needed to go down south? Maybe it was for some kind of special treatment.

He frowned at me, brows rumpled with confusion. "Fine. Why do you ask?"

I put my hands flat on the cold countertop. "Um. You didn't look all that well yesterday and still don't, is all."

He glanced at Haru and then at Summer, who settled on the far side of Haru, before his brown eyes settled on me again. "I suppose I should say thank you for the concern, but we still have something of a headache to deal with."

"An enigma. A puzzle." Haru put his chin in his hand.

Otto shook his head, setting his mug down with a hard clink. "Be serious for once, Haru."

"I am. Dead serious," Haru said, but I'd evidently drawn attention to Otto, and Haru peered at him. "Hey, man, you do look pretty rough."

"So do you from being up all night," Otto retorted.

They were like housemates, bickering and bantering in equal measure, but I saw real concern in Haru's face as he looked at Otto, and, in the corner of my eye, how Summer watched me with them.

Haru shook himself and turned back to me. "I guess it falls to me to be host. What do you fancy for breakfast?"

I sat forward on the stool, trying to see into the kitchen without losing balance. I didn't want to take anything away from Otto or Haru. "What are my options?"

Winter yanked open the fridge door, large enough that I'd need muscles like his to open it. He pointed into the interior as he glowered at me.

"Uh . . . okay." I peered into the fridge from my perch. It was well stocked with cold cuts of meats, wrapped packages that could be cheeses, and branded products; peppy bottles of Orangina next to Tropicana, and some other bottles marked in what looked like Thai script. Honestly, I would've been fine with cereal but I was feeling a little cheeky. If my captors wanted to feed me, then so be it.

Boldly, I met Winter's icy gaze. "What would you recommend?"

He blinked once then grabbed a bottle from the fridge. He twisted the neck with savage force and poured the hissing bottle into a glass. When he placed it in front of me, I half expected him to slam it, so I flinched back a little. "Thanks." I took a sip. "Ooh. Blood orange?"

Winter grunted, turning away.

I licked my lips. "Perhaps that was a yes grunt, but it's fifty-fifty, so that could be a no grunt," I hedged.

Haru stifled a chuckle. "That's a yes grunt. The no grunts are more pronounced." He looked exactly as he had in the bar when he asked for my number, smiling and confident, and my stomach flipped.

Even Summer and Otto smiled, and Summer gave me a more considering look. Winter turned away and hacked at a thick granary loaf, sawing through it with terrible intensity. I winced, but the bread was uncrushed with his apparent anger. He speared the two slices, laid them on a skillet, before shoving it into the mouth of the ancient looking oven.

"Is that an Aga?" I'd always loved the sound of the oven and home heating system I'd heard of in Britain, which sounded great to me. Cooked food and kept you warm? Bliss.

Otto turned his gaze to me, his brows rising, an impressed look mixing with his nauseated one.

Winter grumbled again, the same timbre as last time.

"A yes grunt," I diagnosed before leaning closer. "Wow, I've always wanted to see an Aga."

"Well, now you can," Haru said, voice grim again as he reminded everyone of my predicament.

"*Debes estar bromeando.*" Summer swallowed a glug of his orange juice and set the glass back down firmly. "She's not going to get a guided tour of the house looking at pipes, Haru. That's the last thing we should give a would-be burglar."

"I'm not a burglar," I grumbled, picking at the sleeve of my robe. "I didn't steal anything." Technically. I just put it into another room of the house. Although if they all led to different places in the world, who knew where that key was now?

Not that I gave a shit.

Summer pushed back from the counter. "I have to meet with the consulate today."

Otto perked up a little. "I can come. I—"

"No, Otto. Stay here. Rest, *amigo*." Summer shook his head at the other man.

Otto curled in on himself with a heavy sigh. "I suppose I could use another day to recover. I'll be in the library."

"We know where to find you." Summer said. "Haru, you're on the ascent, so, as much as it pains me to say it, Ms. Intruder is your problem while I'm out."

Hurt flashed over Haru's face for just a moment, so quick I almost thought I imagined it. "It pains you to say what?"

"That you're going to have to contain her." Summer glared at me. "And if you try anything, *chica*, you're toast."

A plate of toasted bread landed next to my hand with a clang, and this time I jumped. Winter scowled at me before setting out jellies, honey, and butter on the counter. Actual yellow butter, served in a dish that looked like a cow.

I raised my eyes to meet Winter's gaze, but he was already moving away, busy tidying up.

"I can take care of it, Summer. It doesn't need to pain you to say it." Haru's voice was light, but underneath even I could hear the undercurrent of hurt.

Summer focused on me, that smoldering gaze like a lit fuse. "This is your one and only warning, Ms. Intruder, or should I call you an escape artist now? Although I admire your handiwork on Haru, I wouldn't suggest laying a hand on him again. I will make you regret it."

Summer walked away without a backward glance. Man, that arrogant asshole just rode roughshod over everyone.

Haru looked around desperately. "Winter, what are you up to today?"

"Busy," Winter mumbled, glancing over at Otto.

The latter tumbled off the barstool, weaving on his feet, and I grabbed his chest in case he fell. "Whoa there. You okay?"

"Uh," Otto gently placed his arms on my shoulders, steadying himself, "feeling a little under the weather, it seems." He had a solid weight to him, leaning in against me. We were pressed chest to chest, and I swear I heard his heartbeat trembling against mine. One hell of a body must be under all that tweed . . . *Stop! Hell, I was so attention starved I was melting at my captors? Jeez.*

Winter was suddenly opposite me pulling Otto to him, that stony gaze accusing as if I'd hurt Otto or something. Otto let me go with something like curiosity in his face. As if I were a puzzle he had to work out. He kept his gaze locked on mine as Winter led him away. Hell, they were the puzzle, all scattering with half stories littered behind them. I was no closer to answers, and there was nothing for me to do today.

Haru let out a long, low breath. "And then there were two, and I guess I'm in charge for the day." He buried his head in his hands.

Chapter Nine

I checked my black leggings again. They definitely fit, and there would be no riding down and eventual chafing. They were something Haru had dropped off for me right after breakfast along with running shoes, a sports bra, and a tank top—all my size. *Interesting.* Did they have a full wardrobe on hand, or had he gone out to get these?

I headed to the bottom of the stairs to find Haru already there waiting for me. He wore a pair of sneakers and basketball shorts, but on top he was . . . shirtless. His broad shoulders topped a wide chest, which dipped into a chiseled stomach with abs I tried not to count, eventually tapering in that delicious V we all know and love. The crook in his nose was still there from me breaking it, something that would probably stay with him for life, yet it only accentuated his stark features rather than detract.

Damnit. I break his nose and somehow it makes him look even better? And, somehow, he never had any bruising! How? I had no idea but probably more witchcraft and trickery. Screw him and his disarmingly good looks. My gaze traveled back up his marbled muscles to find his mirth-filled eyes staring at me.

Holy crap. This stairway was about to become a slip'n's-lide if I didn't stop staring.

"Just on time," he smirked.

"And what exactly do you have planned?" I folded my arms and cocked my hip, and to my annoyance it took every-thing in me not to smile back. I was still pissed at all these men for holding me hostage, but there was an ease being around Haru. Something I rarely felt around others and it made me completely drawn to him. Definitely just the ease. He didn't seem to expect anything from me.

Maybe I was just desperate for a break.

"I figured we'd go for a run." His right eyebrow rose. His gaze trickled over my frame, taking in all the places the sports-wear hugged, and damn it to hell if my core didn't heat from it. "What else did you think these outfits were for?" he drawled.

The open-ended question had plenty of both flirty and feisty quips going through my head, but I pushed them aside because I fucking hated running. Although, with how much I had been doing it recently I could understand the confusion.

My workout routine was inconsistent due to juggling two jobs, but I still preferred weights over cardio. My ideal form of 'running' was actually roaming the outskirts of these grounds while on duty. I snorted to myself because it was to look for potential security breaches. Surprise! It ended up being me.

I narrowed my eyes. "And what exactly makes you think I want to go for a run?"

He shrugged.

I grimaced. "Weren't you all gung-ho about trust or some-thing? This seems like something that should be simple to answer."

"Fair enough." Another one of those goddamn butterfly-inducing smiles. Although, it didn't reach his eyes. There was a hesitation there that wasn't there before, and I was the cause.

My stomach soured, comparing the Haru in front of me with his walls up versus the one I met at the bar that was so at comfort with the world. I wished for that Haru back, but I couldn't let him go thinking we were friends either.

He continued, "You are ex-Army, one of our guards, and seem to take your life very seriously." He paused and shrugged. "Maybe a little too seriously."

I glowered at him.

He waved a hand at me. "I figured you could use some fresh air, and I hate being cooped up in the house all day anyway. Plus, there's still a few things I should take care of. I figured you might want to join me on my own run." He turned his back to me. "That is," he called out as he began walking, "unless you'd rather stay here."

"No!" My feet hopped into gear, scurrying after him. "No, no. I'm coming." Hopefully this 'run' would actually turn into a brisk walk because there was no way I wanted to stay cooped up here.

His shoulders shook with what I could only assume was a silent chuckle.

Shit, I had played right into his palm. Again. First my family and now a run. Seems holding my cards close to my chest wasn't going to be as easy as I thought, especially around him.

My feet tingled with anticipation and I memorized every single turn we took. Left, straight, right, left, straight, right. *The front door! The beacon to my freedom. Yes!*

I tried to keep my pace even, not showing my excitement and being one step closer to eventual freedom once everything got squared away. . . until we walked right past the front door. My steps faltered, slowing in surprise as he headed toward the hall where I had first entered the house. The window I snuck through was now closed, shaded until afternoon sun would filter through it.

Haru must've noticed my hesitation because he stopped and turned back. "Something wrong?"

"Uh." My attention flitted to the front door, and I frowned in confusion. "The front door? The run?" I mean, I knew he seemed to go a million miles per hour, but there was no way he forgot already.

The corner of his mouth tilted. "Wanna play a game?" His head cocked to the side, studying me as he awaited my answer, a lock of straight, dark hair falling across his forehead.

"A game?" I placed my hand on a cocked hip, and his eyes followed the movement. I bristled from the attention. Great, my hot babysitter now wanted to play some Guess Who or Monopoly. A game of tag, perhaps?

"Truth or dare." A playful smile spread across his face, and this time his eyes crinkled a little. Even though I wasn't twelve, I couldn't help but be intrigued. Although there was no way in hell I was giving up any information up that easily, trust be damned.

I squared my shoulders, a power pose. "Dare."

He crooked a finger at me. "Follow me."

He turned, walking again down the hall, and of course my feet had a mind of their own, not giving my brain a chance to decide if I wanted to play along, and followed him. It seemed simple enough. What I wasn't expecting was for him to reach back and slip his hand into mine, sending a jolt through my heating skin, as his pace picked up into a jog. *Ugh, here we go.*

"Wha—"

My words cut off as he flung open a door and led me straight into brightness. On the other side, it wasn't that it was an afternoon sun instead of a morning sun like it should be in Vermont. It wasn't that we ran on cobblestones past people riding by on bikes or past crowds of people enjoying drinks at a corner cafe, the lilt of conversation unintelligible to me. The smell was of a city, smoky and real. What struck me dumb was when we rounded a corner and the mother fucking Eiffel Tower glistening in the sun.

"I—is that—" *Holy fucking shit!*

"Come on, Mari," Haru urged, although there was a knowing smile on his face. "I'm in the mood for a game. Let's see if you can guess where we are before I take you to a new place, hm?"

My steps faltered on the cobbled pavement, sun glaring in my eyes from a car windshield. This was real; somehow I was in fucking Paris! "How are you doing this?"

"Don't be worried about how and just enjoy it!" He circled back to me, the smile turning concerned, reserved once more.

He slackened his pace to match my much slower one and put his hand on my shoulder. "Look, I promise it's not harmful to you. I wouldn't do that. But you've got to lighten up a bit. The answers will come with time." His fingers gently squeezed in a reassuring touch. Every time his skin grazed mine, it numbed my mind of almost everything else. The temptation of him, of how he made me feel, was something I couldn't afford.

No. Kidnapper. He was my kidnapper, I reminded myself and I slapped his hand away.

His smile disappeared again. "Please, Mari. Just try. The situation is what it is and you can either make it better by loosening up or keep your walls up and make everyone miserable. The choice is ultimately yours."

Easy for him to say.

Still, the temptation took hold of my heart. For the first time probably ever, I knew my family was being taken care of. And it didn't involve me working multiple jobs or giving up my own dreams. All it meant was living in a house with four ridiculously hot men. Honestly, probably the easiest thing I've had to do in a long time. Maybe it didn't have to be *that* bad, especially if they were willing to take me to freaking Paris.

Looking into his eyes, I caught hold of my galloping breath, forcing myself to relax. He nodded encouragingly, as I took deeper breaths of the hot salty-sour air, cars honking in the street alongside us.

He beckoned me further. "Come on. If you really want, I'll take you back to the house, but . . ." his gaze turned teasing before he continued, "I'll definitely consider that as you forfeiting the dare."

"Not on your life," I responded, straightening.

"That's right. Atta girl," he said, turning tail and breaking into a run. I groaned before following as closely as I could. My breathing soon became labored with my heart hammering in my chest as we raced down the roads. Couples passed arm in arm, teenagers on their phones, and no one really took notice of two tourists sprinting down the Parisian streets. We passed tantalizing coffee shops, tall trees, and a gaggle of children talking excitedly, their joy universal and undeniable.

Haru slowed to pull out a key, ducking into an alleyway. He motioned me closer, doing a quick head-turn to make sure we weren't followed. His chest was heaving too, sweat standing out on his collarbone and warmth radiating from him.

I couldn't stop staring, but it was short-lived when Haru led me through another door. We were back in a hallway in the house, and Haru raced down the corridor, swiping a card into another door and opening it for me.

I followed, and this time pushed to the max as we ran up and down extreme hills in between houses set close together.

Fuuuuck. If I wasn't completely enamored by the places we were going, I would've collapsed and waved a white flag.

The sun wasn't as high here. In fact it was barely rising.

The streets were quiet, and the signs and shop notices I saw were in English with recognizable brands.

I gasped, "Right . . . it's early here, so a few time zones west of Vermont." I turned to him. "Unless you can time travel too?"

He shook his head, reaching out to me. I let him take my arms, and he moved me out of the path of an early morning sweeper along the sidewalk.

"Sorry!" I called back to the man, but he didn't seem to hear me, focusing on his work rather than the fact that I'd just appeared from Vermont. I guess the man couldn't tell that at all. This was marvelous! I could see how Haru and the others could just walk around the world easily and not cause a stir, but it wasn't as if the guys were utterly unremarkable. They were all gorgeous.

I shook my head. "Thanks. Um, somewhere in America or Canada?"

Haru picked up his pace, kicking his heels up the steep hill. "It's not twenty questions, Marigold. But the way back is coming up fast."

Argh! Quick, I needed more clues! I was so sure I'd seen this place before, but I hadn't traveled at all despite wanting to.

At the top of a hill I saw a red behemoth gliding above gray water, the scent of sea salt smacking me in the face.

"The Golden Gate Bridge!" I whirled to face him. "San Francisco!"

He raised his arm for a high five. "Got it!"

I slapped his palm, grinning through my short panting breaths. "I mean, I got it eventually."

Through another door and back into the hall. Up the stairs, another swipe of the card and onto the next, and this time I followed at his heels. Where next?

The sun was similar to Paris, but it definitely wasn't French vibes. The streets heaved with people and cars, incredibly busy, and at first I couldn't make heads or tails of where we were until a hill off in the distance caught my eye. I had stared at pictures of the creamy pillars of this ancient ruin for hours in a book from the library, obsessed with mythology when I was eleven.

"That's the Acropolis!" My voice caught in my throat. We were in Athens, Greece, and my lifelong dream was coming true.

He nodded eagerly, then frowned, studying my face. "All okay?"

"I . . . yeah." I swallowed hard, coming to a halt. "It's just overwhelming, actually being here at last." I used the moment to release the stitch from my side with a stretch while admiring history I never thought I'd witness in person. My heart swelled and a smile wriggled free.

He nodded, sidling up next to me. "I've had time to get used to it. I suppose I got a bit numb. It's nice seeing the concentration, surprise, and then joy on your face." He glanced at me, perhaps to see how that landed. "You have an expressive face."

I was choking up, rubbing my eyes. "Yeah?"

"Yes. They say some people wear their hearts on their sleeves. I reckon you hide yours, but then you wear yours right out in front, when you're relaxed enough to show it."

What could I say to that? I had spent years repressing, well, me. Joining the military was a way to follow my dreams in a way that made sense, but even that fell to the wayside so I could stay close to home. My father leaving, my mom's work schedule, being the eldest, it meant I had to grow up fast. Who I was and who I wanted to be had become secondary.

Now, here in front of me, was a man that seemed to see through it all. The way his dark eyes penetrated me, like he could see past all the walls I had built up to find the real Mari and he was coaxing her out. He was asking her to come play.

When was the last time I allowed that? I took in the sights and smells, casting my eyes over the horizon to the sky.

Haru led me to another alleyway at a much needed walk. He crowded close behind me, quiet as he listened for any passersby. Could he hear my fast heartbeat underneath my ragged breathing? Hopefully he'd think it was from the workout.

"Okay, let's go." He reached past me to grab the door handle, arm flexing as he twisted it. And yes, his eyes darted to my lips.

I turned and led him into the house. "Which way now?"

"Hmm . . . here." Haru opened the next door.

"Oh, so somewhere in Greece?"

"It doesn't quite work like that," he said with a smirk, "but nice guess."

The sun had set in our new space, but the sky was still light enough. The humid air made my already sweaty skin even stickier, and the bite of the air came with a spice I couldn't place my finger on.

"So, somewhere really behind us time-wise, or in front. Australia?"

Haru shook his head. "I'm needed in the northern hemisphere. I can't go south yet."

"Why not?"

He put on a burst of speed. "A door isn't that far away, Marigold!"

Argh! Was this early evening, or a bit later? Between my feet and my mind running with whatever this travel tech was, it took me a moment to catch the greens, reds, and golds of the building we circled.

"Oh!" I came to a halt. "This is the Wat Pho temple! We're in Bangkok!"

"Yes, ma'am!" Haru came in for another high five, the slap of our palms ringing in the quiet parkland.

Sweat poured down my face, which I doubt had a luscious pink tinge to it, and even though my heart felt like it was about to pound out of my chest and it took way too much focus to keep my breath quiet and even so Haru didn't think I was about to keel over and die, a wide smile plastered on my face. Never in my wildest dreams would I imagine having a run like this. If my lungs didn't burn and my knees didn't feel like they were about to snap, I could envision enjoying running if it was like this. I still wasn't exactly sure what it was, but these phenomena were exhilarating. Tears pricked my eyes as my heart squeezed so tight my chest ached. I had just run through cities I had spent years dreaming about, places I daydreamed of visiting, that I would calculate how much it would cost to go there in my fantasies before redirecting it towards bills. Places I had all but given up on ever seeing in this lifetime and allowed to stay as nothing more than a dream I once had.

My throat closed up, unshed emotion crawling into my mouth. I refused to cry. My breathing became more ragged, slowing Haru down as he took me through another door. We left the beauty of Bangkok behind and reentered a hall in the house. Our pace slowed to a walk, but Haru didn't stop, leading me to one more door.

Walking through, I cleared my throat and wiped my eyes. Perhaps this would be London, as that was another one of my bucket list cities to check off. Instead, a sundrenched glade spread before us with a crystalline pond at its center. Birds chirped in the warm air, still with a tinge of cool current from spring that had yet to fully settle. Large deciduous trees loomed above, their bare trunks brown and striped silver. As Haru walked under the naked limbs of the trees, buds sprouted, unfurling to light green leaves to condense the foliage within a blink. New grass sprouted from underneath his path, dotted with a bright splash of color from a daisy or buttercup.

Holy shit. I really wasn't sleep or oxygen deprived. *This was happening. There was no way this was some kind of futuristic technology. No, it was magic. Real freaking magic.*

"What are you?" My words were uttered on a breath that could have easily been taken by the wind.

"*What* am I?" Haru *tsked*. "That's rather rude. I think you mean who."

I shook my head. "I mean—yes. Of course. Sorry." My embarrassment turned my rambling worse, and it wasn't until Haru chuckled that I realized he was joking with me.

"Isn't it obvious?" He crouched down, running his hand over a sprout which stretched up toward his palm, yearning, until a yellow wildflower bloomed beneath his fingers.

He looked up at me with a smile that caught my breath. "I'm Spring."

My eyebrows twitched together and I huffed a surprised laugh. "Right, sure," I said. What else was I supposed to say to something like that? But then it hit me as hard as a smack in the face, and I took a staggering step back.

Summer. Winter. *Spring.*

All my travel research flitted through my mind like scrolling through the internet and it landed on the Japanese word for Spring—*Haru.*

I swallowed. "Does Otto happen to stand for something?"

Haru rose from his crouch, amusement flickering across his face. "Autumn, of course."

My jaw worked itself up and down, but nothing came out. Where did I start? What did this mean? Did they—were they—

"Are you gods or something?" I finally stuttered. The glade around us was real, of that I had no doubt. So were those other places. The possibilities swam around me.

Haru barked out a laugh. "I wouldn't go that far."

"I don't understand. How are you . . . seasons?"

"That's the big question, isn't it?" He sighed, quick eyes scanning me for my reaction. "I wouldn't call us gods, but we influence our surroundings and help keep balance in the world." He grinned at me. "Plus a few extra tricks."

He held his palm flat and mimed a spiral with his other index finger. Another plant leapt into life, stretching toward him as if he were the sun.

I stared at it. "And the house?" I asked, looking behind us. The door was still open. I could see the lintel and the corridor inside it, but the surroundings held a small shack, not a huge mansion. I gulped. *What was that place?*

Haru smiled at it fondly. "It's the only place we can all coexist." Haru hunkered down, coaxing the plant off his fingers. "Whenever we go to an area, the season will change due to us being there. The house is the one place we can all truly rest. The one place we can call home, what with being somewhat . . . different."

I paced around the shack. From behind it was a wooden structure like a small shed. I put my head inside the door, twisting my head to either side. Long corridors filled with doors like some kind of never ending filing system. If I squinted I could just about see a shimmer in the air like a heat wave.

My heart lurched in my chest. My knees grew weak, but I wanted to know more—no, I wanted to know everything! "So you what, travel around the world like this, making seasons happen?"

He beamed, patting the soil around the small questing tendril with affection. "Yep."

"Beats long haul flights for sure." Not that I had much experience with them, but that was what people said and being so far from home was a major reason I hadn't left.

His eyebrows raised. "I've always wanted to try one. What's it like?"

I grimaced. "Squashed and painful. Trust humans to make international travel uncomfortable. Not at all like this." I stared out at the glade with fresh, sweet air utterly devoid of any human influence. We were truly alone out here, far from anywhere I knew. My heart pounded and palms tingled. "This is . . . wild."

"Yes." Haru stood up slowly, eyes on the little plant he had just rehomed. It wafted toward him as if pushed by the breeze, then turned to seek out the sun. "But it can get a bit lonely. I can't take any of the other seasons with me, for example. We can't be in the same place as each other except for a very limited time of year."

The warm wind brought with it a honeyed smell. An ease had settled through me, from the run and Haru's openness while answering all my questions. Somehow it was like the tension of my life had melted away. I looked to the man that was the cause of this feeling. I wanted to know more. "Two of you were chasing me across what must have been a Japanese city, right?"

He winced. "Yeah, and it caused problems, but we needed to get you back so you wouldn't get lost out there."

I blinked slowly. He had been genuinely worried about me, not about themselves or the weather. My skin warmed even further, but not from the sun. Maybe they weren't as horrible as I presumed. I mean, could I blame them for being cautious with *this*, all the seasonal magic and enchanted house stuff? "What'll happen if you try to be in one place at the same time outside of the house?"

He rubbed the back of his neck. "A clash, weird weather patterns. They're usually violent too. A freak snowstorm in the middle of summer, that sort of thing. If we do it too much, things would really get messed up."

My mouth was open, ready to ask more, when he kicked off his shoes, thumbs hooking into his jogging pants.

"What're you doing?" I asked.

He eyed the clear water and a smirk pulled at the corner of his lips. "Let's go for a swim." He gave me a wink and slipped the shorts right off, nothing underneath.

I gaped, his naked frame confident as he sauntered away from me and into the pond. His shoulder blades flexed with the swing of his arms, showing the lithe muscle in his back. His thighs swelled with every step, and his sculpted ass, which I could bounce a quarter off, curved deliciously and—I was definitely staring. My eyes dropped to the ground as I bit my tongue.

A splash rang in the air, followed by a soft sigh. "Come on, Marigold. The water is great!"

I kept my gaze on my trainers, wiggling my toes as a distraction. "Isn't it cold? It's barely spring."

His soft laughter flitted to me, causing a stir in my belly. "It's a hot spring mixed with the snow melt. It's the perfect temperature after a run."

I glanced around the grove, waiting for someone to pop out from behind a tree and catch us like we were teenagers doing something we weren't supposed to. "What if someone sees us?"

"We're in the middle of a National Park in Tennessee. No one is going to find us."

I looked over my shoulder at the small shed housing the door, a clear sign that people came here.

"We built that," Haru explained, leisurely swimming from one side to another, arms rising and falling like waves. "Sometimes having a quiet place to get away is nice. Come on," he urged, "it's okay to have a little fun."

Fun. What a weird concept for me. When was the last time I did just that? Where I wasn't focused on training, working, or finding ways to make my family's situation better? I had been forced to grow up young. I didn't have hobbies. I didn't even know what I found fun anymore. Every second had a purpose, and the thought of just existing, screw the consequences and relish the moment, was so foreign to me that I didn't know if I could have fun anymore. But seeing the peace settling on Haru's face, his pure enjoyment of being in such a beautiful place, made me realize I wanted that.

Kicking off my shoes, I slipped out of my leggings and socks. I kept my underwear on, and pulled my shirt down to help cover my thighs a little more. I didn't want him to see how they would rub together, how the thicker areas had cottage cheese skin, especially when Haru sure as hell looked like a god even if he didn't consider himself one.

I ran toward the water before I could second guess myself and dove in. I waited for the bite of snow melt, to feel my lungs squeeze with shock as the cold smacked me. Instead, I was met with water as warm as a May day, the perfect temperature between hot and cold. As Goldilocks would say, it was just right.

I surfaced to find Haru beaming at me. "I told you it was perfect," he said.

I tilted my head back and to my surprise laughter bubbled out of me. "Holy shit, this feels amazing." I twisted to float on my back, letting the sounds of the world wash over me to just be.

I gently glided through the water, moving the surface from one side to another as the breeze skated over my skin. Leaves threw a pattern of light and dark in patchwork above me, and small chirping birds chased one another from branch to branch. Watching them, my shoulders relaxed and my mind cleared enough to be present in this moment.

There was a familiarity here. Maybe Mom had taken us to a lake like this once? I was sure I had seen a face like the one in the bark of a tree before and the same collage of branches creating patterns against the blue sky. I had never been to

Tennessee to my knowledge, and I didn't think there was anything like this in Vermont. The aches in my body from the run left me, and, for the first time in what felt like forever, my mind was quiet.

With a sigh and knowing reality had to come back eventually, I straightened to tread water.

Haru sat on a rock, his body dry and back in his shorts, wet hair hanging in his face. A droplet of water rolled down a lock of hair and dripped onto his notebook page, his hands taking long strokes and sweeps across the page. I didn't know when he had gone to retrieve it, and I was surprised he had left me alone at all to do it. Man, I guess I had been in my own head more than I realized.

I swam over to the rock, pulling myself up beside him. "Whatchya drawing?"

He startled and tilted the pad away from me, his cheeks staining slightly. "Nothing."

A small smile pulled at my lips, but I didn't push. I turned my head back to the glade, basking like a flower in the sun, the knots in my stomach easing as I took in its beauty.

Speaking of flowers, plenty had sprung up around Haru, including bunches of the ball-like yellow flower with the old lady style skirts in red that I knew so well.

I sighed, patting one to bob in the wind. "By the way, I prefer to be called Mari rather than . . ." I pointed mutely at the flower, my namesake.

Haru slid his sketchbook to one side, focusing on me. "I happen to like plants, in case you couldn't tell."

"Yes, the house is covered in them."

Now he really did look embarrassed, the color in his cheeks a darling splotch of red. "Ah, yeah. They aren't supposed to be, um, all over quite like that."

"I guess they got away from you?" I recalled the east wing entrance hall with huge thick vines choking the columns all the way to the ceiling, and that door completely overgrown with harsh briars.

"Something like that," he murmured.

Hmm. Maybe something else to ask him about, but later. The soporific sun blazed overhead, and my muscles were loose, tension sliding off my shoulders like the water droplets from my swim. "Flower-lover or not, nothing makes me feel like a toothless grandma than being called Marigold."

He grinned back at me. "Well, then, that would just make me say it more."

I nudged him gently in the side with my elbow, and he threw his hands up, dramatically falling to one side. "Alright, alright, Buttercup."

"*Buttercup?*" I repeated, aghast. "That's a declaration of war. Now I have to find a nickname for you."

"Perfect," he chuckled, sitting upright. The sun glinted through his dark hair, highlighting shocks of blue-black and tawny browns. The depths of his brown and gold-flecked eyes were endless, amused like he saw something funny in every-thing. Maybe he did. It must be nice to see joy wherever you went.

I lay back on my elbows, toes in the water. "I love it here," I whispered.

"You do?" Haru glanced up at me from his paper. "Me too. Wild yet open, quiet and full of life, warm waters and cooling air. It's the perfect balance, really. I mean, someone I once knew described it as that."

By the expression on his face, it seemed like he really missed whoever that was. Questions circled around in my head like the birds above our heads in the sky. Next to Haru, all I could feel was joy. I couldn't not, and I didn't want it to end. I could pry later, but right now, I wanted to just be and talk about me for once.

"So," he turned to me and rested his chin in his palm, "do you still 'fucking hate' me?"

I couldn't smother my wince at the words, which, based on the knowing glint in his eyes, was answer enough.

I didn't. I wanted to and part of me hated what was happening, but after today and learning who they were and everything that they could do, I couldn't fully blame them. Still, I had cards and too many were shown already, so I concentrated on his other question on how I felt about this place.

"I can't place my finger on it," I said, "but it feels right. Like a peace settling into me, almost like I've been here before, which I know I haven't." I tilted my head with my eyebrows raised. "You know that yearning? Like your current home is just where you live, but you know there's something more out there. Like there is somewhere else you need to be, or someone you haven't met. I feel like I've spent my life searching for something . . . and being here settles that side of me a little." I shook my head with a dismissive laugh. "Sorry, I don't know how to explain it."

Haru's silence, not even a chuckle at my ramblings, unnerved me enough to look at him.

His wide eyes stared at me, mouth slightly open, like I had said something absolutely absurd.

Shit. I had said too much, revealed yet another piece of me, even if this time it was how I truly felt instead of what or who mattered to me. I clamped my mouth shut, berating myself for thinking I could open up like that. I let the moment get to me and let my walls slip a little. Now he was looking at me like *I* was the lunatic.

Well, guess what, bucko? You're the one with scary ass magic, and because of it I can't even go home to my freaking family.

I popped up, jittery. I'd said too much, been too weird. I

bustled over to where my pants and shoes were and shimmied them on. "We should get back."

Haru still stared at me, and it wasn't until I walked toward the door that he scrambled to follow me in a flurry of movement.

My heart sank as we walked in silence. *So much for opening up; that'd teach me.* It was a first, and definitely not something I planned on repeating anytime soon.

Once back inside the house, Haru locked up the door with a twist of the key, still lost in his own thoughts.

I stared as he locked the door, locked me inside . . . again. That was my place. I could only leave under their watch. I still wasn't in control of my own life. Instead, I jumped from the frying pan into the fire.

I turned and walked away without another word and went back to the room they *allowed* me. My throat closed from the tears I refused to shed.

Chapter Ten

The next morning I trudged downstairs to the kitchen. Each step lit my legs on fire. Stupid run. Stupid, mind blowing, and breathtaking run.

I'd barely slept, and I was starving. I loved food and was never one to miss breakfast. It truly was the most important meal of the day for me. I couldn't get my family out of my head. I wanted, no needed, to know how they were doing. You could take the problems away from the girl, but not the girl away from the problems.

I couldn't believe Chris. Why would he gamble his education, and, more importantly, his life like that? If he'd been caught with the Adderall . . . Then to leave my mother to pick up the pieces despite the crazy hours she worked.

I entered the kitchen. It was quiet, and no one was there. I grabbed a mug from the counter and went to the shiny, silver contraption on the counter that seemed more artificial intelligence than coffee maker.

"Why can't they just own a normal coffee maker?" I groaned, closing my eyes to calm my irritable nerves. I was tired and annoyed, and I just wanted some damn coffee.

Sighing, I put the cup down and went to sit at the table, shoving my face into the palms of my hands as I rested my elbows on the smooth wood.

That was a bad idea. Images inundated my mind, the other main reason I didn't sleep well last night.

Behind closed lids, I watched Haru strip down and jump into the pond. I heard his laugh and watched how the water droplets slid down his toned body. I imagined my fingers trailing the same path. I watched his lips quirk up with his easy smile, imagining if kissing him would be as soft and effortless.

Shit. It had been way too fucking long since I'd been laid. Clearly. Sure, the attraction to him had been there when we first met, and yes, he had literally taken me around the world yesterday which still had my heart pounding. But then I saw him close up. I felt my own hesitation again, witnessed the distance grow between us until I had left for my room and didn't leave until now. And yet all night long I just kept imagining his perfect body, the way his laugh stroked across me, and wondered what other pleasurable noises he could make.

There was a clank in front of me and I jerked.

Instincts took over and my hand shot out, grabbing a tattooed wrist that had one finger wrapped through the handle of a filled coffee mug. I blinked at Winter whose blue eyes widened with surprise.

"Now I understand what happened to Haru's nose."

I dropped his arm, stomach swirling. "Sorry," I muttered.

He grunted in neither a yes or no way, returning back to the Winter I'd come to know. "For you." He nodded at the coffee before placing it on the counter.

How had I not heard him?

He walked away, our conversation clearly over. I took the time to watch him as he pulled out plates and pans. Soon eggs were thrown into the pan and he snagged a spatula off the counter to stir them. A buttery scent with herbs from the bottles he grabbed and dumped into the pan filled the air. I had never had rosemary in eggs before but it smelled divine.

His biceps flexed with every movement in his white t-shirt that clung to his massive frame above loose gray sweatpants that sat low on his hips. There was a bulge in the front that left little to the imagination, but the imagination side said, "there is no fucking way it can be that big." Beneath the fabric, more dark markings made their appearance across his large shoulders and muscled back.

Fuck, I could climb that man like a tree.

He looked over at me. Flushing, I turned away and took a sip of my coffee.

Voices broke the silence, and I turned to see Summer, Otto, and Haru walk into the kitchen. Summer was smiling at Haru, stealing my breath with how powerful it was, but it fell away when he spotted me at the table. The air grew thick with the four hulking men filling the space, and yet I found my appetite only growing.

"Mari." His tone was reserved, as chilly as the way he looked at me.

Otto looked up from the book his nose was in and gave me a little nod. "Good morning."

"Morning," I responded. They all took their places at the table after grabbing their own cups of coffee, the machine effortlessly whirring to life with a few pushes of a button.

"Breakfast," Winter barked from the stove. He put plates of cheese omelets and toast down, placing mine a little harder than necessary in front of me. Summer watched him carefully over his cup of coffee as Winter walked to sit in the furthest seat from me possible, ignoring eye contact with everyone.

I guess my checking him out hadn't gone unnoticed, and clearly he did not appreciate it.

Cutting off a bite of egg with my fork, I decided to eat in silence. The stabbing pain of hunger was too harsh to ignore, and I refused to let his sour mood get to me, especially after the horrible night sleep I had.

A burst of cheesy goodness erupted into my mouth and I closed my eyes to savor it. "Holy shit! This is so good," I moaned. After swallowing the bite, I opened my eyes ready to dive into the rest, but paused to see everyone staring at me with wide eyes.

I gulped as nerves fluttered down my spine. "What?"

Otto was the first to recover, clearing his throat before giving me a soft smile. "We just aren't used to having a lady in our house."

"Really?" These four men weren't used to having women in the house? They were the most beautiful men I had ever seen; I assumed they had women falling at their feet. A tiny pang lanced through my stomach, but I pushed it aside. If they were gay it might explain why it was only them in this giant house. "Huh. I mean, however you all swing, I support you. I'm an ally of all sexualities."

This had Winter choking on his water, Haru's head falling back with a burst of laughter, and Summer stilled, watching me with such an intense gaze that my stomach swooped.

"There may be some swinging," Otto noted primly, "but I can assure you that we are all very attracted to the female sex."

I nodded, filling my fork with more of the divine omelet. "Of course." I eyed Haru who smirked at me. He had asked for my number. Again, his rock hard abs and v-shaped hips traipsed through my mind. Then my brain decided to hate me and imagined a thin woman trailing her long nails over him. I shoveled toast into my mouth, trying to ignore the pit of jealousy I seemed to have curdling my gut.

Summer's eyebrows arched. "How'd you sleep?"

I met his eyes. They burned like a wildfire, as if he knew the answer. "Fine."

"Fine?" Haru wagged his fork in my direction like a finger.

"No good ever came from a woman saying fine. Tell us the truth, Mari, if we are to build any trust here." He met Summer's eyes. "And all of us should be remembering that."

I pressed my lips tightly together to smother my laugh, both at him calling me out and how he stood up to Summer. Plus his demeanor helped erase some of the tension I'd been feeling, which only reduced more when Otto gave a small nod.

"Speaking of trust," I trailed off as I stared down at my plate, "I understand I am here for the time being and all of that, and I've accepted that. But considering recently you've trusted me enough to take me out of the house and all around the world, literally, I was hoping I could have a visit to my mom's. Check in. Maybe get my cell phone back so I can check in more often."

"Absolutely not." Summer didn't even have the courtesy to look at me when he denied me.

My awkward hope turned into flaming anger. It burned through my veins, lighting my nerves on fire until it made it difficult to keep my voice even when I spoke. "I'm sorry?" I tried to breathe through it. Perhaps I had misheard him.

"Summer?" Otto's face pinched into confusion. He wasn't jumping to conclusions either, waiting for an explanation.

Summer placed his silverware on the sides of his plate with a deliberate clink like a manacle before dabbing the sides of his mouth with a napkin. "You are staying here until the consulate and I can agree upon what exactly shall be done with you. Your time outside of this house interacting with the others has only increased your security level, and therefore your threat level, and you're unvetted. You're a witness now of exactly what we do. We need to minimize contact with those you are closest to and ensure nothing slips out that could put any of us at risk."

My mouth bobbed open and closed in disbelief. I looked

across the table at Otto whose face had gone slack, saying nothing. Based on the sorrow in his gaze when he finally met mine, I knew he understood Summer's reasoning enough to agree. Winter, of course, said nothing. Didn't even look our way, because forgetting my existence was clearly what he planned to do. I bet he couldn't wait to get rid of me.

Finally, I turned to my left in hopes of Haru having my back.

His hand gripped his fork so tightly his knuckles turned white. "Summer, that's not fair. She agreed to stay. There is no reason to punish her, or her family, any more than necessary."

"She should have thought of that before she broke in," Summer grated, giving his Spanish accent an edge. "And then broken out . . . and broken a nose."

"She broke in under orders!" Haru insisted.

"Whose orders?" Summer flung his arms wide. "Why would I, the person who works with CSON for them to protect us, order her to break into our house?"

"You?" Otto asked archly, and even Winter glared at Summer. "CSON came to us and we all agreed and oversee the contracts."

"Ack, you know what I mean," Summer fumed, twisting his napkin in his lap.

"We can trust her," Haru insisted, putting his hand on my shoulder.

His touch set me ablaze. Gone was the walls built between us after our adventure, and instead I seemed to find an ally beside me. The one who flirted with me at the bar. The one who helped rescue my brother, and the one who helped ensure my family would be taken care of. In all honesty, Haru was the only one who could've convinced me to come back here.

Summer breathed in through his nose. "Haru, we discussed this," he said between clenched teeth.

"We didn't *discuss*," Haru said quietly. "You ordered me around."

Summer's eye twitched. "That's our dynamic," he growled.

"Not . . . not everywhere," Haru said, raising his chin.

Summer turned his glare onto me. "You might have Haru wrapped around your little finger, but you won't get past me. You aren't going anywhere!" he thundered.

My calm blasted away. "Who do you think you are?" I slammed my hands on the table, the movement jostling Haru's arm from my shoulders. "This is my life! I have done nothing but try to be a good Shield and do my job. I realize you are worried about how I'll disrupt *your* life, but what about mine? What about the people who depend on me?" My throat tightened from my anger, tears brimming in my eyes. I hated crying in public, and I hated when people watched, especially when they were the cause of it. "I see no mutual trust. To be clear, I'm not even asking to leave. All I want to do was make sure my mom and brother aren't being *evicted* or aren't *starving*. You say they're being taken care of, but how am I supposed to know that? For all I know, they might have had the electricity turned off because I wasn't able to pay the bill before getting stuck here." What did they care? They had all they needed. Whatever their weird deal was, they knew it made them valuable. I could see the sense, but it galled.

Winter barely twitched, but Otto looked positively seething at my anger. His eyes glinted behind his glasses and I realized he was probably feeling it. Summer looked ready to match my fire with his, and Haru . . .

Haru looked lost.

I collected myself and stood slowly to survey them all. They stayed seated, as if rooted to their chairs by Haru's plants. Four faces gazed at me, four pairs of eyes unblinking.

I looked down at Haru. "I won't go anywhere else and I'll

stay in the room, if that will lessen the risk of me talking about stuff and let me check in on my family. I didn't ask to be taken anywhere, if you recall. You did that."

I wanted to shout more—Screw you! Screw trust!—but settled for throwing my napkin down on the table and marching out. Tears blurred my vision. I couldn't see any of them, couldn't see any of their reactions, and I didn't give a damn. Silence was what greeted me, as empty as my chest.

No one tried to stop me from leaving.

I DIDN'T KNOW how long I paced my room or how many times I remade my bed after picking up a pillow to throw it against a wall. I used it as a punching bag for a good long while, getting satisfying noises but nothing lessened the dread in my chest. I had to get out.

A knock thudded on my door. I was calmer but had zero regrets about what I'd said. "What?" I kept my voice firm.

"It's me." Haru's soft voice was hesitant, remorseful, and I hated how it tugged at my heartstrings.

"Come in," I said, folding my arms across my chest and leaning against the post at the end of my bed.

Haru opened the door slowly and stepped inside. He raised his eyes to meet mine, which I knew had to be hard. I had perfected my resting bitch face.

"I'm sorry," he said. "Summer had no right." He waited for me to say something, anything.

I didn't.

He took another step toward me. "You came, on your own accord, and now are being punished for it. You shouldn't be."

I continued to stare. Waiting for what, I didn't know.

He bit his lip, shifting on his feet before taking yet another step. "Your request isn't absurd. I saw your house, the state of your brother, and your mother's fear. Of course you want to check in on them. It isn't an insane request at all. By no means do I want you locked in this room, and eventually the others will realize the absurdity of that too. I want us to build trust. I told you during the run that we could make this enjoyable or miserable, and you chose to let go. Our run was amazing, the pond was . . ." His eyes glistened at the memory. "Amazing," he whispered after a moment. His gaze found mine, true sorrow dampening them. "I'm so sorry, Mari. I will talk with the others, and I promise they'll come around. You've started to open yourself up, and in time I just know the others will too." When he finished, he stared at me. The amount of pain mixed with hope etching his perfect face and his crinkled forehead had my heart battering against those walls I'd built.

"I can't say I feel bad for what I said," I finally said.

"You shouldn't." His eyes sparked with a mixture of relief and apology as he took three more steps toward me, closing the rest of the distance. "Summer should've listened to your case before saying no. I know I would have. Otto would have—"

I snorted. "And I'm sure Winter would've frozen me before I could've gotten the words out. Summer would lock me up and throw away the key if he could."

I didn't know what it was I said, but Haru stopped midstep. It didn't even look like he was breathing.

"Haru?" Worry furrowed my brow.

"Yeah, I just, uh," He squeezed his eyes shut and took a breath. "It's nothing." When he reopened his eyes, a smile spread across his lips, although it didn't fully meet his eyes.

"Summer should've heard you out. None of us realized how much you being here affected anyone but you. I'm so sorry. I wish you had told me sooner about wanting to check in on your family."

My head dropped to hide the tears threatening to break through. "The worst part is, none of it was an exaggeration. What if my mom thinks I abandoned her like my dad? I didn't have time to explain much." It was such a deep fear; a dark truth that I hadn't fully realized was inside of me until I said the words aloud. Admitting it made it real, and I couldn't hold back as silent tears poured down my face.

Haru pulled me into his chest, wrapping his arms around me securely as if nothing would touch me. He smoothed my back, giving me space to snot and sob into his shirt until it was thoroughly damp.

When there was nothing left in me, I pulled my head back. "Sorry," I sniffled, wiping my eyes.

"Don't be." He rubbed my cheeks with his thumb, leaving a trail of warmth. "We should be the ones who are sorry. And thank you for trusting me enough to share that with me."

His words were so kind, so genuine, that tears threatened to burst all over again. Instead, I leaned in and hugged him. Breathing in his honeysuckle scent, I burrowed into him like I could somehow step away from bills and reality and everything that made my life so messy.

"The worst thing is," I mumbled into his chest, "I've been worried about them, but it was nice. My whole life I've taken care of them, put off my own dreams, and focused on how to make money to help around the house. So, to literally run around the world, forget my day to day, and just enjoy life—" My throat clogged, blocking the rest of my words.

His hand stroked my hair, following it all the way down to my mid back. "You're young. You should be allowed to enjoy life. You shouldn't feel ashamed by any of this. You have taken your duty seriously as a daughter and sister, arguably too seriously. But you should never feel bad for wanting to live your own life and fulfill your own dreams. You are human and should be allowed to do those things. Families are complicated. It's not always sunshine and rainbows. It can sometimes be a mixture of heartache and resentment, along with loyalty and love. That's nothing to feel bad about, it just is. It's part of having meaningful relationships sometimes."

My breath caught. He framed my feelings in better ways than I could ever explain, that deep taproot of love and the struggle to survive with a burgeoning desire to be swept free to float on the breeze. I would never want to abandon my family, but I also wanted to live a life of my choosing, and the competing needs pulled at me.

His quiet voice went on. "It's admirable what you have done for them. They're lucky to have you. I just know you being here is bound to make our lives better too. I can feel it."

His words, his acceptance, his understanding, his kindness —all of it pulled at me. Haru was just being Haru, and I knew what I wanted in that moment. I wanted to feel something more than resentment. I wanted to put aside my anger and do exactly what I'd been daydreaming about since I'd met him.

My lips found his.

His hands paused on my back, surprise freezing him in place, but he quickly leaned deeper into my kiss.

My arms roved up his hard chest, weaving around his strong shoulders until they wrapped around his neck. He pulled me tighter against him. Our mouths molded and moved, the perfect mix between sweet and intense. I had never been kissed like this. Like there was a need not just in me but in him; like he'd been waiting years for this kiss.

His tongue stroked along my bottom lip. I opened up for him, allowing it to slip inside and tease my own. I moaned into his mouth, which riled him up more. His hands slid to my thighs and gripped me tighter.

A short gasp escaped me when he lifted me. He did it so easily, I lightened our kiss from surprise. I wound my legs around his waist. He moved until I felt the pillar on the bed press against my spine.

His hardness strained against his jeans and against my core. Despite the fabric that separated us, a spike of pleasure built inside of me. I moaned from how his body moved against mine, rubbing in all the right spots. The sensation built until it was hard to concentrate on anything but the tingling reaching toward its peak.

One of his hands moved over my hip and up across my stomach until he cupped my breast. His thumb rubbed through the material of my shirt across the peaked nipple. More pleasure built, along with a barb of adrenaline at his touch. My hips moved, craving more, as my need continued to build.

I bit his lip as I tried not to ask for more and he groaned into my mouth, which only made me kiss him harder. I wanted more. I wanted all of him. I wanted to forget all the pain and heartache. I wanted to feel his skin against mine. I wanted him to know how wet I was, and how badly I wanted to feel him inside of me.

AND WITH THE reverent way he touched and kissed me, I could only assume he wanted the same. This only made the pleasure grow until it was spreading from between my legs outward until I could feel it bloom into my fingertips. I was so close.

"Mari," he breathed against my mouth. The word was light, filled with such desire I thought his words alone could give me an orgasm.

I broke the kiss and found his gaze. There was so much need, so much heat, that it took my breath away.

His heavy breaths splashed against my face. "I've been wanting to do that since I met you at the bar."

Fuck, so had I and so much more. "I want you to—" I began, when I glanced over his shoulder as movement caught my attention.

There, standing in the door, was Summer.

I tensed, squeezing Haru's shoulder until he turned his head to look behind him.

"Summer," he said, slowly lowering me down his body to the ground. My shirt rode up along the way, and as soon as my bare feet touched the smooth floor, I pulled it down to cover up my stomach. My face heated, embarrassed like I was a teenager caught by their mother.

Summer looked between the two of us. His eyes were hard, mouth set in a straight line. "I came to apologize. I didn't mean to interrupt." His eyes found mine again, and they were so intense I didn't know what to make of it. The air thickened with heat that radiated from him. "Carry on." He turned and walked out the door.

I made to step toward him, but stopped. I didn't need to explain myself. Even if he came to apologize, I was a grown ass woman. So what if Haru and I had been making out?

"I think he might be a little peeved." I gave a forced chuckle, side-eyeing Haru who still stared at the empty doorway.

He returned a knowing smile. "I don't think peeved is the word I would use."

Chapter Eleven

Peeved was the word to describe me at least. Mood doused, I expected Haru to leave immediately. What had I done? This wasn't a time to give into my desires. Give in to one of the men who held me hostage. This wouldn't bode well with trying to see my family, I was sure. I busied myself straightening the covers of my bed. The bed they had given me in this cell of a room.

He came to stand next to me. "Are you alright?"

"Not really," I admitted. "I still need to check on my family." Should I apologize for kissing him? He had seemed into it, his swollen lips mere inches from mine.

"Can I touch you?" His hand hovered over my arm, dispelling my doubts.

"Yes." *Please.*

He stroked my arm from my wrist up to my elbow, leaving a wake of electricity behind the trailing finger which thundered into my very being. His pupils dilated a little, lips parting with want . . . Then he cocked his head to the open door. "Want to go talk to Summer? I think he might be, ah, receptive."

Hope surged in my chest. I didn't want this moment to end, but my family came first. "To me calling home?"

"To you in general." Haru chuckled and the deep chime tickled across my skin creating goosebumps. He rested his chin on my shoulder, breath tingling the shell of my ear. "We should go talk to him now."

"I'm not so sure." That look Summer gave me had been unreadable. I didn't know what to make of it, and I sure as hell wasn't prepared to face it again. "So . . . How long have you known Summer?" Perhaps he would argue my case for me?

"Summer came into his powers before any of us. He found me first, so Otto and Winter look to me to sort of manage him."

"Manage him, mm?" Shit, I shouldn't be flirting with him, but Haru was easy to tease.

"You've seen what he's like. Unilateral decisions, snap judgements. I know he just means to protect us. I'll talk to him."

The thrill in my stomach was matched with a pulse of light in my core. "If you could, that would be wonderful."

His breath was so hot on the back of my neck. "Just so we're clear, I'm going to be thinking about that kiss, Mari."

My skin pebbled. "I shouldn't have done that, it was probably a mistake. I—" I ran out of words, because it had felt so good, so perfect. And I wanted more.

"Did it feel like a mistake?" His fingers slid across my shoulders as if he was preparing to give me a massage, eliciting a shiver deeper than goosebumps. "How about this?"

"I . . ."

He dropped his hands quickly. "I only want an enthusiastic 'Yes' from you, Buttercup, so have some time to think." He took a step back, giving me space.

That yes nearly tore from my throat, but some space was probably for the best. An internal shiver wracked me, my hands desperate to bring him right back and moan all the yeses in his mouth. Clamping down my confused feelings, I said, "Alright. Good luck with Summer."

He nodded once and left, but with an encouraging smile. As he left through the door, he touched his lips as if in salute, and I heard him whistling down the hallway.

Had I done that to him? Made him that happy? I took to my bed, lying flat and trying to breathe, but my hands were twitchy and my lips kept sliding over each other as if trying to recapture the warm, eager press of his lips to mine.

Groaning, I rolled off the bed. I needed to move again, to get this prickly energy out, and began a workout alongside my bed. Pretty soon I lost myself in a storm of push-ups and squats, closing my eyes and pretending I was at the Shield gym, shedding my top so I didn't sweat through one of my few pieces of clothing.

Sinking into the workout was what I needed. I'd given in for just a moment, but had I fucked everything up again by not accepting Haru immediately? Haru seemed to be thrilled by the kiss, and thinking of him sticking up for me when I was not in a position to do it myself just made it better. He was saying and doing all the right things.

I pushed harder on my jump squats. He had been completely sincere since we met at the bar and I gave him my number, and cheering me on slapping down that asshole. Even tracking me down and convincing me to come back to the house he did so carefully, and it was clear he hated doing it.

And the others too. Summer, Otto, and Winter, all with their own kind of magnetism. The whole mind-blowing secret of this house and what they could do, their powers, was only the start of it, I was sure. I needed to know more—wanted to know everything.

A rap on the door made me slow. "Yes?"

"It's me." Haru opened the door, putting his head around.

His eyes widened slightly at the sweat streaming down my chest, gaze definitely locking on my breasts constrained in my workout bra. "Hello," he breathed, and joy filled me to the brim at how he swallowed hard, hands gripping the door as if it was the only thing holding him up.

He physically shook himself and smiled. "Summer said yes."

"Yes?" My heart thudded in my chest.

"You are going home to visit your family."

My jaw dropped. "Really?" *At last!* "I'll be ready to go really quickly, I just need to hop in the shower."

"Sure." Haru chuckled and was that a hint of nervousness? "I like showers."

My heart thumped again, the image of him standing in the lake with water rolling down his gorgeous torso flashing back at me. "Mm, yes, but I think that might slow me down just a bit," I said, wiping my face with a towel from the bathroom and grinning at him over it.

He allowed that with a sunny smile that made my stomach swoop. "Afterward, then. Consider it something between a truth and a dare. A promise." He winked. "I'll wait right outside."

My legs were trembling as I washed, but I quickly mastered myself. I was going home!

Dressing swiftly, I grabbed my purse and stepped outside my room to find Haru leaning against the wall, arms folded. In the dim light, he seemed to glow, making my heart skip, but his eyes were sad when they met mine.

My steps slowed. "What's wrong?"

"I . . ." His gaze dropped, and my stomach curled. *Oh, shit, does he regret kissing me?* "You congratulated me like I'd talked Summer round, but actually, he had already put things in motion." He trailed a hand through his hair. "I kind of wish that I *had* had the chance to talk Summer around. It's not easy convincing Summer of anything. He has to think it's his idea." He shook his head, pushing away from the wall. "But this isn't about me. This is about you. We can go when you're ready."

"Ready." Eagerness to see my family flooded me along with tendrils of anxiety. Were they okay? "And I did promise I would comply, so you don't need to threaten me with anything."

"No, that's Summer's gig." He lowered his voice and in a husky tone added, "You'd better be a good girl."

A shiver raced across my skin. "Or what?" I tried to keep my voice even, but *damn*. The way he gazed into my eyes as well, like he was searching through my most intimate thoughts . . .

A bloom of moss trickled up along the walls surrounding us, and Haru snatched his attention away. "Shit." He rubbed the back of his neck ruefully. "That, uh, worked a little too well." Before I could respond, he let out a low annoyed breath, and a small sprinkling of clover popped up ahead of us. "I don't mean to come across desperate. Otto was right. I need to calm it down a bit. Play it cool."

It tickled me that Haru had talked to Otto about me. The quiet librarian was probably hiding something in his desk. A riding crop, maybe. "I'd like to talk to him too."

Haru led me down the stairs. "Well, good, but for today, you're mine."

And that made my heart beat a little harder.

Haru continued, "Otto headed off early but he wanted me to say he'd be taking you to the southern hemisphere for breakfast tomorrow, if you're up for it. It might not be breakfast food due to time differences, but I have no doubt it'll be delicious. We could probably go for a run beforehand, if you wanted to get up early."

I groaned, causing Haru's brows to bunch together.

"I thought you enjoyed it." His voice was light, but edged with hesitation.

"I did," I quickly assured, wanting to rid the somber look on his face and in his eyes. "Sort of," I added, wanting to divulge the truth.

He frowned.

"I'm just not much of a runner," I admitted. "I'm more of a weights girl if anything. But I loved seeing the sights! I'd just much rather do it at a walking pace and with plenty of moments where I can sit on a bench and enjoy it from a seated position every once in a while."

He released an easy chuckle. "Noted. Leisurely strolls from now on."

My heart fluttered with the idea of getting to see more sights of the world, and at a pace I could bask in and appreciate the beauty a little bit more.

Haru's eyes traced the sketch of the scales on the stairs as we passed.

"Um. Everything okay?" I said automatically before my brain could stop me.

"One day, I'll finish this," he sighed.

I nudged him with my hip. "Why don't we do that? Put on an audiobook and paint away." I tucked my hair behind my ear. "Maybe . . . everyone could pitch in?"

He chuckled and looked at me with a subdued smile. "Sounds good, Buttercup." He slid his arm around my shoulders, tucking me into his side. "We might argue for years over which audiobook to put on, though."

"I'm sure Otto has a list of suggestions." I expected Haru to lead me to a door, but instead we went past the kitchen and the plant-filled sunroom, down a further corridor. This was where the frozen door was, I thought I recalled, but it wasn't here now.

Haru walked in time with me as we passed a few open

doors. Inside one was a literal game room, filled with ranks of arcade machines around a pool table as well as a giant flat screen tv, a gaming console sitting on a stand beneath it. They were all silent, bright colors muted, and a dim bar lay shadowed along the back.

I pulled Haru to a halt. "Whoa now. This has been here the whole time?"

Haru blinked at it. "Yep."

"Are there other facilities I should be aware of?"

Haru counted on his fingers. "Bar, games, pool room. As in swimming pool. Sauna and spa. Rooftop garden with bar . . ." He laughed at the expression on my face. "These are Summer's projects. I prefer running along streets with people and swimming in the wild."

"Yeah, naked," I teased.

"Of course. What else?" He skated closer to me, and fuck me, but I wanted him naked right then and there. I bit my lip when a deep vibrating roar came around the corner. My grip tightened on Haru, pulling him behind me and dropping my purse to raise my fists toward the threat.

Haru burst out laughing and laid a gentle hand on my shoulder. "Thanks for protecting me. That's another of Summer's projects. Let me introduce you to Betsy."

Cheeks heating, I muttered, "Just doing my job and making sure you're safe."

His eyes flickered desire as deep as lake. "Our shield, doing a great job." He kissed my hand, leading me onward, and I followed with my ears ringing.

I poked my head around the corner to see an immaculate garage space. Seriously, this garage had carpeting. Four cars gleamed in a row, the paintwork shimmering with care and attention.

The one closest to us, purring with a dangerous tone, was all sharp edges in matte black and glistening chrome. The wheel detailing looked like ninja throwing stars, and the sleek car hovered low to the ground, windows completely blacked out.

I had to lean into Haru to reach his ear. "What is that?" I asked, pleased as he bent lower for me.

"Who is that, you mean." Haru nodded toward the floor.

From underneath the car of midnight rolled Summer. He was lying flat on his back on one of those mechanic rollers in a tight white shirt. Well, it was once white. Now it was stained with oil, along with his bronzed arms and thick neck.

He eased up to standing, rubbing his hands in the grease rag hanging from his black suit pants. He gave the car a fond smile, and damn, he was beyond gorgeous.

"Nice to look at, right?" Haru grinned at me, slinging an arm over my shoulders to pull me close against his side. I flushed again, imagining Summer pressed just as close, but on the other side of me. Summer's eyes found mine, and dark desire speared through me, making me suddenly afraid I'd spoken that desire out loud.

"Hm? Oh! Uh," I looked frantically at the car.

Summer switched off the ignition. "This is Betsy," Summer said, his voice as low as the car's growl had been.

"I see." And see I did, as every knead of his fingers in the rag sent a ripple of muscle up Summer's arms. I focused on the car, which was almost as beautiful, with sleek lines I wanted to run my fingers along. "I haven't seen this before."

One side of Summer's lips twitched. Was that a smile? "She's a Bugatti Voiture Noire."

"Uh, duh. Of course. But how did you get it? There was just one made, right? Unless this is a knock off."

Summer looked completely stunned, and Haru laughed at his reaction. Summer regrouped to say, "It most certainly is not."

Wow. The world's most expensive car, and Summer worked on her himself, getting down and dirty doing it.

Speaking of . . . I looked Summer up and down. "Are you coming with us?"

He glanced down at his grease monkey attire. "I can't, that would interfere with the local weather system. Besides, I'd have to throw on a shirt."

And be all filthy underneath. My legs wobbled a little, not gonna lie, at the idea of a greasy Summer getting me all dirty. Sheesh, conceding to more than one guy at the same time? What was up with me, apart from being mega thirsty? "Don't worry about it. One person escorting me to my mom and brother is probably enough. Besides, I'd prefer to protect you guys one at a time, or my duties will be split."

As I spoke, Summer's gaze grew more and more intense, his shoulders bunching as though he was holding himself from moving. "Next time, then," he said, his voice a promise. "I'm great at meeting family."

I just bet he was all smooth charm when he wanted to be, hiding the smoldering intensity behind civility.

Haru held out his hand. "Alright, hand me the keys, please."

Summer hunted in his pocket, his hands roving deep into those tight pants, and pulled out a card. "Don't make me regret this."

"You won't. Trust me," Haru said.

Summer rolled his eyes. "I trust you, Haru, but . . ." He glanced at me, then back at Haru. It was clear that he was worried about me being a problem.

I walked over to the passenger side to show how compliant I was being, and Summer's hand swooped in to grasp the handle and open the door for me.

I peered up at him, not doing a good job at hiding my surprise. I didn't think a man had ever opened a car door for me before, which I had never thought much about because I was usually all 'I am woman hear me roar'. But it was kind of nice.

As I settled myself, I said in a rush, "Hey, thanks for sorting this out. I really do appreciate it."

He gave me an unreadable look. "Your sincerity is appreciated, but it was really nothing."

Nothing, when my family meant everything to me. I clenched my fists. *Asshole.*

Haru laughed, sliding behind the wheel and turning that playful grin on us. "Sure, because four hours on the phone to multiple countries is nothing."

Oh, wow. Summer had hauled his butt through actual work? His chiseled jaw ticked with annoyance as Haru outed him.

"Thank you," I said again. "Maybe you're not so bad."

He scowled, but I'd pierced his calm at last. "You'll change your mind on that," he vowed, voice dark and dripping with promise.

I squeezed my legs together at the zing tingling through me at his voice. "Can't wait," I returned.

Haru laughed as Summer shut the door, and I joined him as we both heard a burst of Spanish, probably swear words given the delicious emphasis he put on them.

Once Haru calmed down, he asked, "Ready?"

"Yep." I had my seat belt on and gripped in both hands.

I watched Summer, his hands on his hips watching us leave, as Haru eased us out of the garage. "Look after her," he bellowed, and Haru saluted as he picked up speed down the long, curving driveway. Betsy was low but extremely comfortable, every inch oozing wealth. It was much too grand for someone like me.

Haru pulled up behind the huge gates. Bishop and Lilian scrambled to open them. This was the first time a Shield had to ever let anything through, so I wasn't surprised that they had no idea what to do.

"Friends of yours?" Haru asked.

"Yeah. Lilian looks tired." She might have been doing double shifts, asked to haul ass because I'd disappeared. She was worried. I went to the bathroom and never came back. She had probably pulled all kinds of alarms about my disappearance. What had she been told?

Haru looked at me sadly, and that look on his face catapulted me back to just a few days ago when I hated him.

"I know," I reassured him. "Unvetted, all that. It's not like I didn't have to pass some background checks to get this job, you know."

"I know, and I trust you," Haru said. "Summer did a lot of work just now to reassure himself, but I trusted you from the get go." He nodded to Bishop and Lilian. "If you want to tell them you're okay, I will take the heat from Summer."

The idea filled me with a surge of reassuring warmth, loosening muscles I hadn't realized I'd tensed. I could meet them halfway as they were going to great lengths for me. "Thank you, Haru, but I wouldn't do that to you. We'll talk about it. I appreciate the safety concerns, as this affects all of you too."

He tapped the steering wheel, still waiting for Bishop to open his side of the ornate gates. "Alright, one at a time. Very sensible, Mari." He moved forward gently and, once we were clear of the gates, accelerated down the lane. I jerked forward, grabbing his arm, and he chuckled. *Asshole!* The car seemed to cling to the road as tightly as I held his wrist.

The roads flickered by, Haru finding all the perfectly-sized gaps to overtake. He didn't ever go over the speed limit, but the car would roar ahead on the slightest touch of the throttle, making it seem like we were on a racetrack. I put the window down and the breeze played with my hair, blonde strands whipping in my face. It was hard to stay removed from the reality of my day to day as it all flashed past me. Work, chores, the grind of the day in day out tidal movements of life that was my rhythm. My heart was pounding, face hot, by the time we pulled into my street.

With everyone else packed along the uneven sidewalk, there was no parking available on the street. Haru circled for a while looking for a space, and I had time to let reality sink in. This crowded apartment block was my life. That spacious house with all its amenities was theirs. I rubbed my cheeks of embarrassment, refusing to feel ashamed of our circumstances. They were what they were.

"Maybe we should find a parking structure," I offered.

"Got one." Haru put his arm around my seat to help him twist around to see out of the back window. He scowled. "Tiny windows, all tinted black, no good for maneuvering."

I smiled at him, but the fact was he had four cars in his garage to choose from. Mine was probably still in the CSON parking lot.

I hurried out, impatient now that we were here, and ran up the stairs. My hands fumbled with the keys in the door, and then we were in. "Mom! Chris!"

"Marigold!" Mom cried out, hobbling over, mouth open in shock. Chris's bedroom door flew open and he barreled in for a hug.

He hadn't done that since he was about ten years old, and I pulled him under my arm, squeezing tight. "Oh, Chris. Chris! You're okay!" Then I put him at arm's length, inspecting his face. He had a small bruise and his eyes were puffy like he'd been crying, but he seemed okay, if not quite looking me in the eye.

Mom wrapped her arms around us both. "He told me everything, Marigold, and while we are going to get through it, I am very, very shocked."

Chris hung his head.

"And you?" Mom whirled to me. Wow, she'd gone from 0 to 60 being pissed at me, and I raised my arms as if surrendering. "Where have you been? Not even a call or a text?"

"I—" I shot Haru a quick look as if to say, "See?", and he had the grace to look torn.

Mom rolled her eyes. "Your new boss told me all about your new assignment. I didn't know you'd need to be completely blackout or in the dark, or whatever it's called, Marigold."

"New boss?" Summer must have called them. I was right, he wasn't all bad. I suppose "new assignment" wasn't untruthful, but still.

Chris held on for one more second, then turned to face Haru. "Who's this?" he asked accusingly, eyebrow arched.

I extracted myself from Mom to make introductions. "This is one of my new charges, Haru."

"Hello. It's nice to meet you," Haru said with a little bow.

"Haru, this is my mom, Beth, and my brother, Chris."

Mom gave a simpering smile, kind of glassy-eyed at Haru's perfection, but at least it distracted her anger and worry. "Mari, you should have said you were coming, and with company! I'd have tidied up at least."

"Mom, can I talk to you for a moment?"

Haru didn't even glance my way. His trust in me was absolute.

Chris bristled. "Great. I need a word with this guy."

"Chris," I admonished. What was this about? It was adorable seeing my little brother get protective, but it was hellishly embarrassing.

Haru placed his arms politely to either side of his body. "I'd be delighted to talk," he said. Chris grunted and led the way to his room.

I rolled my eyes and pulled Mom aside in the back of the tiny kitchen. "I'm sorry, Mom."

She put her hands flat on the kitchen counter. "What is going on, Marigold?"

My throat dried. "I . . . I can't tell you. It's a secret assignment—"

She waved her hand. "Oh, I know *you're* okay, Marigold. I meant with our Christopher." She shook her head. "Adderall? Drug dealers? He is going to a good school, Marigold. I never thought he'd get caught up with that sort of nonsense! Where did I go wrong?"

I put the kettle on the stove out of habit. "I don't know, except, I think maybe he felt the pressure."

Mom rubbed her forehead. She knew what I meant. "Oh, Marigold. It seems like we've been walking uphill, and it keeps getting steeper and steeper. But this is our life, and it should be for living!"

I dried the dishes while I waited for the kettle to boil. Movement helped me think. "Yes, but . . ."

"But what?"

I put the damp towel down. "Money. Real world stuff."

"Real world stuff came knocking down my door, Marigold, and if drug dealers and goodness knows what else is part of that, I don't want it." She sniffed, and I couldn't help my smile. My tiny mom, ready to beat down the dealers herself if it came to it.

I scrubbed at the counter with furious strokes. "But we can't just ignore that we need money, Mom."

Mom took the towel from me gently. "We're constantly pushing, Marigold. I know life is hard, but there are meant to be sweet moments as well." She sighed and pursed her lips. "When was the last time we ever slowed down to smell the roses? And now Christopher is picking up on this attitude." She touched my cheek. "Don't think I haven't missed what you do for us, sweetheart. I know we've gone through some hard times recently, and you've done ever so well. Thank you."

"Of course." My nose stung, and I wrinkled it savagely. I wouldn't cry. I couldn't.

Mom smoothed my hair. "You're so responsible. You've had to grow up so quickly, and for that I'm sorry. But, well, perhaps this new opportunity will be really good for you, Marigold."

The twist in my stomach loosened slightly. "Yeah. Maybe." A chance to finally travel the way I had dreamed of, but in a way that didn't involve planes or money. All it cost was my freedom, giving me a different kind of freedom in return.

Was she right? Was there an upside to my situation? They hadn't hurt me, and it struck me that Haru kept trying to reach out, even when I slapped his hand down repeatedly. He didn't want me in this situation as much as I didn't want to be in it, but at the same time, that nascent attraction kept bubbling between us.

Her eyes twinkled as if she could tell where my thoughts had wandered. "Is that Haru guy a celebrity or something?"

Scoffing, I refilled the dishwasher. "Super classified, Mom. Suffice to say he's really important. They all are."

"They?" Mom waved her hands as if to remind herself. "I won't ask any more. Just . . . Marigold? I didn't get a very good feeling about your new boss, okay?"

New boss? I straightened upright slowly and lowered my voice. Chris and Haru were only on the other side of the small apartment. "What do you mean?"

"Your boss dropped off the money you sent us."

"Oh?" My stomach churned. I had no idea what the hell she was talking about, and I suddenly wasn't sure it was Summer she meant. "Remind me? It's been a long few days."

She blinked at me. "Well, I suppose if I was protecting that, uh, Mr. Haru, I'd forget ten thousand dollars too." She winked at me.

Ten thousand dollars? "Oh," was all I could say faintly.

"I have to say, he's not the same caliber as Mr. Haru here." Her nose wrinkled. "A bit suspicious if you ask me."

"Anyone dropping off an envelope of 10k is going to be suspicious, Mom." My stomach was really roiling now. What was Summer up to? Of course they could hand out money like sweets. They had to have serious assets given that huge magical house and the luxury cars, but it still rubbed me raw. Plus he said he couldn't leave the house because it wasn't his season.

"And your father's debts are gone!" she abruptly added.

"What?" I went slack jawed, while internally wincing at the 'your father' bit. Personally, I typically liked to think of him as Mr. P.O.S.

"Yes, I got a call to say we were cleared."

Did Summer . . . Oh shit, was it the shady guy? Did they give ten grand to my mom and then use the rest to pay off the debt? Technically I completed the mission, so I should receive the money. Suddenly my heart accelerated. *Of course!* It had to be the higher up from CSON, although it was shitty of them to use it how they saw fit. Must be a way to pay me without the IRS getting on my ass or something.

I glanced quickly at Chris's door to make sure Haru wasn't standing there or our trust would be burned to the ground before it had even begun. Mystery guy had given me the creeps too, but he was one of my commanding officers. I had no choice but to obey, right?

Mom frowned. "Is everything okay with you? He said you wanted us to have it, and you were on a deep mission. It sounded exciting, like I knew you wanted, Marigold. But I do want to hear your voice."

"I'm fine, apart from missing you two." I looked around. The cupboards had sufficient food, the light in the corridor was replaced, and everything was swept nice and clean.

She kissed me on the cheek. "Good. Now, go talk to your brother, please."

"Sure." I wasn't sure what I was going to say to him. Or scream at him most likely. I went into Chris's room in a storm of feeling. Textbooks had been left open on the bed next to Chris. Haru sat at his desk, both absorbed in staring at the computer screen.

"So now we have a shared realm set up, and . . ." Chris noticed me. "Oh, hi."

I leaned against the wall. "Hi yourself." The atmosphere was stilted, tense as soon as I came in, like Chris knew he'd been caught doing something wrong. Which he had been, but hopefully not right this second.

Chris' cheeks flushed with guilt. "Anyways, Haru, the Minecraft server is all ready, so just hop on whenever."

"I will, thanks." Haru stood, clutching a piece of paper with a string of letters and numbers on it. He beamed at me. "Your brother introduced me to his server. He has some really amazing projects on there!"

"Computer games?" I raised an eyebrow at Chris.

"Engineering computer games," he mumbled.

"Look, Buttercup, it's spectacular!" Haru tugged at my arm to show me Chris's computer.

My brother squirmed. "I'm meant to be studying."

The dark circles under my brother's eyes really tugged at me. He shouldn't be putting himself through the wringer. That was probably how he got caught up in this mess in the first place. "Chris, we need to talk."

"That's my cue," Haru said, letting go of my arm and bowing before making his way out. "I'll be right outside."

"Okay, Haru." It was good of him to give us this privacy. I waited until the door shut, giving my best impersonation of a pissed off sister by glaring at Chris's ear. He swallowed hard and dropped his gaze, closing the textbooks on the bed with a soft finality. Tall and lanky enough to be fully grown, he still had the little flick of hair that fell in front of his ears. In a few short years that hair might blend into a beard if he let it grow out. It was like I could see him at every age all at the same time; the scowling teen from a few weeks ago to the eager twelve-year old ecstatic he got the scholarship, to the nine-year old who patted every cat and dog he could, down to the three-year old asking me where Daddy was.

As soon as the door clicked closed, I crumbled. I tapped his arms, his shoulders, pulled back, then grabbed him again, testing for any breaks or bruises as if I'd just yanked him from those fucking drug dealers all over again. Tears soaked my cheeks, pattering over my lips. I was a mess and I didn't care. "Are you really okay?"

He was stunned. I had never, ever cried in front of him. "Ye—Yeah, Mari, I'm okay."

"Why did you do it? Why?" My shoulders shook with the force of the sobs wracking me as I imagined what could have been. As if the horrors of that night were fresh in front of me. Instead of a scowling little brother, I might not have one at all. "We could have lost you!"

He stared at me, mouth agape. "Well, you didn't?" he offered, but even he knew it was lame. Sitting heavily on the edge of the bed, he dropped his head into his hands.

I wiped my face, pulling myself together. He was fine. He wasn't badly hurt, and although it could have been a different story, the truth was he would live to learn from his mistakes. "Didn't you know how stupid it was?"

"Looking at it when you saw it, yeah, I did. But it didn't start out like that." He pressed the palms of his hands together, tension strumming along his arms.

I faced him, leaning down a little so I could meet his eyes. "Tell me what happened, Chris."

He was quiet for a long moment while he thought, then just as I was about to speak again, he began in a quiet voice, "I had a friend who was flunking, and suddenly he wasn't. When

I asked him for study tips, he said, 'Take one of these.' And it was great! I could retain information like I was reading it from the back of my eyeballs, and I was focusing no matter what else was going on. I could block out everything and it would just be me and the math, you know?"

I sat next to him, hunting my purse for a tissue. "Pretend I have the same relationship with equations that you do and that I'm nodding along."

He shrugged one shoulder. "Alright, like . . . weight training. I know you do it mostly for work, but I've heard you say you can just sink into the movement and be you for a while."

That hit me hard and I sighed. "Yes, I suppose. Okay, so you're vibing or whatever, but you're smart; so, so smart, Chris. You should have known—"

He put up a hand, and I closed my mouth. I wanted to understand. I'd only do that if I really listened. "Yeah, I'm smart," he said, but his voice was disparaging. "Smart and on a scholarship. If I slip, even a few marks, the teachers' eyes zoom in on me and they're asking me 'what's wrong? Do I need to see the principal? Is everything okay at home?'" He shook his head and huffed. "Like, just because I take the bus to school doesn't mean we aren't doing fine, you know? Except when we aren't doing all that great. But we're still okay."

The stubborn loyalty to our family warmed my heart like nothing else.

"So . . . I did great and aced the next few tests. I just wanted to use it as a tool, like noise canceling headphones, but my friend said he couldn't give it to me anymore and to see a guy called Darren after school. He would be down the street on a Tuesday. I knew he wasn't a student or anything like that . . ." Chris paused then shook his head. "I know it was stupid. I know. But it didn't seem that bad to start."

"Yeah." Although by no means on the same scale, I could see how a small trickle could turn into a flood. That had happened with me trying to juggle two jobs and giving up everything in between.

"And then he wanted me to sell, because he didn't want to keep coming up to the school. He thought he could have me do the runs, and he'd give me a cut."

Cold crept into my stomach. I waited, barely breathing.

"I . . . said yes, but I turned around the same day and told him no. That's when you caught up with us and, well . . . You know the rest."

"I guess." I let out a low breath. He had been tempted by the money, but he hadn't gone through with it. "And now you see how dangerous they are and all that."

"Yeah, but," he flashed me a small, hesitant grin, "they were no match for you."

I shook my head with a small laugh. "Nope, not that many all at once." I really had been about to be overwhelmed when Haru intervened. Wiping my eyes, I gathered my thoughts. "So what's next?"

"A detox program," he said in a small voice, his eyes unfocused on his computer. "Mom said we've come into a bit of money, so it won't impact us too much."

Correct, but the ten thousand that was dropped off wouldn't go very far with treatments. "Good. Great." I put my arm around his shoulders. "Talk to us, okay? We're in this together."

"Right. Though Mom said you'd be busy on a new assignment, and you couldn't say too much about it." Chris leaned into my side, smiling softly. "Don't worry, I'll step up and help Mom."

I could see the steely determination in his face—propping himself up but not running away—and pride bubbled in my chest.

I nudged him gently. "But you do need some downtime. Let's see the, uh, computer pixels."

He beamed like I'd given him the sun. My little brother balanced between kid and adult. "Thanks, Mari."

HARU and I played video games with Chris while Mom made snacks, something I'd heard was common for teenagers but I couldn't exactly remember when we'd been able to do that before. Mom even joined in for a four player racing game. Chris and I had never heard her laugh quite as madly as when she threw bananas to blow up our races.

Haru and I went out to the lounge for soft drinks, and Haru opened a can for me before grabbing his own. Somehow this amazing guy fit into the tiny apartment that was my life, expanding it to make it seem so much bigger.

He took a sip. "Feeling better?"

"Yes," I said, giving him a genuine smile.

"I can tell." He closed his eyes. "I sense a lot of worry in this house, but it all stems from a place of love. There is a lot of love here, Mari."

Love. Good. My stomach warmed.

His head drooped. "I know our house can seem fraught. Everyone has their work to do all the time, and we rarely make time to just hang out ourselves. It wasn't always like that. Once it was fun and full of love . . ." He rubbed a hand down his face, sighing. "Life is to be lived, experienced, not just gotten through. Even if it's something small that brings you joy, we need to nurture it. We've forgotten all about that."

"Right." That resonated with me. "I have certainly let the nurturing of fun fall to the wayside while real world things took over." I flicked through the latest bills on the counter, frowning.

Haru glanced over my shoulder. "Summer can take care of those."

I scrunched them in my hand, the paper crinkling. "No. These are my family's personal finances." But wouldn't that be great? A huge windfall; breathing space bought by these guys.

I searched his face, but of course there wasn't any deceit. He was sad but resolute, and he was sincerely giving me this opportunity.

He moved closer, his hand a whisper on my shoulder. "I . . . There's something going on, and I know you can feel it too. I want you to be with us. I want you to trust us." He gently touched my cheek, cupping it in the palm of his hand. "Just let go a little. I promise I'll make it worth it."

He was right. There was something going on, and I had a job to do. Now I knew everyone was okay here, I could focus on the new path opening up in front of us. I could focus on me, and Haru had opened that space for me.

We said our goodbyes after a little while longer. My family was safe for now; I could see that. As we walked to the car, our breath steaming in the late afternoon air, it was getting harder and harder to deny my attraction and need for him. Ever since we kissed, or rather made out in my bedroom, I wanted him in a way I had never wanted anyone.

Haru adjusted the mirror ten or so minutes into the drive. "You've been quiet. Everything okay?" His hands gripped the wheel a little too tightly. "I mean, not perfectly fine, obviously," he allowed.

"Why not?" I responded, watching his face carefully. I had

to wrap my head around the situation because what he offered was exactly what I wanted. A freedom I had never been able to have. The ability to enjoy my life and let go a little. I truly felt I could do that with him, even all of them maybe.

He glanced at me. "Because this is not the way I'd want to do things," he admitted quietly. "I'd want dates, not dungeons."

"Depends what you're into," I quipped, relishing the flush on his cheeks.

"You know what I mean." He met my eyes briefly before concentrating on the road.

"I think . . . We've all got some issues, but I'd like to see where this takes us." My heart raced with fear and elation. I'd ended up in this situation in such a backward way, but maybe it was a blessing in disguise if I let it be. If I took Haru up on his offer and just let go a little.

"Stop and smell the roses," I said with a smile, looking at the receding town of Stowe behind us.

And I swear he tensed just a little bit.

Chapter Twelve

My eyes flew open, my breath coming too fast. The room was dark, and I lay in my bed with sweat beading my forehead. I couldn't remember what I had dreamed about, the images already fuzzy and fading. Only the barest of glimpses remained. Someone screaming my name and intense cold. Even now, despite being drenched in sweat, I was so damn cold. The center of my chest hurt with a piercing pain. I rubbed at it, glancing at the clock.

One a.m.? Shit, I had come upstairs to shower before dinner. Seems I fell asleep in my robe before I made it to the clothes part of things. I guess I hadn't realized how emotionally drained I was, or how much the worry for my family had been bothering me. Now, I could breathe easier. Apparently enough to sleep like I hadn't in probably years. Because even when I wasn't shouldering burdens, I was working the bar.

Slipping out of bed, I fixed the tie on my robe, pulling it closer around me to help fight off the cold that still seemed to chill my bones. My stomach made itself known with a gurgle. "Okay," I told it with a scowl. "I'm going." I went to the door to find it unlocked again, and somehow this small act made my shoulders relax. Seems Haru was right that trust would slowly come. It was definitely late at night, so they should be asleep too. Which meant they were trusting me not to run. And now that I knew my family was taken care of and the side of me that felt the relief of letting things go a little, I found myself not wanting to break their trust.

I followed the same path I had yesterday downstairs to the kitchen, the plants still growing out from the carpet, some with buds now. The house was dark, only a few sconces lit. I crept across the kitchen and pulled open the fridge, which illuminated the room. Staring into the monstrosity of a fridge, which I guess it had to be since it fed four men, my jaw dropped, aghast with how much food was inside. *This would feed mom, Chris, and me for over a month.*

I reached inside and pulled out a container of cut pineapple. It had been so long since I had pineapple, and damn did I love it. It was an indulgence, something I rarely bought for myself with the family budget always on my mind. But, hey, as long as I was here . . .

I closed the door with my shoulder as I opened the lid and popped a piece into my mouth. Its sweet juices filled my mouth, and I let out a moan.

Doesn't pineapple make you taste good? I stared at it, wondering if Haru had eaten any recently. How he tasted. If his cu—

Nope, nope. Not going there. Nope. That damn make out session, and then with him being so sweet, was getting to me. I couldn't help but wonder what else he could do with that mouth of his.

I bit into another piece and my eyes rolled back into my head. Shit, this was good.

"You could make a guy jealous with how you eat fruit."

I nearly choked on the pineapple, barely managing to swallow it, and whirled toward a dark form in the doorway.

Stepping further into the kitchen, Haru closed the distance between us until he was only a few feet away. He was fully dressed, but my gaze still dipped at the memory of his hardness pressing between my legs.

A smile tugged at the corner of his mouth as if his own thoughts had run in the same direction, his gaze flicking down to my lips.

"I was hungry," I mumbled, keeping my head down so he couldn't see my blush as I moved to the kitchen island to sit.

"By all means, help yourself. I just heard a sound and decided to check it out. Can't be too careful these days. Never know who might break in." His tone was playful, matching the twinkle in his eye.

"Ah," I noted while attempting to drop his gaze. The somersaults in my stomach were too aggressive this early in the morning. Instead, I focused on his chin.

Haru frowned and moved even closer, leaning his elbow on the countertop and casually resting his temple against his closed fist. "Everything alright?"

"Yup!" I squeaked before shoving another piece of pineapple into my mouth.

His eyes narrowed. "Something is telling me not to believe you. After visiting your family, you went upstairs and never came back down."

Lowering the container, I met his gaze. "It's nothing. I'm fine." *Except for the fact I now can't stop thinking about you.* I must have felt a bit shaken from the dream I couldn't even remember.

With his free hand, he clutched his chest like he'd been wounded. "Not the dreaded 'I'm fine.' There is no way in hell I'm going to believe you now."

I chewed on my bottom lip as flashes of the way his hands had felt against my body, taking my breast in his large palm. I couldn't admit that to him.

"Truth or dare," he offered. It wasn't in his usual playful demeanor, but for whatever reason the familiar game we'd started unfurled a knot in my stomach.

"Isn't it my turn?" I quipped.

His lips twitched with the threat of a smile. "Truth."

"Boring," I jested. And, of course, our kiss came racing back to my mind and my cheeks heated. Coughing, I cleared my throat. I hmm-ed and haw-ed until I found something that had confused me for the last several days. "Why did you get weird at the glen during our run?"

His brows furrowed with confusion.

"I know saying the place felt familiar might've been a bit eccentric, especially since I've been well, nowhere. But I don't think it was *that* bad," I added, suddenly feeling a bit awkward. I saw no other reason for him to clam up unless I did something.

He shook his head, eyebrows drawing together. "No, I'm sorry I made you feel that way. You just reminded me of something—someone—is all, and it took me by surprise."

"Who?" I pushed, intrigue mixed with a flash of jealousy rearing its ugly head.

"Ah, ah, ah." He wagged a finger at me. "You used your truth. My turn."

I sighed. "Fine. Truth." I wasn't up for a whirlwind run, and my stomach swirled at what else he would dare me to do. I stared at his mouth, his full lips, and bit my lip at the images in my head.

The corner of his mouth quirked up. "What are you doing down here so late? Did you have a nightmare, or maybe a different kind of dream?"

I knew exactly what kind of dream he meant, and no it wasn't that. Instead, I was having very real memories of what he did to me and how he could kiss me.

"Weird dream," I blurted, as if that explained anything. "I

don't remember what happened but . . . I woke up from it a bit thrown off. That's all."

"Oh." His eyes searched mine, his playfulness dropped in the face of my distress. "A nightmare?"

I shook my head as if I could bat his concern away. I didn't need anyone worrying about me. "No, nothing like that, and I can deal with nightmares anyway."

"Of course you can, but sometimes talking about it helps." He came around the other side of the breakfast bar toward me, closing the distance.

"Ah, ah, ah," I mocked him in return, waving my fork at him. "You used your truth, and it's my go now."

He eased back a step, leaning against the wall and folding his arms across his wide chest. The tight black shirt strained over his biceps, and I'd never envied clothing more. "You've got me there," he said. "I'm yours to command. Will you choose a truth for a truth, or," his gaze traced the curves of the sleek robe I wore, alighting on the single knot keeping my rapidly heating body from his gaze, "are you ready for a dare, Buttercup?"

The pineapple container trembled in my hand, and the images crossing my mind were like those of my dream; fevered, frenzied, and oh so wet.

He cocked his head and bit his lip, and fuck me but I wanted to be the one biting it. "Maybe a little longer, hm? I'll take a truth for now."

Damn! Well, then, I'd have to find an awkward subject . . . Recalling how he had been looking at me in the glen, I challenged him with, "What were you drawing at the glen?"

"You."

I speared a pineapple, but I couldn't seem to make my fingers move. "M—me?" I sounded like all the breath had whooshed out of me from the enormity of that. *Drawing me? Why? Just because I was there?*

He nodded, eyes glazing as he recalled our morning. "You were so serene and peaceful. So beautiful."

No one had called me beautiful before, and I knew he meant it. There was no trace of mockery in his face. Hell, no one had ever kissed me or touched me the way he had. I squeezed my thighs together as a surge of desire surged through me.

Haru continued, "You're very pent up, on edge all the time. Understandably so, but it felt like a moment I may never get to see again. So I wanted to document it."

I really hoped he chose dare next because I was definitely going to make him show me those. If they were horrible, I planned on burning them.

"Truth or dare," he interrupted my thoughts.

"Truth." I picked up another piece of pineapple and popped it into my mouth.

"Do you want me right now?" His words were light, but the dark promise they held caused a swoop in my belly.

"Yes," I whispered. I didn't know what had come over me, but it *was* true. I wanted him. More than I wanted anything before.

He came around the counter until he stood in front of me. His honeysuckle scent washed over me.

I placed the pineapple container on the counter, my breath coming in short spurts. "Truth or dare," I gulped, scarcely able to meet his gaze.

A spark of interest alighted his eyes. "Dare."

"Kiss me."

The words were barely out of my mouth before he was on me. His hand twisted into my hair, his other gripping my hip to pull me toward him. He devoured me with his kiss, wiping my mind clean of everything but him. The way his hardness strained against his pants. The way his hands roved over my curves, slipping under my robe as it loosened. His hand palmed my breast until it found my peaked nipple.

He grazed his thumb over it before adding a cheeky little pinch.

"Haru," I breathed. I wanted more, needed more. It'd been so long since someone had touched me like this; since I had felt anything close to his caress. "More," I pleaded.

He groaned against my skin, and with my legs wrapped around him, his hands found my ass. Without breaking our kiss, he walked me to the dining room table and laid me down atop it. He pulled away, and I whimpered from the sudden cold. This, whatever this was between us, had warmed me. I didn't want it to end. For once, I was giving into what I wanted to do. I wasn't overthinking. I wasn't weighing the pros and cons. I was one with the moment, letting my feelings take the wheel, and what they wanted were him.

I spread my legs, slightly, a coy invitation that I never thought I would've done before today.

A dark chuckle emanated from Haru as his eyes wandered over my prone form, the robe barely covering my nakedness beneath it. "Truth or dare?" His voice was deep, trickling across my nerve endings and soaking me between my legs.

"Truth," I choked out.

"Will you regret this?" His gaze found mine and what stared at me was a man barely containing himself. His fingers flexed against the flesh of my thighs.

I shook my head. "No."

His smile was devilish, more sinister than playful, as he sank to his knees. "Hold on, Buttercup, because you're about to be my ice cream cone." His head disappeared under my robe, and soft lips pressed against my calf, his fingers smoothing up the other. Shivers tingled across my skin at his light touch and the way he trailed butterfly kisses up the inside of my leg. When he reached my thigh, they opened wider of their own accord.

His lips were replaced by his tongue, swirling delicate designs until I felt his hot breath against my core. "You smell so good," he growled.

My core throbbed, threatening to cum in a moment. His fingers traced the outside of my thighs, pulling little mewls from me as it danced between pleasure and tickles. My clit throbbed with its need to be touched.

"You are so fucking beautiful." His tongue swiped between my legs, eliciting a surprised gasp from me.

My hands pressed against the hardwood, looking for anything to grasp onto as he expertly worked me. "Mmmm," he moaned, pleased by either my taste or the noises I made. I didn't know, but whatever it was he must've liked it because he did it again. He savored every single curve and dip of my center until he finally landed on my nub.

His tongue circled my clit before he gave it a little suck, and I cried out from the jolt of pleasure. A finger replaced his tongue, swiping through my folds. "You're so fucking wet for me. I knew it."

My chest rose and fell in deep breaths as I tried to hold myself together. My hips shifted, craving more, egging him on.

"Ahhh, is this what you want?" Two more fingers slipped inside me. Pressing his palm against my clit, he curled the tips of his fingers up inside me. "I don't know whose turn it is, but truth."

I ground myself against his palm, seeking out my release he continued to build inside of me. The harder I pushed against him, the faster his fingers moved. My pussy clenched tighter around him with each stroke. "Yes!"

"Let go. Let me see you. I want to see everything you are," he coaxed. "Come for me."

My fists clenched as I climbed higher, my vision blurring

until I could barely see. All I could do was ride the highs of pleasure. Knowing Haru was giving it to me only brought me closer to the edge.

His palm fell away and a protest formed on my lips, but his mouth enveloped my clit. His fingers still worked melodies inside of me, while his tongue was the conductor of the symphony. My moans and gasps joined the music, and with every flick of his tongue and scrape of his teeth I got closer to orgasm.

With a hard thrust of his fingers coupled with a soft swipe at my clit, I came undone. "Haru!" I yelled into the night, my hands finding his head and burrowing into his soft hair as my hips worked through every spark of my orgasm. As I floated down, my arm fell limply to my side.

I opened my eyes and gasped at the sight, sitting up suddenly.

Haru stood, wiping at his glistening mouth, eyes wide from my sudden movement.

All around us flowers had grown and bloomed. From the floor to the chairs to the walls.

"Fuck," Haru muttered, staring at his haywire powers. "Otto's going to be so pissed."

And then I laughed. I laughed so hard from the delight of the beautiful garden that had grown around me during my orgasm. "It's gorgeous." I threw my legs over the side of the table, soft petals brushing the soles of my feet. I walked over to a yellow flower, the epitome of spring, illuminated by the moonlight. I smiled at it as I stroked the stem. "You're amazing."

He stared at me, slackjawed, as though the world around us had disappeared. "Rose?" The word was so light I questioned if I'd heard it.

I frowned in confusion, and I stared at the flower still tucked between my forefinger and thumb. "You mean daffodil?" A bubble of laughter rose up in me. "Shouldn't you know that, Mr. Flower Man?"

He shook his head, eyes clearing like he'd been slammed back into reality. "Right, yes, of course. I meant to make roses for you, of course."

"Huh," I said, looking at the flower again. "I think I prefer daffodils." I pulled the robe closed over my nakedness, tying it tightly as I walked back to him.

His gaze searched my face, as though trying to decipher som code and I had all the answers. I didn't, but the way his attention pierced through me, I couldn't look away. "I should . . . get to bed. It's late," he said finally.

"Yeah, of course." My words were light, airy, and barely there. This man had just given me that best orgasm of my fucking life, and now we were just casually going back to our rooms. As *one does.*

Neither of us broke eye contact. I expected him to clam up like at the glen, for the tension to last forever and us to depart in silence. What he actually did was the last thing I would've expected by its tenderness.

Leaning forward, he kissed me on the forehead, and whispered, "Have a good night," before rushing off.

What the hell?

Chapter Thirteen

I barely slept and in the morning, I came downstairs with tentative steps. I touched the spot where Haru had pressed his lips. It was such a swift, familiar kiss. Like a quick peck before going off to work. Something that distilled a lifetime of love living alongside someone else into a single gesture.

Get over yourself. I had barely met the guy and was already mooning over him? *Stockholm syndrome much?*

My feet crunched on the carpet. Was this moss? I bent down, brushing a cloud of clover. It smelled fresh, each tiny shoot perky and green.

"You're cute, but you don't belong here," I told it. It surely couldn't get enough sunlight despite the big windows.

I trailed a finger on the half-finished painting up the stairs. It was a shame his colors weren't more all over the house, given how bare and cold some corridors seemed. Then again, maybe he didn't have time to paint all the walls. There could easily be hundreds of corridors if this place really did lead anywhere in the world.

If these doors led everywhere, what about door 207?

Where I slid the key? A tendril of fear snagged my heart, like my shirt catching on a nail and dragging me to a halt with an alarming tearing sound. CSON could access the house now. That was a good thing. *Right?*

Walking past the kitchen where Winter stood banging pots and pans around as he put things away, I headed for the conservatory. I stopped short in the doorway, amused. Haru stood shirtless and stained with blue paint like he'd been wrestling a smurf. He was panting like he'd battled something too, but all he faced was an easel. Surrounding him was copious amounts of paper, thick parchment-type that held ink well. I picked one up, trying not to let the edges flutter.

It was a drawing of me, lying face up in the water. My eyes were closed, eyelashes resting on my cheek, and my neck and chest was mainly submerged except for my boobs. Those were drawn in almost embarrassingly pert and perky detail through the wet shirt clinging to me.

I shifted my arms over my chest. Was that really what I looked like? No way. I picked up another sheet of paper to see a slightly different angle of me in the water. This time I was getting out, but overlaid with another figure. I frowned at it. Maybe he used this one as a guide?

I glanced over at Haru. He was focused, using his fingers to make very deliberate strokes as though he caressed the canvas. I cleared my throat to get his attention.

Haru looked over at me, dark circles prominent. Had he slept at all? Yet as soon as he saw me, the shadows around his eyes transformed to welcome then concern. "Did you have another nightmare?"

"Hi. And, uh, no." Hundreds of pages laid scattered all over the floor, some with clumps of moss already crawling across them. "I've never seen an artist at work. Is this the usual process?"

He rubbed a hand over his face and ran his fingers through

his hair, smearing blue paint over his temple and into his locks. It was kinda cute, like war paint of a distracted genius. "I don't know, I guess? Probably. I mean, I'm so excited I can't think straight. Not that I think straight most of the time." He waited as if I was supposed to say something to that.

"Um . . . okay. Maybe you should get some rest?" I motioned to his hair. "Have a shower or something?"

He seemed briefly disappointed, as though I hadn't responded as he expected, but immediately brightened again with a devilish gleam. "Are you offering to come with me this time?"

While the idea certainly had appeal—soaping up Haru to get him cleaned before I made him dirty would be fun—it was clear he was wired with energy. "Look, I think we need some breakfast."

He blinked at me and shook his head after a moment. "Is it morning? At last." He put his hands around his mouth and bellowed, "Guys, get over here!"

A scrape from the kitchen was my only warning before Winter rounded the corner. I backed into a protective stance as he loomed over me, his shadow dark and cold. "What did she do?" he grumbled, glaring at me with muscles extending through his tight black shirt. *Holy shit, Winter was intense up close.*

Haru flapped a blue hand at him. "Nothing, she's fine! I want to tell you something."

Winter grunted, but I shivered under his gaze. Where Haru's gaze was daring as he flirted, Winter looked like he was turning over every inch of me with icy disdain.

Haru looked around. "Where's Otto and Summer?"

"Here." Otto came around the corner at a much more sedate pace, mug in his long fingered hands. His gaze also went straight to me, giving me a small smile like we shared a secret, before he arched an eyebrow at Haru. "Well?"

Haru had trouble containing himself, muscles twitching like he longed to jump toward me. He quickly snatched his attention from me to count the guys. "And Summer, he shouldn't miss this."

"*Estoy aquí.*"A deep wave of heat engulfed my right side as Summer came to stand next to Winter, shirt unbuttoned and also holding a cup of coffee. Bringing it up to his lips for a sip revealed way too much bronzed skin.

I gulped, then realized I was gaping at all of them: Haru vibrating with excitement, Summer simmering next to me, Otto's calm demeanor, Winter's irate shadow.

"And?" Summer's voice was husky with sleep. It made me shiver; that, or it was Winter's presence.

Haru threw his arms wide to reveal his work. On the easel was an outline of me in blue, but the lines were all wobbly. It took me a second to see that drawn on top of the sketch were a lot of different women's faces, all in different shades of blue.

"It's not my taste, but it's nice," I offered, not wanting to seem like a complete savage. Modern art just wasn't my thing.

"See it yet?" Haru asked the guys, his voice reverent.

They were utterly silent. My stomach dropped as I realized Otto and Summer literally weren't breathing. As I watched, the mug slipped out of Otto's hand and smashed into tiny chips that scattered across the smooth floor.

That jolted them alert. Winter staggered as if Haru had punched him. "Are you okay?" I asked him, reaching for him unconsciously.

He shook his head once, opening and closing his mouth, then stormed into the kitchen somehow in a worse mood than I'd seen yet.

Summer took a deep breath, nostrils flaring. "Haru. A word in private," he hissed.

Haru searched his face, his brows knitting together. "What's wrong?"

"What's wrong is that she—" Summer stabbed a finger toward me, "—is an intruder, Haru, and we shouldn't discuss anything around her."

"Right," Otto said, but faintly, like he'd had all the breath punched out of him as well.

"Yes!" Haru clasped his blue hands together. "She found us. She—"

"That's enough!" Summer roared.

The sudden noise made me duck into a defensive stance, but Haru flinched, and I wasn't having any of that.

I rounded on Summer, growling. "Talk amongst yourselves all you like. You only have to ask me to leave or, better yet, just release me. But you will not shout at anyone. There is no reason for it. Do you hear me?"

"I hear you loud and clear." Summer's anger swung straight toward me. The air grew warmer like I was having a hot flash. He stepped closer, his chest brushing mine. "I don't know what you're doing here, what your end goal is, or what your intentions are." He lowered his voice to a snarl. "But I will find out," he whispered, his threat blowing hot over the sweat on my forehead.

I raised a hand, refusing to let it shake, and wiped a bead of sweat rolling down the side of my face.

He glowered at me, glare switching from one of my eyes to the other, as if comparing them.

Otto stepped next to us and cleared his throat. "Summer, what if . . . well, what if Haru has a point?"

What were they talking about? A point about painting?

Summer's scrutiny swung to Haru. "Haru, you're in full swing. Hyper. You're seeing things that aren't there."

Haru bristled. "I might be distractible, but I know what I'm talking about. Don't turn away from this, Summer."

"It's been too long. Move on." Summer waved him away

with a sniff. "I'll talk to you when you've gone out and used some of your power so you are more focused."

"I'm focused now, Summer—"

"No you are not!" Summer thundered. "You're still so desperate, you're clutching at straws! Go out and do your damn job."

"Listen to me!" Haru demanded, flinging his arms out, and the plants hanging from the ceiling whipped toward Summer.

"No powers in the house!" Otto admonished, grabbing me and hustling me to the side. He was strong for a librarian, jeez.

Vines snaked down to crawl around Summer, their lush sweet scents filling the air like an intoxicating poison. The greenery wrapped around Summer's shoulders and Haru paced forward, jabbing him in the chest with a finger. "Listen to me! You might be the oldest but you aren't always the boss around here! Right, Otto?"

Otto adjusted his glasses on his nose, keeping me close to his side. I could feel his heartbeat pounding against my chest, and tucked in the crook of his arm all I could smell was his cedar scent. "Er, leave me out of this domestic incident, please."

Haru scowled at him, and I also gave Otto a raised eyebrow. If he had something to air about how Summer ran this place, he should say.

Summer was literally glowing, heat wafting off him, but then his thin shirt curled at the edges. Otto's sucked in breath was my only warning when Summer caught fire, flames spreading up his arms and shoulders.

"Shit!" I lunged for a blanket lying on one of the couches. "Stop, drop, and roll!"

Otto yanked me back by my elbow. "He's fine, it's us we have to worry about. Summer! Get yourself under control! You have three seconds." Otto flexed his hand as if preparing to grab him.

Instantly the flames went out. "I am in control," Summer snarled. "I am nothing *but* control." He glared at Otto. "Stop trying to calm me down."

Otto lifted his hand and immediately I felt the tension in the air a little more, like it had muted without me noticing but now snapped back at full volume. *Potential fight,* my senses screamed and I slid into a defensive guard.

Summer took a step through the shriveled vines and seized Haru's chin. "See me in my office later," he hissed, his voice full of foreboding.

Haru's eyes flickered with something matching that dark desire. They were locked in some kind of battle of wills, but Haru caved first. "Alright, but you have to at least hear me out."

Otto cleared his throat, wafting away the fumes from the burned shirt. "I've listened in any case, Haru, and I believe we need more evidence. A few drawings mean little. There's no way this would stand on trial, and it is filled with bias."

Haru rolled his eyes. "This isn't some legal hearing or experiment or meeting! We found h—"

"That's enough." Summer cut in firmly, but quietly.

Haru's mouth snapped shut. *What was he about to say? Found something? What?*

Otto looked down at me, lifting his arm slowly. The loss of his touch, that instinctive protection, made my heart sag a little, but I tried not to show it on my face. He gave Haru a nod. "I understand what you're saying, and I will look more into it."

Summer glowered at Otto, finding himself outnumbered with Winter already stormed off. "Fine. But be careful." Then his eyes dropped to me. "I will expose your schemes, Marigold Stewart, if that is indeed your real name."

I raised my chin in defiance, although his choice of words

spoke straight to my hindbrain. *Expose, eh?* My legs wavered a little. "You've got my ID, asshole!"

"Unless it's faked."

Otto shook his head. "It isn't, and I also dropped a line to CSON. She works for them, and was apparently under orders."

I stiffened as Summer swung toward Otto. *He knew?*

"You talked to CSON?" Summer demanded.

Otto's brows drew together. His hand on my elbow tightened a little, almost as if he were . . . scared?

I narrowed my eyes at Summer. It was clear he threw his considerable weight around.

Otto swallowed and replied evenly, "Yes, I talked to them. She is under orders to protect us."

"By breaking in?" Summer said incredulously.

Wait. What? I smoothed my face to show indifference. This was news to me too, but I guess I was being protected by my organization. And my assignment meant I wasn't going anywhere anytime soon. But at least it gave me a job. I wasn't their captive anymore.

"You see, I'm here for my job. To protect you," I said, folding my arms and raising an eyebrow at him. Summer wouldn't intimidate me, and there was no way I was giving away that I had no clue what Otto was talking about. "So dramatic and for what?"

Summer's eyes narrowed. "You literally broke Haru's nose."

Shit.

"He was chasing me. A woman has to know how to protect herself in this day and age," I quipped. For whatever reason there was a thrill with pushing his buttons, and the threat in his eyes like he wanted to bend me over his knee and spank me only made it that much more enticing.

Summer opened his mouth to speak, for what I assume was a rebuttal, but Haru burst into laughter.

"You can't really blame her, Summer," he added between chuckles. "And I'm sure she could've done a lot worse."

I grinned at him. "Oh, I definitely could have."

Haru winked, causing a flurry of bubbles to burst through me.

Otto straightened beside me. "I will take Marigold with me today and I . . . will let you know what I conclude."

Conclude about what?

Shaking his head, Summer dragged Haru out of the conservatory area, barking at him, "Shower, now. Then you've got work to do."

Haru stumbled but Summer righted him before he could fall. "Right. Yes." Haru looked around at me, grinning. "Be right back, Buttercup. Just be yourself, alright? Have fun with Otto!"

Summer shot me a look that struck straight to my stomach. He was pissed at me, but behind the anger was despair.

Despair of what? What was going on?

Chapter Fourteen

"*What is going on?*" I finally voiced.

Otto pulled off his glasses, resting his back against the wall like he was exhausted, and rubbed his temples far more roughly than I thought comfortable. They were all taller than me, but Otto didn't loom like Winter or Summer. He had a more unobtrusive sexiness oozing from his pores. Definitely a wallflower, but those long fingers and the way his rich brown eyes settled on me made me think he could definitely be a freak in the sheets.

Settling his glasses back on his face, he gave me a calculating look that was searching as hell. If Haru was warm enthusiasm, Summer hot anger, and Winter cold indifference, Otto was cool calculation.

"We are going to spend the day together," he decreed. It was hard to read anything from his voice. What that meant for him. Even though he had said he was taking me to breakfast, was he disappointed to be babysitting, or was he as intrigued as I was?

"So . . . you're Autumn. Right?" I asked, setting my hands on my hips.

He frowned slightly. "And where did you hear that?"

"Haru explained that you are, uh, the seasons." I pointed outside the windows to the bright Vermont morning where spring continued to bloom.

"He did, hm? I'll verify that with him." He pulled a notebook out of his jacket pocket, flipped open a page, and pulled out a pen as thin as a toothpick. He used it to make a note, which he underscored with a flourish, but his brown eyes never left mine. As if he expected me to protest or break under his scrutiny.

I pointed at his hand. "That is the tiniest pen I have ever seen."

He snapped the notebook shut, lifting up from the back wall, and gesturing forward. "Come on." His hand settled on my lower back to lead me forward. The touch was light but firm. The flash of memory of him stroking the spine of the book when I'd first met them flashed through my mind. I bit my lip.

"The seasons don't start themselves, you know." He really wasn't giving anything away.

"Uh huh," I mustered, trying not to show how much this minor contact flustered me. He was so reserved, I sometimes couldn't make heads or tails of how he felt toward me. But the way he would watch me with his calculated gaze, it was like trying to piece me together, figure me out. He was definitely the one to watch, because if he did figure me out I'd be at his absolute mercy.

We strode into the kitchen and I peered around for Winter. I was rooted to the spot as I waited to see his accusing blue eyes, and when I didn't I wrung my hands. He'd rushed off pretty quickly earlier when Haru showed his artwork of me. Why was that?

Otto pulled out a seat for me at the breakfast bar and I

took it. I'd better start the conversation before he could ask me invasive questions and get me flustered again. "So, how do you get to be a season?"

Otto pulled off his jacket, and just like the others his muscled frame filled the shirt underneath divinely. He hung his coat on a hook over the unlit fireplace, stirring a fragrance of warm cedar and fresh pine to wash over me. Damn, he was so controlled and latched down, but I could imagine him rolling up his sleeves with a riding crop in hand . . . "Through a great deal of physical, mental, and emotional trauma," he explained, voice still void of any emotion, and my stomach dropped. "Coupled with agony every single day."

My hands tensed on the counter and my heart melted. "I'm so sorry I brought it up, I was being curious and nosy. I'm so sorry you're going through that." I imagined poor Haru with his easy smile and light laughter, masking some horrific event in his past filled with unimaginable pain, yet still smiling through it. No wonder Summer was a constant inferno and Winter was shut off.

Otto winced. "Ah. Don't do that. I was testing you." He slipped his hand over mine, brushing his thumb against the back of it until my hands were no longer white knuckled.

"Don't do what?" I breathed, thoughts flitting away while I did my best to focus on the conversation, which led me to watching his mouth as he spoke.

"Feel so deeply. Goodness, that really hit you hard, didn't it?" His lips were so full, the contours of every syllable felt like poetry he was reading from a book. The accent made it that much more delicious. He pulled his hand away and I immediately missed the steady pressure. I leaned on one elbow as if bending under a weight. Again, the way he memorized me, peering directly into my soul, made me feel that even if I tried to lie he would catch it. This man was dangerous. Not only could he be someone to learn every part of me, but the way my heart yearned to open up and release all the burdens I held made me think I would actually let him.

My nose stung; the precursor to crying for me. I rubbed the feeling away. Why was I unraveling so close to this man? "What's going on?"

Otto pulled the French press closer to us, turning over two clean mugs from the counter and pouring us some sweet, blessed coffee at last. "I suppose you can say I'm something of an empath," he explained quietly. "I sense what people nearby are feeling sometimes, and I can quiet and calm emotions around me."

"Oh, wow." I thought about that for a moment. "So you felt everything they were feeling in that argument? Does it get, uh, heated here often?"

Otto's lips twisted with chagrin. "Sometimes. They calm down on their own normally, but . . . I can give them a head start, you might say."

"So you calmed them down? That's a neat trick."

"Yes, very handy." He took a sip of hot coffee, grimacing.

"Was that at the taste, the heat, or the fact that you have to douse the guys' emotions every now and again?"

He glanced over at me. "Or all three. That's a possibility."

I smiled. Maybe he liked to play too, but his sport was words. "Yep, got me there. Or something else I haven't thought of." I put my chin in my hand. Apparently, my orders were to stay put. Perhaps I should be finding out as much as I could at the same time? A maggoty anxious feeling ate away at me, like I was being disingenuous in liking these guys and wanting to know more about them. But really, understanding my charges could only be good, right? "How do you season places?"

He chuckled at my choice of words. "Now, I have a bit of a dilemma. Your questions can be taken as innocent or as probing." Oh, god, the way his mouth shaped probing was just sinful. I swallowed my body's reaction down hard. *What was up with me? Wasn't Haru enough for me?*

Otto went on, "Of course any inquiring mind would want answers, but so would other factions."

"Do you have enemies? I literally stood outside for years and never saw anything." My instincts kicked in. "Look, if you feel threatened, say so. I'm here for your protection after all."

Otto smothered what looked like what could've been a hint of a smile behind another sip of coffee. "We do not feel particularly threatened by anyone at this time, but, well . . . There are bound to be people who would like to use us. Couldn't you just imagine a hotel mogul capturing Summer to ensure it was always hot in their locale, or Winter to provide a year-round ski experience?"

"Or Haru, to grow their crops," I suggested, mind racing. "You're right, there could be all sorts of threats."

He leaned back in his chair. "But no one really wants autumn all that much. So I am probably the safest of us all to walk around."

"No, that's not true," I interjected. "You should have a bodyguard, too, and I will fill that role."

He looked me up and down, again memorizing every detail of my form. Nerves flared inside me, heart fluttering in my chest. What did he see? More importantly, what did he think of what he saw? He swallowed hard once, then jerked his head back toward the table, drumming those long, decadent fingers against the edge. *What was that about?* His cheeks and throat darkened a little. *Was he blushing?*

Yeah, he was definitely blushing. I took another sip of coffee, contemplating him. Seems two could play at this game, and it wasn't just him causing me to react so strongly. "What do you need to get done today? I know you're technically looking after me, but now I know you might be in danger, I'm going to step up my game too."

He ran a hand over his short hair and—*oh, adorable*—it was trembling a little bit. He was hot as hell but his tenderness made me even more drawn to him. His face grew solemn. "Er, well, I—"

"What?" I pressed.

"I think I can take care of it myself," he finished.

My stomach dropped. *He doesn't think I can do it. That I can help.* I hated when people underestimated me. Whether it was my size, the fact that I was a woman, or that I was poor. It all was stupid and unfounded. My anger flared. "I am a trained professional. I know several martial arts."

"Yes, of course." He pulled back a little, the space between us growing.

"I'm serious!" I scrunched my face and took a step forward off the stool, partially from annoyance and another part to fill the gap forming, like there was a piece of me that needed him close.

He lifted his hands slightly. "I believe you. You're coming through loud and clear." He shook his head. "Well, I *do* have some things to do."

"Then it's a deal." I threw out my hand between us. "I'll protect you on your outings, then." And I'd get to see some more of the world.

Otto stared at my outstretched hand, eyes wide behind his glasses, and he released a breath with a small, deep chuckle. "Deal." His hand enveloped mine, the cool touch quickly warming and sending tingles fluttering through me like when Haru touched me. He watched our hands as though mesmerized before clearing his throat and pulling away. He stood, downing his coffee in one. "Save your appetite, I know exactly the right place for breakfast."

OTTO WAS WAITING by the library for me along the corridor from my room. "Here," he said, handing me gloves and a scarf.

"It's really warm right now." I pulled at my shirt, and his eyes dipped down. Yep, he was interested for sure. I couldn't help the flattered excitement in my belly.

"It will not be warm where we're going. Autumn, remember? While Haru is prancing around the northern hemisphere, I influence the southern hemisphere." He led me along the corridor and stopped in front of a thick oak door. With the twist of a key, we were through.

Purple folds across the mountains greeted us, the air crisp and cool. "Wow," I breathed, my air curling into fog.

"Indeed." Otto gestured. "The San Martín de los Andes. Patagonia."

"It's . . . wow." It was stunning. The conifer trees sprouted other-worldly colors of crimson and lavender purple. It was colder too, but the drop in temperature heightened my focus.

"Anything else to say? Just 'wow'?" he asked, tone disdainful and a little bit pointed.

I blinked, feeling dumb and wrong-footed. "Hey, just because I didn't wax lyrical? 'Wow' gets the message across just fine. It's not every day a girl gets dragged onto different continents within minutes of each other by hot guys." I rubbed my face, surely turning pink not due to the cold. *Did I just admit to finding them hot? Damn.*

"I suppose." He frowned, shifting his weight and putting his hands behind his back. "This will go a lot better if you are honest with me, Marigold," he went on, voice stiff and prim.

Argh. "I prefer to be called Mari."

He gave me another analyzed look. "Too short."

"Hey! I know I'm on the shorter side, but I can't help it!"

He shook his head. "No, I mean the moniker. It diminishes you. Cuts you down. Three melodious syllables is preferred."

"Says who? Otto shortened from Autumn, right?"

"And still the same amount of syllables," he pointed out, a hint of triumph in his voice.

I shrugged my shoulders, the wonder of this new place still gripping me despite his changeable attitude. This was a whole new continent experiencing a completely different season to the one I had just left. It was amazing.

Otto came to stand next to me. "Look, I . . . apologize. If Haru is correct, then I would want to do things far more differently than this."

"Correct about what?" I asked, searching his eyes. "All he showed you guys was a painting with lots of women on it. What's that about? Past lovers?" I waggled my eyebrows in jest, trying to ignore the small spark of envy. "Any I need to look out for? I'm not afraid to take someone down, man or woman."

Otto's brown eyes softened, flickering with pain. "I can't tell you yet, Marigold. We still don't know whether we can trust you."

"And I don't know what to make of you," I admitted with a shrug, completely honestly.

He smiled a little at that, as though he was satisfied with the truth from me. "That will do as a beginning, I think." His sharp eyes scanned the horizon. Next to him, I felt a colder wind than with Haru. Hunching deeper into my scarf, I shoved my hands into my pockets as the leaves faded to tans and vibrant browns.

He frowned lightly then pulled off his jacket, holding it up for me. "Here."

"I'm fine, really." The wind blew again, now with a cutting edge, and cold seemed to seep from the ground through my shoes.

Otto shook his head in exasperation and draped the jacket around my shoulders anyway. "Not much longer, then we can go back." He shoved his hands into his pockets.

His jacket was warm and reminded me of curling up by a cozy fire with a blanket. Not that I'd ever done that. I'd never had the opportunity. I breathed in, pulling the lapels closer to my cold cheeks. It smelled of him, which for whatever reason helped me settle even more. The jacket really did ward away the cold, like being wrapped in a warm embrace.

"And done," he said, turning around and gesturing back to the door we'd come through, this one hanging in midair.

I peered at it, curious. "So you just turn up, and that's it? Do you only have to stick around for a certain amount of time?"

He chuckled, the sound enthralling me. "I welcome questions, and you'll get the answers as soon as we've established that trust, I promise." He glanced down at me, adjusting his glasses. "In truth, we're leaving now because I can tell you're cold. I'm glad my jacket is helping."

Mm, yes, helping. I snuggled deeper into it.

After Patagonia we went through another door down the hall, the roar of traffic smacking into me before we even walked through. My heart rate leapt as Otto grabbed my arm and pulled me out of the way of a cavalcade of cars, horns bleating. "Belo Horizonte," Otto shouted over the noise.

"Belo-a-what?" I called back. I might have done my fair share of daydreaming and learning about places around the world, but I couldn't tell if what he just said was a random greeting, a place, or something else entirely.

"Brazil. Sixth largest city in the country."

My eyes widened, and I took the time to admire the city around me. The streets were set out as regular as New York but with palm trees poking out along a lakeside. I kept my arm wound with his, and he pulled me toward a neon blue sign. "*Pão de queijo, obrigada,*" he said to the lady behind the counter and received a package of warm, cheesy smelling goodness in return. He passed me the package, then leaned in, putting his cheek close to mine. "Cheese bread," he explained, his pace slowing to match mine. We walked arm in arm, me clinging to him and the package which was slowly soaking through with delicious grease.

We walked down long streets set out in the grid structure all the way down to a rectangle of green. "It's a well-organized city," Otto noted.

I chuckled. "Is that all? No lyrical poetry about the straightness of the streets, the size of the sidewalks, the bulge of the buildings?"

He let a small crack in his poker face shine through. "Straight sizable bulge, eh?"

My hand flew up to my face, package and all, as heat flooded my cheeks. "I didn't mean it like that!"

He laughed, a full-throated, gut-busting belly laugh, and holy crap was it beautiful. A deep tenor that shook me to my core, and I couldn't help but laugh too.

We meandered into a park. Joggers zoomed past and walkers strode by, talking into the cell phones pressed to the sides of their faces. Just like any city park, then, but different. The language, the colors, the subtle differences in fashion, even the smell of the air was new and exciting.

Otto settled on a park bench, stretching his long legs out in front of him. "Well? What do you think of the *pão de queijo?*"

"I, uh, haven't tried one yet." Grease was coming through the white paper bag, coating my fingers. It smelled heavenly, but . . .

"A moment on the lips, a lifetime on the hips." My mother's voice rang in the back of my mind. It didn't matter how hard I tried to find confidence despite how society saw me, I still caved every once in a while. So I went without the dessert, determined to live up to her expectations.

"I'm not hungry," I said.

His eyes narrowed slightly. "That's a lie, Marigold." He leaned forward, pressing his palms together. "Why lie about that? Do you think I'm trying to poison you?"

"No, no. I mean, you could have done that with the coffee, and you didn't."

"Food allergy? If so, why not just say so? I won't be offended." He looked from the packet back to my face. "What is it?"

"It's pure grease and cheese. I can smell it from here. It's heavenly, but . . . I shouldn't."

"Shouldn't." Otto rolled that word around his mouth like it tasted bad. "Well, it's a popular breakfast food in Brazil. Probably the most popular, but there are other choices."

"I'll bring these back for the others," I said, my voice coming out small.

He stood up suddenly. "Come. We're getting the full works."

I trotted along beside him, confusion and curiosity warring in my brain. When we got to the crosswalk, he held his arm out for mine. Feeling slightly silly, I took it, walking in step with him. Strength flexed in the arm I held onto for sure. *Damn, he was probably lifting heavy tomes all day every day for guns like these.*

We went along to another shop where Otto ordered *Api Morada*. Two violently purple drinks came to us in tall glasses. "Wow," I breathed.

He rolled his eyes but smiled at me, as if he was starting to like the word. "Cornmeal smoothies flavored with cinnamon and sugar. They pair beautifully with the cheese breads." He beckoned for the package.

I passed them up and he took out a small bun—much smaller than I was expecting from the grease stains on the packet. He turned the pale round ball this way and that, then bit into it. "Mm. Perfect."

I brushed some crumbs off my pants. "Yes, well. You're Mr. Attractive over there. I only have to look at a raisin to put on weight."

He swallowed the mouthful, frowning slightly. "Ah, is that the 'shouldn't' is coming from?" He took a sip of his drink, watching me, but this time instead of searching for cracks he seemed genuinely prepared to listen.

I bit my lip before I tried my drink hesitantly. Warm and thick, it was delicious, like pure sugar. I swallowed my sip and huffed a laugh. "Wow that has to be hundreds, if not thousands, of calories."

He put his cheese bun down, wiping his hands on a napkin. "Marigold, I'm going to insist you increase your vocabulary from 'wow' and 'calories' to new heights and new sensations. You are as decadent as this dessert. It's about time you act like it. As you said yourself, it's not every day you cross continents."

I tried not to dwell on his passing compliment, afraid I'd show my hand at how it made my heart stutter. "So, YOLO?" I said, a teasing smile on my face.

He gave a theatrical shudder. "Oh, help me," he muttered with a wink, and I laughed.

The flutters in my stomach took on a new dance. He was being so sweet, when he really didn't have to be. What could I do in return?

I picked up the cheese bun. "How do you say this again?"

Chapter Fifteen

I traipsed through the halls of the manor, admiring the craftsmanship of the doors as I searched for one of the boys. Well, Haru or Otto preferably. I was hoping I could choose our next outing, either where to run with Haru or eat with Otto.

The whirlwind of everything had finally caught up with me. Or maybe the whirlwind of my life. I had spent a week relaxing, going on walks with Haru, having Winter make me breakfast, spying on Summer as he worked in his garage when he wasn't on the phone in his office, and reading with Otto. It was the closest to a vacation I'd ever had and it was nice.

Allowing time to settle, letting go a little like Haru had suggested, felt like a weight being lifted. Knowing my family was being taken care of allowed me to be a little more present. It gave me time to want more for myself, for my life. This situation came about in a shit way but it was like a blessing in disguise. And these men, their camaraderie, were slowly weaseling their way into my heart, especially Haru. I mean, how could he not? With his easy demeanor, kindness, and hilarity. He had a way of making me see the world differently and showing me it could actually be fun! I wanted more of him. Of this.

I still didn't have my phone, but Summer had assured me that I could use the house phone to call whenever I needed. It was probably a safety measure on their end to help ensure I wasn't going around spouting how I was living with four magical men. Not that I would anyways. I was here on a mission.

My stomach squirmed at the thought. It actually didn't sit right with me. As a trained soldier, I wasn't paid to think or have an opinion. I was trained to take orders. But if my position as a shield was to protect them, why did they have me conduct a major security breach? I didn't think much of it at the time, but the more I was here, the more I understood them. The more the nagging feeling in the back of my mind about the key card I slipped under the door bothered me.

They hadn't noticed the missing key yet. At least, not that I knew, and that only made me more concerned. There had to be something. An important reason for safety on why CSON had me do that, right?

Turning a corner, I was met with the ice door again. Had it moved somehow, or was I more lost than I thought? It was definitely the same door though, locked deep in a glacier so it was just an inky smudge through the layers of rock-hard ice.

I had seen this door and the one covered in plants. Why were they locked away like this? It had to be them using their powers, right? Where did those doors lead?

I swirled around, marching into the house, and quieted my steps. I wanted answers. For their safety, for myself, I didn't know. But trust needed to be earned somehow.

"Haru!" I hollered. "Otto!" My voice echoed through the mansion. You'd think it'd be easier to find them despite this place being a maze, but I guess when it was connected to every end of the Earth, them being "anywhere" was an understatement.

"Mari?" A messy-headed Haru peeked out from behind a doorway, blinking against the light filling the hall, a sharp contrast to the dark room he'd poked out of.

I halted. "Were you asleep?" Haru was always more of the first one up kind of person.

He stepped out of the room—shirtless. Sweatpants hung low on his hips, showing off every plane of his smooth chest and swimmer's shoulders. *Yes, a swimmer's body was the perfect way to explain his physique.*

I tried not to stare, but I definitely took time to soak him in. I needed to find the pool he'd talked about and give it my gratitude because damn this man was fine.

"Long night," Haru yawned. "No rest when it's your season."

"Right," I said. Actually this was perfect. I didn't want to seem like I was prying, but I wanted answers. I cocked my head to the side. "Truth or dare?"

Haru's head perked up, a small smile fluttering to his face. "Naughty thing. Trying to take advantage of me after I just woke up?"

"Maybe," I said with a shrug and a smile.

He chuckled, stepping aside and lifting his arm to the side. "By all means, Buttercup, come on in."

The playful little nickname had a smile creeping onto my face, which I hid with my hair as I entered his room. It was dim, and I had to strain my eyes.

"I'll get the drapes, one sec," Haru said, moving away from me. As he moved away a glow intensified along the ceiling. I craned my neck back to see sea green and ice blue bioluminescent fungi flare to life, little caps curling.

"Oh! I'd forgotten about those," Haru breathed, stopping in his tracks and craning his neck back.

"They're pretty," I offered. "Good mood lighting."

"Yes, they are, and they're coming back." Excitement tangled his voice, causing him to trip over his words. With a sudden flourish, he pointed at the other end of the wall.

With a crack, plants started to move, curling up one another like writhing snakes, pulling the drapes apart. I gasped, and Haru did too, as light illuminated the room.

Shade-loving plants trawled up the walls, his bed in the center of a mossy carpet. The sheets looked to be cotton at least as opposed to a blanket. In response to the sunlight, dormant seeds started sprouting from everywhere, blooming into a wild meadow of pinks, yellows, oranges, and cornflower blue.

"Ooh," I breathed, pulling in the fresh air.

Haru turned to me, his eyes bright like I'd brought him Christmas morning instead of just a wake-up call. "I can do it!" he told me. "I can control them again!"

"You couldn't before?" I cocked my head at him. "Didn't you use vines against Summer?"

He waved his hand. "I was just angry and the plants reacted. Now I've got fine control again." He beamed at me. "All because of you."

I blinked. "Me?"

His eyes widened slightly and he nodded. "Yes. Having someone special in our lives," he said, but my gut said he was hedging slightly.

Haru leaned against the wall, a grin of triumph in his face. "Truth."

Phew. I definitely had no dare planned, and based on the way Haru's eyes tracked me, studied me, I had a feeling he knew I was using this game of ours for something other than fun. It was as though I could feel Otto's logical brain ticking inside of his mind instead.

"What do the seasons do when it's not their time of year?"

I asked as I moseyed around his room, trying to stop myself from snooping inside of drawers and closets. I wanted to know everything about him. About them.

"Whatever they please, really. We are mostly confined to the house. We can make quick stops in places if it's on the cusp of our season. But that can still cause problems like the earliest snowfall a place has seen in years. Although, it's become easier to handle over the past two hundred years or so."

What? "Two hundred years?"

Haru nodded. "The World Wars and all that, global warming, and climate change. It makes it easier to cover our tracks because people chalk it up to climate change. The world is sensitive to our presence, especially Summer and Winter."

Two hundred years. Two hundred years? Maybe that shouldn't be the detail to focus on, but that was baffling to me.

"How old are you guys?" I gaped, failing to hide my surprise.

Haru chuckled and shrugged. "Old."

"Do you age?"

"Not once we become a season."

"So, you're . . . immortal?" I pressed, beyond curious.

Haru smirked. "You could say that."

My eyes narrowed. "So, you are gods." *I knew it!*

Haru chortled, the deep vibration warming my insides. "No. We've never been worshipped, and our presence is known through a natural scientific phenomenon. The Seasons have never considered themselves gods, nor do we have any desire to do so."

"Are there female seasons?" Now that I had started, I couldn't stop my questions from tumbling out.

Haru pushed off the door and stepped toward me. He shook his head, a glum glint filling his eyes. "No, nothing like that for us."

It was hard to imagine four delicious immortals going through life celibate. Although, the thought made my chest pinch. Imagining Haru laughing at someone else's joke as he gazed adoringly at them, Summer protecting another with his looming presence, Otto with his head in a woman's lap as he read, and even Winter's chilly self melting as he got close to another. I downright hated that idea, and the fact it bothered me so much only made me confused on top of it. Neither feeling I enjoyed.

Still, I couldn't stop the next inquiry. "What about your love life then? It's hard to imagine you four being alone all this time."

His Adam's apple bobbed with a swallow. "We haven't been alone."

My stomach soured. *Damn, I should've left it alone.*

Haru inched closer to me, circling behind me as I stood there in silent contempt. "But when we find someone—someone very special to each of us—our loyalty and love knows no bounds."

Was he trying to tell me something? Alluding to something?

Haru walked up behind me, placing a hand on my hip. "Well?" His voice was serious as his thumb swirled circles on my side.

A shiver ran down my spine. "I have a job." My voice was breathy as my heart hammered against my chest.

"Of course. A very important role."

Without meaning to and only realizing when it was too late, I leaned back against his hard chest. I wanted him. More than I'd ever wanted anyone. He was a man who had lived hundreds, maybe even thousands, of years. Of course he'd been with others, but right now, he was here with me.

Nuzzling his nose behind my ear, he whispered, "Dare."

I clenched my thighs together as way too many dirty

thoughts played through my mind. I knew my panties were soaked already.

Taking a steadying inhale to help clear my foggy brain, I breathed, "Kiss me."

He turned me, catching my breath, and his mouth was on mine before I found it again. His hands moved over my hips, raising my shirt until my bare stomach was pressed against his. I wound my hands around his neck as I relished in his taste of orange blossom and honey suckle. He was sweet and earthy, both grounding me and lifting me to greater heights. He bit my bottom lip and I gasped. Using the opportunity, his tongue slipped inside my mouth as he devoured my moan. He kissed like a god.

Suddenly, I found myself thanking all the women who came before me for giving him the practice and talent to play me like a fiddle.

Chapter Sixteen

I couldn't think about the other women in his life anymore as his hands became urgent. He tugged at my shirt, opening the buttons with quick flicks of his fingers.

"My loyal protector," he murmured into my mouth as his hands traveled over the cotton restraining my breasts. His thumb pressed over my left nipple, and I mewled at the delicious shock of feeling straight to my core.

He pulled my shirt back and down, exposing my upper body at the same time he pinned my arms behind me. He drew back a little, studying my face. "Truth time. It seems you like that. Do you?"

I had to admit, it was a new sensation, being at his mercy. The tingle in my core suggested I did indeed like it, tempered by the trust we shared. I knew I was safe in his hands. Admitting to what I liked was also new to me, but I knew he would treasure the knowledge, not kink shame me. "Yeah, I do."

Haru's smile widened. "I knew you would. Wait 'til I tell Summer."

Although he was mentioning someone else when we were

getting heated, it felt somehow right, and very, very hot. The idea of Summer's smoldering gaze raking over me like fingers on my back turned me on and then some.

"Truth," I gasped. "Do you . . . ever do this with any of the other guys?" The comment about sexual fluidity last week hadn't escaped me, and I'd been curious ever since.

Haru's eyes brightened. "Oh, yes. I'll be more than happy to show you."

I knew it. The way Haru and Summer interacted with one another seemed more than house mates. Haru's enthusiasm made me smile. "Okay," I breathed, flushing with a thrill I wasn't expecting.

"Truth," Haru said, and my stomach flipped. "I can sense your desire. I want to touch you. Can I?"

"Please touch me," I begged.

Haru moaned with a shudder. "I've waited so long—" He swallowed back what he was going to say. Perhaps it had been so long since he had a woman as opposed to one of the guys. Whatever the reason, his eyes clouded with pain briefly before his sunny, self-satisfied smile broke through. "Thank you," he said, capturing my mouth with his and sliding his hand down my stomach.

Normally I didn't like to be touched on my stomach knowing it wasn't flat by any means, but I trusted Haru, and he seemed to like my body.

He cupped my breasts through my bra. "I want to see all of you."

"Is that a dare?" I asked, my heart beating harder. I wondered if he could feel it through the fabric separating my skin from his palms.

"No, no games for this," Haru reassured me, and his sweetness had my eyes prickling with tears.

He saw and covered me with his hard body, reaching around to open the clasp of my bra before sliding the straps down my shoulders, his fingers gliding down my arms. My skin pebbled under his touch. When my breasts were finally freed, he bit his lip and looked up at me, pupils blown with desire. His breath was coming faster, face flushed. I reached out and pressed my palm against the hard length straining against his pants. His eyes rolled and he groaned. "Do that again." He grinned at me. "I can dare you, if you want."

"Oh, I want." I loved how he wasn't pressing or forcing me into anything. How he was letting me take this at my own pace while still being playful and just *Haru*—pure gentle encouragement to grow. Spring did not force but coached, letting everything come in its own time.

Speaking of come. "You seem fairly close," I surmised as his body twitched against mine.

"I was close when you walked into my room," he said, shuddering with desire. "It's only my superb will that's keeping me in check."

"Maybe you don't need to hold back," I whispered, stroking him through the rough fabric of his sweatpants.

Haru groaned, then tipped me back onto the bed, soft cotton and prickly moss pressing against my back. The tendrils on the walls shivered, but far from being weird, it was exciting. His lips stroked mine and then his mouth journeyed lower, tongue skating over the tendons of my neck and up over my breast. Wetness swirled around my left nipple, and I arched my back to give him more. He took my nipple in his mouth, tongue flicking and lapping over my nerves, sending shockwaves to my core. His hand cupped my right breast, the pad of his thumb pressing over my rigid nipple, each pass making me groan.

"Haru," I gasped.

"My turn," he said. "Truth, although I can tell your body is singing to me. Do you want more?"

"Yes, more," I cried out.

"That was emphatic." Haru's appreciative smile warmed me further. He slid his hand lower, fumbling with the button of my pants. "Do you want this?"

"It's my turn," I gasped. "You already had a go."

"Oh, I haven't had a go yet, and it is your turn. I'm going to send you to such heights, you are going to ascend this peak with me and I'm going to guide you safely back down."

I was shaking now, trying to buck my hips against him for friction, needing something between my legs where a fire was burning. "Haru," I said, my voice begging, pleading.

"What do you want? I'll give it to you, anything at all." He shot me such a mischievous grin, face hovering between my breasts. Wetness gleamed on the left and his fingers played my right nipple as if lightly strumming.

"Dare," I said. "I want to come."

"You don't have to dare me for that. It's yours." His fingers delved under my pants, searching, sliding through my slippery wetness. He shivered. "So wet. So soft." He leaned in, lips at my ear. "I want to taste. May I?"

"Yes!" I cried.

In moments, he had pulled my pants off, my ass against the mossy cover of his bed. It was warm, so warm when he covered me, sliding backward and sinking to his knees with reverence.

"So beautiful," he said, voice adoring, and his fingers swiped into my folds. I was naked, strewn over the bed, panting and aching with need. I felt powerful, desirable, to have such a man at my side and wanting to share these delights with me. *Me.* Mari, too busy and too stressed to do anything except work, and he had plucked me out from the rut of my life and nurtured me.

His mouth finally landed where I wanted it, tongue questing into me and straight on my throbbing clit like he was laser guided. I cried out, grabbing his hair.

"Too much?" He mumbled around my mound, slowing.

"More," I insisted, pulling his head closer.

He chuckled, the vibrations doing amazing things to the heat around my clit, and he swirled his tongue with confident strokes. My thighs clamped around his head. I pressed him closer, closer, as if we could meld and this pleasure reverberated between us both, pushing us higher and higher. I crested the peak, my muscles tensing, and I cried out as my awareness splintered and scattered, my orgasm pulsing through me.

Haru lifted his head, a smug smile in place. His face was utterly covered in moisture, cheeks glistening as if he had been swimming. Best of all was the triumph in his eyes.

"Mm. I think you enjoyed that," he said teasingly, "judging by the way you nearly crushed my skull like a watermelon."

My hands flew to my mouth. "I'm sorry, Haru."

"Don't be." He stood, falling forward into my embrace, and pressed his head against my chest. "Mari," he whispered, his words piercing straight to my heart, as close as he was to it.

"Haru." I pulled him close, but I wanted more. Something I couldn't define. Just more. "More," I told him, trusting him with my wants and wishes. "Do you want more?"

"I crave everything you want to give me," he said, lifting his head, eyes shining with adoration.

He rose and hovered over me, easing me back to nestle against the covers. They were even pricklier than before. Tingles ran down my back, vines surging from underneath me and snaking across the bed. Far from being scary or strange, I relaxed against them. This was Haru, and he wouldn't hurt me.

Reaching down, I pulled his sweats down. His gaze, full of awe, held mine, and his penis jutted proudly, the tip resting on my mound.

I opened my legs wider, wrapping his hips with my legs, and he eased in as he pressed deeper. "Mari," he whispered, and flowers bloomed all around us in a riot of colors and scents, royal blues and sky blues and blues as deep as the ocean depths. He buried himself in me, sliding his arms around my shoulders and lifting my upper body up slightly to hold me. "Oh, Mari," he groaned.

"Dare," I said, and his eyes fluttered closed with a smile.

"I know what you want," he said, hips beginning to move and sliding back and forth. He entered me, filling me. It was precisely what I needed—the right friction, the right rhythm. Harder and harder with each stroke tapping a spot that made stars spark in my vision. Vines writhed against my bare skin and he tipped his head back, panting, and met my eyes. His gaze was tender with a shine that edged toward euphoria as he cried his release, "Mari! Mari!"

I came as he did, crying out his name while ripples darted from my core inside as my walls tightened around his cock. He arched back, then curled forward, fingers gripping my shoulders as if he would never let me go. We floated in the moment for a while, his weight reassuring, as the flowers turned to face me as if they sought the sun.

I smiled up at him. "Are they going to know what we did in here from the new plant life?"

He winked, wiping a bead of sweat off his temple. "They're gonna know what we did in here because they could hear you clear to Timbuktu."

I lightly smacked his arm, and his bright peals of laughter shook the petals of the spring blossoms.

Chapter Seventeen

Rolling over, a soft smile warmed my face as I hugged the down-filled pillow. Haru's honeysuckle scent washed over me as I inhaled deeply, relishing in how relaxed I felt. I wished to lie here forever but with such a great night's sleep, I was well rested.

I opened my eyes to find the bed next to me empty. I hadn't heard Haru get up. Pressing onto my elbows, I sat up with a frown.

Resting on the bedside table on his side of the bed was a tray with a rose, a cinnamon roll, and a folded note with my name scrawled across it. Grinning, I crawled across the king-sized bed and picked up the orange rose and note. The soft petals tickled my nose as I took a whiff of its subtle sweetness and I unfolded the paper.

Mari,

Duty calls this time of year. Stay as long as you like.

Haru

Biting my lip as though that could contain my excitement, I placed the card back on the tray and flower stem in the water then picked up the roll. To my surprise, it was still steaming, like it was fresh from the oven, and icing dripped off the side from the warmth. Careful not to get any on the white sheets, I took a bite. Sweet cinnamon, brown sugar, and a hint of clove burst across my tongue.

"Ohmgo," I murmured through a muffled mouthful. It was clearly homemade, and for whatever reason, I had a feeling it was Winter's harsh hands that made this fluffy delicacy. It didn't take long for me to finish it off, relishing in every bite until I was scooping the cream cheese frosting from the plate with my finger.

Stretching, I rose from the bed, and yet another smile broke across my face when I found a colorful silk robe folded at the foot of the bed. The base color was a beautiful bright blue with pink cherry blossoms decorating it. I slipped it on, enjoying the lightness and soft texture as I tied the belt around my waist. My breasts and hips were extra voluptuous in this, leaving little to the imagination, but I didn't care. Last night Haru had made me feel like a goddess with how he devoured all of my curves with his eyes, touch, and mouth, and I planned to ride this high for as long as possible. I didn't think I'd ever felt more beautiful or desired in my entire life.

I didn't know I could feel this way. I wished every woman that was considered plus size would have their moment of feeling irresistible, hot, and sexy, because we were. All of us. We all deserved our Haru, and screw anybody else that made us feel otherwise.

Whether it was last night, or maybe over the past week, something had changed—shifted. I now couldn't envision my life without Haru's lightness or Otto's reasoning. Even Summer had me intrigued, especially with the way Haru talked about him last night. Imagining those two together . . . *damn.*

There was a tingle between my legs, my sex drive ramping right back up like a beast finally let out of its cage.

I frowned at my lower half. "Down, girl."

Before heading to the door, I remade Haru's bed and grabbed the tray he had left me. I planned to keep the note and flower, but I could at least take the tray and dirty dish down to the kitchen.

I took my time in the halls, allowing myself to enjoy being in the moment. I had stayed because of Summer wouldn't let me leave, but being in Haru's room, it felt like I was always supposed to be here. Like I would've found my way here even if I hadn't been hired on as a shield.

"Yeah, okay, Mari," I laughed at myself. Seems multiple orgasms had loosened a screw in my head. It may feel different with Haru and even Otto, and while I was definitely intrigued by Summer, Winter was a far cry from wanting me here.

The house was quiet and walking through halls with no windows and Haru's curtains having been pulled shut, I had no concept of the time of day. I guess in a house where you traveled to differing times all over the world that was bound to happen. I'm surprised they managed regular meals of any kind with their crazy schedules. I could only assume it was those who got left behind that managed the daily household needs and helped the working seasons keep some kind of schedule.

I glanced at the door numbers. 205. My gut clenched. Up ahead loomed the door I had slipped the keycard under. My gut twisted as guilt took hold of my innards while passing 207. *Knowing what I knew now, would I still have done that? Should I have asked more questions about the orders?* I was trained not to question authority, and the money alone had been such a strong driving force. Yet knowing these four and what they're capable of . . . Even if it was my boss, who was tasked with protecting them, it didn't sit right with me.

Determination settled low in my belly. I would call her. I needed clarification on my role because right now, it didn't seem like I was doing much protecting. If this was by any means shady, I'd rather resign than to—to . . .

To backstab Haru and the others.

My face paled. *Is that what I was doing?*

"No," I whispered to myself as I shook my head. That was ludicrous. If they had wanted to have someone seduce the men for whatever reason, I doubt I would've been their first choice. What had progressed between Haru and I was different. It had to be.

The handle of the door twisted—the one I had slipped the key under. My eyes widened and I moved closer to it.

Was it Haru? Otto? I guess they had multiple keys, or maybe it had already been figured out and they received the key back from CSON. It was just above my paygrade to know—

The man, the one from the bar who paid the tab and gave me my orders, stepped through.

"Wha—" My words cut off as he grabbed my wrist and pulled me through. The tray clattered to the ground, the vase shattering and water soaking the note. The other side was a warehouse, all concrete floors and dark green walls, and behind me the door slammed shut. I was thrown against it and instinct took over.

I kicked out, using the door as support since I was off centered. The man was ready and easily deflected the kick. I didn't wait before taking a swing. I caught his chin, surprising him. It was enough time that I dropped and swept out my leg, not caring how my robe flew open and left nothing to the imagination.

My hit hadn't been strong enough because he had enough wit about him to jump and bring his knee up to crack me under the chin. I fell backward, catching myself before my skull slammed into the wooden door. Glass cut into my palm.

A hand wrapped around my throat, pulling me up off the

ground. My air cut off, and I scrabbled against his unyielding grip.

Pressing me against the door, the man snarled through his bloodied lip, "Stop. I'm just here to talk."

Despite the fact I couldn't breathe, my fight or flight mode calmed enough to where I could make sense of the situation. I did my best to nod against his hand, and he dropped it.

I took a few staggering breaths, my throat already sore. "What the fuck?" I wheezed. "Ever heard of a phone?"

"We didn't want to risk communication over something that could be traced or recorded." He straightened his suit, ignoring the blood on his swollen lip. "Although, we didn't expect such a . . . physical response in person."

"I'm trained in combat and a man pulled me through a door with zero warning," I pointed out. "Who wouldn't view it as an attack?"

He cleared his throat. "Understood. But it wasn't as if we had time to provide an official invitation without heightening the risk of one of the Seasons seeing us."

I rolled my eyes. "Whatever. What do you want?" I folded my arms over my chest, using the position to help keep my robe closed as the tie had loosened in the kerfuffle.

He looked me up and down. "You seem to have successfully inserted yourself."

"Inserted myself?" I scoffed. *What the hell was that supposed to mean?* "I had *orders* to stay put, and as a shield I assumed it was to continue what I was hired to do. Protect them," I clarified.

He pulled out a phone, scrolling the screen for a moment before shaking his head. He peered up from the phone, his eyes moving over what I wore and then landing on the flower on the ground. "I will take the current circumstance as a success. Smith will be pleased."

I didn't like this, not one bit. They were making me feel

like a whore. Like I was some ploy and this was meant to happen. Everything that had happened was because of *my* choices, *my* actions. Last night was my decision.

"For the next part of your assignment—"

"No," I stopped him. "I was hired to protect them. I don't want to do any more of this work. No more sneaking, no more keys, none of it."

He leveled a look at me. "You were hired to follow orders for their protection. You are expected to do just that."

"If it's anything beyond protecting them, I refuse," I said, my arms tightening around my midriff.

"We were afraid of this." The man cleared his throat. "If you want your family to continue to be taken care of, you will follow our orders. It is not just your life at stake here, but the livelihood of your family. Which is exactly why we came to you with this proposition instead of someone else."

My face paled as my breath was sucked from me. "The livelihood of my family?" The words felt loose on my lips as I tried to make sense of them.

He nodded. "The money."

"You assholes." My teeth ground together. I had hoped it had been Summer but, to my dismay, my gut was right. This man, my CSON boss, had been working me into their web, bringing my family into this and—and they knew. They knew why I took the proposition. They knew what they were doing when they offered it to me. I was a puppet and the worst part was they had me right where they wanted me.

That was why they had used the rest of the money to pay off the bookies. Ten thousand was beyond helpful, but it wouldn't solve our problems long term. They wanted me to keep working so they'd keep sending my mom money. It was so fucking manipulative my blood boiled. But then I saw my mom being able to take less shifts and getting the medical help she needed. Chris being able to focus on school and not feel the pressures I had when I was his age to help out with money problems. Damn it all to hell, their tactics were working. My family needed this, and I couldn't rely on the pay out of six figures any more.

"Well?" The impatience in his voice was clear. "We need to finish the conversation soon so we do not risk them noticing you missing."

"And if I say 'no'?"

"You will lose your job and your family will lose their money. In fact, CSON owns the building your family lives in, so they will lose that too. We will be sure you're blacklisted from any job. We can erase you, or we can help you. It's your choice."

This was a threat. They were blackmailing me into doing what they wanted. The moment I showed any kind of question, curiosity, they were ready. Ready to trap me so I had no choice but agree.

I bit the inside of my cheek. I didn't want this, but . . . It was my family. And now that I knew how screwed up CSON was and the rose colored glasses had been removed, maybe I could protect the Seasons in a way I couldn't before. Perhaps I could still help my family and find a way to keep them safe too. Because if I lost my job I didn't know if they'd let me stay, and how could I protect them then? How could I help anyone?

"What do you want me to do?" I sighed as my stomach sank like a rock to the bottom of the dark depths of the ocean.

"You must lure Winter over here to us."

A burst of laughter flew from me involuntarily. "I think you have the wrong idea of how I've 'infiltrated' the house." Yes, I used air quotes and everything.

The man's face stayed somber, not showing any amusement or annoyance. "He's the dangerous one."

"Grumpy, maybe," I retorted.

His lips pressed into a hard line. "Look. Do your job. You

are a Shield. You are meant to protect them. We don't care how you convince him, but we need Winter here." The judgment in his gaze at my outfit made my insides sour. "You need to do it. If you don't believe us about the dangers his powers possess, ask them what happened here one hundred and fifty years ago."

I frowned. *What was that supposed to mean?*

He checked his phone. "It's been too long. You need to get back." He shuffled toward me, and I instantly went on alert, but he just reached past me for the handle. With his hand on my back he ushered me through the door despite my protests.

"You have two weeks," he said before shutting it in my face.

"Crap," I whispered to myself once alone in the hall. I had forgotten dropping the tray, the letter ruined in a puddle spreading across the floor like the dread seeping deep in my chest.

Chapter Eighteen

Rubbing my throat, I thumped down the corridor toward the kitchen, the cinnamon roll souring in my stomach. I had to get towels to tidy the mess upstairs, right outside the incriminating door, before anyone else found it. Of course there wasn't a door labeled "housekeeping." Just rows and rows of numbers, all blurring as my eyes watered.

I refused to cry. Digging my fingernails into my palms, mindful of the fresh and fortunately not deep cut, I opened my eyes wide to dispel the threat of tears. The stairway blurred into shades of blue as I failed to contain them.

There were bangs and clatters coming from the kitchen. Great, Winter was there. I snuck up to the open side of the corridor to observe him.

He bent over the countertop, knife in hand, muttering as he sliced through some greens. I knew Germanic languages could sound fairly aggressive, but he seemed to be cussing out the cabbages.

Was he dangerous? Sure, he ran full tilt at me, but I was the intruder in the situation. I loitered, watching some more.

He finished chopping the leaves and scraped them down the chopping board with the flat of the knife, dropping them into a pot to a pleasant hiss of frying. His muttering started repeating, and sounded almost lyrical.

Singing? His deep voice, guttural and rusty, rang out of the kitchen, wafting along with the pleasant scent of frying greens and garlic.

I stepped up to the bar, my silent steps second nature. If I could just get the cleaning stuff without him knowing, that would be best, but I had no idea where it was.

Eventually, I cleared my throat. "Sorry to disturb."

He jumped, literally leaping like a scalded cat. "What is it?" he grunted, not turning around. He straightened up, stirring the pan.

"Sorry if I scared you."

"You didn't," he muttered, ears going red. "Well? Hungry?"

"No, I'm fine." The last thing I had eaten, that lovely treat, sat heavy in my stomach after my encounter with the man handing me my orders.

"Then what?" He still faced away from me.

"I'm looking for the cleaning stuff."

"Room not good enough?" he asked.

"It's fine. I just dropped something."

He grunted again. "Where is it? I'll get around to it."

Was he the home maker? "I can do it. I just need to know where the cleaning stuff is. I want to help out around here where I can."

His shoulders loosened a little, the tension bleeding out of them. "Out of the kitchen, turn left, third corridor on the right. Second door, red." He tutted. "At least it was recently."

I tried to remember his directions, walking a little closer around the bar. "What do you mean, 'recently'?"

"House moves sometimes. Doesn't stay the same."

"Oh." My head reeled. "So, every now and again, you get new . . . corridors? Rooms?"

"And they rearrange." He cleared his throat. "I probably can't tell you too much, *Flicka.*"

"Flicker?" I tried to verify, but I knew I was already butchering the language. I had no idea what he just said or what it meant.

He made a series of grunting noises. I wondered briefly if he was choking until I realized he was chuckling.

I pressed my lips together, annoyance bristling my nerves. "Thanks for the directions," I said before turning and making my way out of the kitchen quickly.

He didn't come after me, and I was thankful for that.

Was he really all that dangerous? Big and scary, sure, but those big hands kneaded dough gently. I'd always wanted to be handled with the care of someone who knew my limits, who used their strength with care. He could probably turn me over his shoulder with no issues, and tan my backside—

Whoa, what was I thinking? I glared down at my thirsty lady bits. Still, it was true what the Brits said: stand around all day waiting for a bus, then two arrive at once. Or, in my case, four.

I stopped in the corridor. Wait, had I already gone down the third corridor on the right? Or was it the left? Damn, but I'd have to go back and ask Winter again.

I turned and ice blue caught my eye. This corridor was the one that was partly frozen. The ice had receded a bit, leaving cracked wood in its wake, but the door at the end of the corridor was still locked behind ice.

"What are you doing here?" Winter snarled behind me.

It was my turn to leap out of my skin. I spun, but my foot slid on the ice.

He grabbed my forearms, wrenching me up. "Well? This isn't where I told you to go!"

I looked between his steel blue eyes, teeth bared in his snarl. My breath came short, puffing in the air between us. "I took a wrong turn. I—"

"Keep the fuck away from these doors," he said. My body slid against his hard frame as he set me down on my feet slowly. I peered up at him, still flush against him, barely breathing.

"Are they . . . Are they dangerous?" I looked back over my shoulder. "Did you do that?"

He hooked his finger under my chin and turned my face back to him. His breath was cool against my face, an icy breeze. My nipples peaked under my shirt and the way he quickly glanced down told me he felt the change.

I wrapped my hand around his wrist, locking him in my grip and found his piercing eyes. Maybe he was dangerous. If he could freeze a corridor for all time and not break a figurative sweat?

His gaze darted between mine as if searching for something, dipping to my lips then over my cheeks and forehead. He reached out and lifted my chin with a finger. "What happened?" he asked, breathless, as if he was the one gasping in the cold.

"I don't know. I'm asking you," I said, pulling my head back and out of his fingers.

He let my chin go but wrapped his huge hand around my upper arm. "You're hurt. What is this?" His face darkened. "Tell me what happened. Who was it?"

Oh, hell. I probably had a bruise or two from face planting during the corridor fighting what I thought was an intruder. "Nothing. I slipped."

"Slipped where?" His eyes darted up to the jagged icicles looming from the ceiling. "Here?"

"No, I only just got here. I got lost." I met his eyes.

His expression softened for a moment, running his teeth

over his lips. "What happened?" he asked, voice so calm and soft my heart rate slowed.

I dropped my gaze. "I fell in the shower, alright? I'm such a klutz."

"The shower." He took a deep breath, closing his eyes. "I'll sort it," he said, firm and strong, like he was promising his ax to my cause or something.

I was so tense and that image was so funny, the idea of him dressed—or at least partly dressed—in furs, lifting an ax across his palms and up to me, made me giggle.

His eyebrows knitted together. "What's so funny?"

"It's just, you said that like Gimli from Lord of the Rings."

He cocked his head. "Gimli says that in The Lord of the Rings? I don't recall reading that."

"Oh, no, in the movie." My brow raises as I take in his confused expression. "The Peter Jackson movie?"

"Oh." He shrugged. "We don't really watch movies."

My jaw dropped open. "You don't?"

"No. Too much to do when in season," he grunted.

"And when you're off season?"

Winter ran a hand over his bound hair. "Got an ever-moving house to clean."

I giggled again, and this time he grinned at me, briefly, as if he rationed his smiles for me and I was allowed one for the first time.

Somehow, that made it just as special.

We walked back toward the kitchen. "I still need that cleaning stuff."

"Right. Here." He opened a door, and I finally got my hands on some rags and a squeeze bottle of cleaner adorned in Arabic script. I sniffed the end gingerly. "Mm, lemony fresh." Some of the chemical must have leaked a little, because the cut on my palm started to sting. "Ouch!"

Winter snatched the bottle out of my hand. "What is it?"

"Nothing."

He grabbed my wrist. "Oh, really?"

"Ow, big guy, gentle," I reprimanded.

He glowered but loosened his grip for me to pull away. "Show me."

I turned my palm over. "I cut myself on some glass when I fell. Klutz, remember?" I felt like a fraud, an actor in a pantomime, being way too ridiculous to be believed. Winter would call me out for lying any second.

He was breathing heavily. In the close cleaning cupboard, it was tight and warm, but the temperature was dropping rapidly.

"Winter?" I asked.

His eyes flickered with pain, then he backed away. "I'm in control. I am." He beckoned. "Come on."

"Not without the supplies."

He rolled his eyes and grabbed a bucket, slinging rags and another type of cleaner in it. "Let's go," he insisted.

He led me into the kitchen. "Otto!" he yelled.

"He might be out or sleeping," I protested, waving for him to quiet down.

"Otto! Get out here."

"I think he's out," I told him when we heard no answer.

Winter paced the kitchen for a moment then grabbed a basket from a cupboard. "First aid kit," he said.

"Okay." I flipped open the lid of the kit and ferreted around with my good hand, sliding onto a stool to sit. They had antiseptic and Band-Aids—the usual stuff.

He loomed over the bar, shadowing his supplies. "M— may I?" he asked quietly.

I looked up, and up, and up—dude was so tall—at him. "May you what?"

His eyes widened slightly, nostrils flaring, and then he held out his hand.

I lifted mine toward him slowly, and he took it. The contrast between his skin, pale as death and covered with deep black tattoos, and my tanned skin, made me catch my breath.

He glared at the injury as if it had called his mother a whore. Pulling out a tube, he squeezed it onto my hand, fingers gently stroking it back and forth to massage it into the cut. I winced, and his fingers tightened around mine, keeping me in place.

"Sorry," he muttered. "Has to hurt to heal."

"Sure." I bit my lip through the rest, staring at him to take my mind off it. A lock of hair fell from the knot at the nape of his neck and slid across his forehead, briefly obscuring those intense blue eyes. He picked up a bandage and tore into the packet with his teeth. He pulled it out carefully, as if it were a butterfly.

Fierce strength, gentle care. That was what he reminded me of.

"There," he said.

"Thanks." I curled my hand over the dressing.

He shrugged again, then whirled to the sink to wash his hands. He went back to his cooking, lifting a huge pot onto the stove and glaring at the contents as if making sure they were behaving.

"What was the song you were singing?" I asked.

He frowned at me. "What?"

I put the lid back on the first aid box, careful of my hand. "You were singing something. It was nice, in a Eurobeat kind of way."

He shook his head angrily. "I don't sing."

"Uh huh. You don't sing, and you don't watch movies."

"Busy," he said, and I guessed that was the end of our conversation.

I took the cleaning supplies up and dealt with the mess, glaring at door 207 as if it might open again.

"Hello? Earth to Mari."

I looked up into Haru's smiling face. He was waving at me. He'd probably been there for a while, and I'd been lost in thought.

"Hi," I returned, my heart rising to see him. And something else.

He smiled back, sliding to squat next to where I scrubbed the floor. "What are we doing here?"

"Oh, uh, nothing." I stood up hurriedly, brushing off my hands. "I dropped the tray you left me. I was just clearing up."

"Oh, okay." He glanced again at the door, then put his thumb toward it. "Want to see what's behind it?"

I grabbed his arm. "No! No."

He frowned at me. "Mari? What's up?"

"I—uh, I fancy a night in." I walked my fingers up his arm.

"Of course. I *was* thinking we'd go out, though. I need to visit Paris. I know we've been there but I want to do it slowly this time, and—"

"Yes!" I yelped, leaping at the chance not only to visit Paris again, but also to get him away from that door.

He chuckled. "Come on, then. Let's freshen up and go." He held out his hand for mine, but I didn't take it as I stood, in case he saw the bandage.

On the way to my room, I did take Haru's arm, though. It felt natural, but it also kept the burgeoning bruise on my cheek away from him. "Are there any countries you can't go to?" I asked.

"Not really. There needs to be enough of a population to allow us to appear and not cause suspicion though, so we tend to only go to doors in towns and cities."

"Are there any other doors you can't go in?" I asked.

His steps slowed. "What do you mean?"

"I saw a frozen door. Behind ice. What's that about?" My heart rate climbed, throat closing.

Haru blew air between his lips. "Well, those are . . . Well, they're personal."

"Those?" I asked carefully. I'd seen the other doors, of course.

He flushed. "Yeah." He looked down. "Look, they're personal. I don't actually know what's in everyone else's, but . . ." He shuddered, putting his arm around me and pulling me closer to his side. "I can't talk about it yet. One day. Okay?"

What did that mean? What were those doors about? From the way Haru spoke, there was one each.

Where did they lead?

I looked at Haru. "Are they dangerous? I need to know, to do my job."

"No, nothing like that." Haru's mood had been doused. "I, uh, I'll see you in half an hour." He gave me a kiss on the forehead, pressing his lips against my skin as if he were leaving an imprint of his soul with me. Then he hurried off, arms wrapped tightly around his chest.

I went into my room and put my back to the door. What was behind those doors? Winter had been angry I was anywhere near it. Was that what I was here to find out?

I licked my dry lips, undressing. What about Winter himself? He made the air colder wherever he went, stealing the warmth from the room. But I didn't get the sense he was dangerous. Or, really, that he meant to be dangerous.

Turning that over in my mind, I went into the bathroom and turned on the shower. Stepping in, I felt something soft under my feet.

I looked down and found a non-slip mat decorated with pebble shapes. They massaged my feet as I stood under the hot water. When had that appeared?

I turned my hand over, touching the Band-Aid Winter had pressed over the cut in my palm. He was the only one who knew, who thought I had slipped in the shower. He must have taken the time while I was cleaning to put this mat here.

So I wouldn't slip again.

My eyes blurred with tears. This time, I let them flow.

Chapter Nineteen

When Haru met me outside my room, his boundless energy lifted me up a notch, but not completely. He noticed immediately and frowned. "What's the matter? Missing home?"

I shook my head. "No."

He ducked a little, looking into my face. "Are you okay?" He touched the bruise now really showing on my chin and sucked in a breath. It seemed my makeup job was substandard, or at least not up to Haru's scrutiny. "What happened?"

"Oh, it's nothing. Winter—"

Haru went stiff. "Winter hurt you?" he barked, and the corridor shivered around us. The wood started to warp, trembling in the lintels.

I grabbed Haru's arm. "He patched me up. I fell in the shower." The lie hitched in my chest, but it didn't hurt as much as Winter's gruff concern. "He fixed the issue. He didn't cause it."

"Well. Good." He closed his eyes and the corridor stopped quaking. He grabbed my hand with the bandage on it. "Great. Let's go back to Paris then."

My stomach clenched as pain shot up my arm, mingling with my information from CSON. *Ask them what happened 150 years ago.* "Haru, you jumped to a pretty big conclusion there. Is there a concern around Winter?"

His smile flickered, but he shook his head. "Let's not talk about boring stuff. I can't wait to see your face when I show you my favorite hangout spots."

"That sounds fun, Haru, but I want to talk seriously for a moment."

He grinned more widely. "You're way too serious, Mari. This is about helping you relax and welcome in more fun."

"Fun? I also have a job to do. Keep you safe."

"Ooh, yes, sure. My valiant protector." He winked at me.

I bristled and dropped a hand onto my hip. "You *are* taking me seriously, aren't you?"

His eyebrows dipped. "Of course." He tugged my hand. "Let's not talk about this now. Let's just go see Paris. I've been looking forward to this!"

He was hiding something. My gut tingled. I pulled my hand from his, massaging the band aid back into place. "What aren't you telling me?"

He ran a hand through his hair, leaving it sticking up. "I just want to relax with you."

"We can't relax all the time, and I certainly can't relax if I don't have the full picture. Having unknowns doesn't put my mind at ease."

"You sound anxious. Want a massage?" He smiled hopefully at me.

I hadn't had a massage before, but I really didn't feel like piling on a new experience whilst overwhelmed with everything else. Besides, he was trying desperately to deflect. "Haru, I'm being serious."

With a heavy sigh, he folded his arms and seemed to curl into himself. A tendril of fear curled around my stomach like a leech, this time about the relationship. This was still so new. What if he found me boring and this thing we had withered before it even began?

The idea of losing him hurt more than I ever imagined it would so soon after meeting them. My world had been turned upside down. How could I go back to working every hour of every day, knowing this house and these unique guys were right here, out of reach?

I seized his hand. "I can see this isn't the right time. Right?"

"Yeah." His gaze darted up to mine, and his smile spread. My heart gave a relieved thump at the look in his eyes; doting and with laugh lines making their appearance.

"Let's check out Paris, then, if that's where you need to go next," I said.

"It is and it isn't. I just can't wait to see your reaction to my favorite spots." He took my hand, the one with the band aid on it, and led me down the corridor.

I followed, feeling like a deflated balloon slumped at the end of a flaccid string. This should be one of those Instagram shots, the gorgeous guy excited to show his girlfriend around the world, but I felt like a fake. *Liar.*

I didn't even look the part. I wasn't some beautiful jetsetter. *Fat.* How could I possibly interest these cultured immortals, with this amazing house and all these cool opportunities? Not to mention their awesome powers. I was a dumpy mortal. A brief butterfly in their lives.

I didn't want to lose this chance with them. It was selfish, and I was sweating trying to align it with my orders to justify this situation, but I had a sinking feeling one day it would conflict. For now, I wanted—no, needed—to stay, to follow Haru and tease out what he was hiding from me. Winter's words floated back to me: *it hurts before it heals.*

Haru was avoiding something.

He slowed a little to let me draw level and put his arm around my shoulders. His warmth flowed over me, soothing the tension in my neck muscles. "There's this gorgeous cafe right on the Seine, and then I want to go to the Gold Museum in Venice. It's hardly known so there will be barely any crowds. For lunch we can go to Bruges. Those little chocolate box streets are gorgeous this time of year." He took a deep breath as if already breathing in fresh air. "Ah. There's just so much. Where to pick first?"

We went down the stairs, and I trailed a hand on the headless dragon on the wall. "I suppose with so many choices, you're out all the time."

"When it's my season, yeah. Twice a year, north then south." He tugged me past the painting.

I planted my stance. "So you have three months off every three months, essentially. Stuck in this house." I looked up at the towering artwork, spiraling up the stairs. "This is all you, isn't it?"

His eyes clouded briefly. "Yeah, sort of. I led it."

"And the others joined in?"

He shrugged. "No. This is a me project."

"Do you ever do stuff together? You all seem like ships passing in the night."

"We used to. We kind of do." He shook himself. "We will again but, for now, you're all mine."

For now? My brain latched onto that key phrase. Were his thoughts already taking the same track as mine, only enjoying me for as long as I was here?

We passed into Paris and my brain was as busy and loud as the streets, filled with fears. I had orders to lure Winter to door 207. Haru might already be bored with me. They were locked in the house for half the year, and they'd grown used to each other's company. Of course I was a novelty. Just like a toy, I would wear out and fade and fall apart, and they wouldn't.

The unfairness of it grabbed me around the throat, choking me with angry tears.

"Mari?" Haru's warm concern enveloped me just as his arms did. He stopped and pulled me into a hug. "Is it all too much?"

"Yeah," I said shakily. "But I don't want to spoil your fun."

He cupped my cheek in his hand. "If you're not having fun, Buttercup, I won't push it."

I curled my fingers into his shirt. "I'll cheer up in a moment." Would distracting myself work? I still knew problems loomed, waiting for me when I got back. It was like an elephant sitting on my chest. I closed my eyes. When I felt like crap, doing something nice for someone else was always my go-to. It made them feel good and grateful and made me feel useful.

What could I possibly offer a powerful immortal?

The idea snapped into my head like it was dropped there. I opened my eyes, invigorated, when I spotted the stranger. Over Haru's shoulder, a man caught my eye. I'd never seen him before, but the way he was looking our way—at Haru—tingled my senses.

He lifted his hand and touched his ear, speaking into his wrist. I couldn't read his lips to understand what he was saying since he was likely speaking French, but he was definitely up to something.

I pressed my lips to Haru's cheek, out of sight. "Someone noticed us and is reporting on it," I whispered to him, lips brushing his skin.

His eyebrows dipped but, to his credit, he didn't immediately turn around and gawk. "Oh, great."

"Who knows who you really are?"

"CSON," he said, but bitterly. "Not at Shield level, but higher up. They call themselves grandiose things all the time. I don't know what they are this decade."

Decade? "And . . . You don't like us?" I asked.

"I have no problem with the Shields, they are just doing what they are told. There's more classified levels of knowledge and with that sort of knowledge comes a desire to use it. Think about it. If you had the seasons in your pocket, wouldn't you want to use them?"

"So are you . . . trapped by CSON?"

"Trapped?" Haru snorted. "We can go anywhere we want in an eye blink. We choose not to all go together so we don't cause hideous weather patterns. It's kind of a stalemate."

"Sounds very tense."

"Yes, and boring. So let's just go. He'll be harmless."

Would he? The way the operative was glaring at me made my chest squeeze painfully. Was he pissed? I was interpreting everything as the worst case, anxious tension twining in my gut. What if he was reporting that I'd isolated Haru instead of Winter?

What if they were going to make a grab for *him*?

I took Haru's arm. "We have to lose our tail, now. Where's the nearest door back?"

"Back to the house?" Haru looked way behind us, back toward the street we'd come from. Right where the operative was just full on following us, hands in his pockets. "It's about a mile back that way." He grinned at me. "There's also another door in the Louvre."

I didn't want to pass that operative. "That one. Let's move and try to lose our tail."

Haru leaned in close to me. "Let's."

Lacing my fingers with his, I tugged him down the street and then into a side alley. Although it was a busy Parisian street, this seemed to be residential with beautiful light blue shutters thrown open on the windows and ivy festooning the walls. Pulling him close to me, we flattened along the side of the wall.

"Ooh, this is exciting." Haru's hands roamed, setting my bare arms tingling. He breathed deeply next to my forehead and the plants around us shuddered, leaves unfurling and widening, flowers budding and blooming. "Oops. Getting a bit too excited," Haru murmured, his hips sliding flush with mine. I was caught between the hard pressure along my back from the wall and a hard length in front from Haru.

A thrill thrummed through my stomach, but I had work to do. "Can you hide us?"

"To a point." Haru glanced at the ivy. More tendrils burst from the stem and feathered into the sky. "It will soon get too big for itself and die when I leave," he said sadly.

I didn't like the heartache in his voice, but I liked the idea of that operative tailing us even less. "Stop for now. That might be enough."

We watched the alleyway. The operative made it to the alleyway entrance, then stopped dead and frowned, scanning the alleyway and turning in place to sweep the street with his gaze.

I chuckled under my breath. "I bet he hadn't expected me to move very fast at all," I whispered to Haru. *Score one for me.*

"Or evade him, since he is technically there for my protection." Haru's hands slid up to my chest, under my shirt. His warm fingers smoothed across my skin feverishly, pushing up underneath my underwired bra. "Fortunately, I have you to watch over me."

"Haru," I breathed. "Stop distracting your Shield."

His eyes, shaded by the narrow walls and plants, went darker still. "Gotta function under pressure, darling." His hand slid lower, dipping into the waistband of my pants. His urgent movements excited me like nothing else.

"We're in a street, Haru. Being tracked," I reminded him.

He nibbled my earlobe and kissed my neck, causing spears

of desire to strike my core like he ran a current from my pulse to my pussy. "Mm. Yes."

I gently shoved at him. "This isn't a game, Haru."

"Isn't it?" His fingers slid down, parting my lower lips and stroking my bud. "It's exciting, anyway."

My legs trembled as he strummed me. "Haru. This is serious."

"Mm, yes. Very serious." He captured my lips, his kiss urgent and assertive, making me open to him.

I moaned into his mouth, unable to do anything other than melt for him, but I kept an eye on the operative.

And he was approaching the rustling ivy.

Oh, damn! I twisted my head away from the kiss. "Haru, he's coming."

"Are you?" He smiled, banding his arms around me and trapping me against the wall as he plucked once more.

And I loved it. Sensation crashed over me as I shuddered around his fingers, panties soaked, and he tipped his head back with satisfaction.

Breathless, I grabbed his wrist, pulling him out of my pants, and ran.

We burst from the cage of ivy then we were running as fast as we could. Haru whooped, keeping pace with me. I swung my head over my shoulder to check on the agent.

He looked stunned, raising his wrist again to speak rapidly into his watch.

My gut clenched. Was he organizing troops to cut us off? The bliss of my orgasm blended into the sharp sting of fear.

We burst from the alleyway on the other side, and I tugged Haru across the street. People in sharp suits strode here and there, the skies gray, and tourists clattered along chattering to one another. Cars honked as they slammed to a stop right beside us, angry streams of French directed at me.

"Whoa, Mari, I like a touch of danger, but this is a bit

much." Haru followed me anyway, waving cheerily at the irate drivers.

The high pitched whine of a motorcycle bearing down on us filled my awareness. I pulled Haru to a stop and tossed him behind me. *Was the rider going to try to abduct him?* I raised my fists, ready to defend my boyfriend.

The rider skirted past, gesticulating, but Haru was unharmed. His eyes were wide, though. "Uh, Mari? Is everything okay?"

He couldn't trust CSON, but I couldn't tell him that. I couldn't tell him they were after Winter.

Or could I?

"Haru, I want you to trust me."

"I do. Of course I do." He clung to me. We were marooned in the middle of the road, cars zooming by either side. "Whatever is going on, you don't need to explain it. I'll follow your lead."

"Great." I saw a sign for the Louvre. "Let's go."

We waited for the traffic to ease then dashed across the road. The French Shield operative tried to follow, heralded by the screech of brakes behind us. I picked up the pace, and Haru streaked alongside me. As we passed the street cafés, flowers bloomed and bushes heaved up, cracking their pots. Cries of alarm followed us, but Haru just chuckled.

We made it to the glass pyramid and I barked, "Where is it?"

"Somewhere in the old building."

I pulled up my collar, looking behind us for the operative. I couldn't see him. "Pretend to be tourists. Let's buy tickets and go in."

We got in the queue and sure enough, the operative sprinted by us, barely glancing at the throng of tourists. My belly tensed, then slowly unknotted.

"Deux, s'il vous plait," Haru said to the clerk, paying. Haru flourished the tickets at me. "Et voila," he said with a wink.

I took the tickets and his hand. "I'll have to learn French. And Japanese. And Spanish."

"And Norwegian for Winter." Haru slung his arm around my shoulders.

Guilt stabbed at me, and we walked into the greatest art museum in the world.

"Mm, tasty," Haru said, gaze sliding lovingly over the Botticelli beauties. "Buxom, plentiful, and gorgeous."

"Plump," I returned. "They aren't today's beauty standards."

"No? Then the world is missing out." Haru licked his lips as his gaze travelled from the statues to me. I shivered, goosebumps raising.

Smooth carvings of marble passed me by and my stomach was slowly relaxing. We had lost our tail, and the door home was in here somewhere. Haru seemed to be in no hurry, wandering here and there among the old masters.

"This takes me back," he said, pausing at a painting. A nude black haired woman was being chained to a cliff by unconcerned villagers.

I read the title. "Andromeda Chained to the rock by the Nereids."

"One of Summer's favorites," Haru murmured, sliding behind my back and enveloping me in an embrace. He grasped my wrists gently.

I gasped at the tingle racing through me.

"I think he'll want to play with us soon. He's shown remarkable self-control." Haru kissed the side of my neck. "Same with Otto. They keep pretending, but they can't hide it from me. You should see the way their eyes are drawn to you whenever you're in the room."

Those two as well? Could I have all three? "And?" I swung to face him with a raised brow.

He quirked an eyebrow. "I know you're interested too, and I want to reassure you. It's fine. More than fine." He lowered his voice. "Whatever you want, whoever you want, I want to make sure you get it. Ever had multiple partners? I tell you, it's the best fun you'll ever have." He kissed my neck, nipping softly. "This from me, coupled with Otto's meticulous fingers. Summer holding back until he can't take it anymore. Then he's opening, demanding, brutally brilliant."

My breathing quickened. I could imagine it. Summer's smoldering smirk as I unraveled in front of him, Otto's gorgeous arms around me.

"You really wouldn't mind?" I asked, the question strangled as the idea gripped me.

"Mind? I'm encouraging it." His fingers slid to the front of my blouse, tweaking the buttons. "What are you imagining?"

I gulped. "You, kissing me. Summer, stripping me." I shuddered in his arms. I would feel so exposed to his controlled gaze, watching the fire in his eyes blaze out of control. "Otto, between my legs." He would be attentive and responsive, studying me intently and smug at every twitch and gasp. "Winter, watching." His cold glare softening, melting . . .

Haru's breath hitched. "Well." He swallowed hard and cleared his throat. "We can build up to that. Let's start slow." He grinned down at me. "Come on, then, Mari. Let's go home."

I smiled back, but I couldn't help but feel his mood had cooled slightly when I mentioned Winter. Haru wasn't ready to talk yet, but there was something he wasn't mentioning.

Something he was afraid of.

Chapter Twenty

I didn't like that Haru was holding back. Well, maybe not sexually, and despite his free spirit—something I admired—he was being cagey about something.

I was worried it was me. I couldn't help it. Years of my mom prattling about losing weight, that I needed to be nicer, what man would want a woman in the military, and whatever else was hard to ignore sometimes. I liked Haru, more than I'd liked anyone before. It was easy being around him, something that felt flawless. It was like for the first time in my life I could be myself and someone saw my worth. With how he made me feel, the snarky girls and my mother's comments shouldn't be there in the back of my mind worrying me. But he had spent so much time talking about trust, and yet, I had my own secrets and I thought he still had his. There was something shut off tightly, and I couldn't help fear it was me.

I traipsed the halls in search of someone who I thought might be able to help. "Summer," I sing-songed.

Nothing. I knew he had to be here somewhere because it wasn't his season, but this place was ginormous and I hadn't fully figured out any of the guys' usual spots. Honestly, I kind of avoided finding out because I was a wee bit nervous of running into Winter alone.

Summer had to be here somewhere. I knew he and Haru were close, and I was hoping he'd help me come up with a plan. A way to repay Haru for everything he's done for me and how welcome he has made me feel. But, secretly, I hoped it warmed him up a little more to me. Maybe even help get me some answers.

Voices reached me from the next hall.

I quickened my pace and the closer I got, the more my gut twisted.

"It's unsafe!" Otto shouted.

My feet scuttled to a stop just short of the library entrance, shocked that Otto would ever raise his voice.

"We don't even know if it's her!" Summer retorted, equally as angry. "*Esto es absurdo.*"

"You're being absurd!" Otto didn't hesitate to respond. "Why take the chance? Again? If it is—"

"If it is, we would have noticed! One hundred and fifty years! It's been one hundred and fifty years since he—"

"Stop." Otto cut in. "You don't need to say it. I was there."

"Then why? Why indulge this insane idea? We were finally getting over it, working through it, accepting the reality," Summer pressed.

"You call the last few decades getting over it? Ah yes, with Haru avoiding anything serious, you holeing yourself up with work, and Winter avoiding any emotion all together."

"*I'm* holeing myself up with work?" Summer scoffed. "*Que rico,* coming from you."

"Yes, because the four of us really bond these days." The disdain in Otto's voice made my skin itch uncomfortably.

"How would you even know, considering you never leave the library?"

Grinding my teeth and hearing enough of their petulant fight, I stomped around the corner and into the library.

Their heads turned to me in unison. "What're you doing here?" Summer spat, a warm blast of air radiating off of him.

I swallowed. "Looking for you."

"Why?" His words were short, annoyed.

Otto glared at him. "Why're you being such a twat? She hasn't done anything."

"You mean besides breaking into our house?" Summer's attention returned to Otto.

They stared one another down, and despite the deep breaths they both took, the room just grew hotter, angrier. Suddenly, it was like there was a barrier of heat separating me from them.

"Summer," I called.

He didn't respond.

"Otto?"

Nothing. It was as though I was a ghost and they could no longer hear me.

"Uh oh." Haru moseyed up behind me, pressing his back into my chest and resting a hand gently on my waist.

My brows furrowed at him. "Uh oh?"

He cleared his throat. "So, uh, Otto is usually a pretty calm and collected person."

"I've noticed," I whispered. The two of them didn't even acknowledge us. By this point I was waiting to see who would throw the first punch. As a Shield, was I expected to jump between the two of them? If they used their powers, what help would I be anyway?

"There's a reason for that," Haru continued in a whisper. "Otto can calm people's emotions, but if he gets riled up, so do others."

"Right," I said, although I couldn't say I fully understood. "What about us?"

"All his anger is directed toward Summer right now," Haru explained. "I think he's using part of his powers to block you, but if this gets any worse, we're gonna be in real trouble."

I frowned. "How can we help?"

"We can take bets on who will win," Haru jested with a shrug.

I twisted my head to glare at him, which elicited a small chuckle.

"Yes, yes, no time for games." He sighed, eyes focusing with thought as he became suddenly serious. "I have one idea."

"What is it?"

"I don't know if you'll be game. You might want to leave and let me take care of it. After all, what if it doesn't work?"

I twisted in his arms and folded my arms across my chest. "I'm not going anywhere. Tell me the plan."

There was a twinkle in Haru's eyes, one akin to the look he got before a dare. "We need to relieve some tension. Have some fun and calm down the situation. A distraction, if you will."

"Alright." I waited for the punchline. "And how exactly do you plan to do that?"

"Last chance to leave," Haru stared at me, eyebrow raised. Again, with such intensity it was as though he was trying to call my bluff.

"Nope."

Haru reached out, wrapped his hand around the back of my neck and pulled me toward him in a flash. My hands fell flat against his chest as his lips found mine. My gasp was cut off as his tongue slid into my mouth. His free hand wrapped around my waist, squeezing it before sliding to my back to pull him flush against him.

I pushed against his chest, creating enough space to break my lips free. "Haru, I don't think this is the time or the place."

"Are you sure?" Eyes smoldering, he looked over my shoulder and inclined his head.

I followed his gaze to see Summer and Otto staring at me once more. But this time their faces weren't contorted with barely contained rage. There was surprise and . . . interest.

My cheeks flushed.

Haru's fingers traced designs on my lower back, drawing my attention back to him. He smiled down at me, his expression knowing. *Asshole.* I shouldn't have told him about my fantasies yesterday. This wasn't fair.

He leaned down and whispered in my ear. "Relax." The light movement of air over my ear made me shiver. "They like it. Do you?"

I gulped, and, after a brief pause gave the slightest of nods. "Good girl."

My legs could've given out with those two words.

A rumble sounded from behind me. "That's not for you to say," Summer interrupted with a growl.

Haru looked up and smirked. "Then what is, sir?"

"Cup her ass," Summer demanded.

Haru, without hesitation, moved his hand over my curves until his palm securely grasped my left cheek.

My core heated, enjoying how Haru touched me, and I was beyond turned on by the fact that Summer had ordered it.

Bending his head, Haru took my mouth once more. His body pushed against me, and I hadn't realized he had moved us until my backside hit a firm wall behind me.

I pulled away from his delicious kiss with a gasp of surprise.

It wasn't a wall behind me but Otto, whose hands now rested on my hips.

"*Bien*," Summer noted from off to the side. "Continue."

I couldn't see Summer as Haru bent over, filling my world and running his tongue along the curve of my ear. His touch sending thrills through my body until goosebumps rose. His knee pushed my legs apart, the space soon occupied by his thigh.

Otto used his hands to guide my hips, grinding me against Haru's leg, and between the movement and pressure, pleasure swirled inside of me. He made a soft noise in his throat, a sound that rumbled in his chest behind me and sent shivers straight to my core.

Haru kissed down my neck, and I leaned my head back with a sigh. When I reopened my eyes, Otto was staring down at me, his lips slightly parted as he took me in. Reaching up, I grabbed the back of his head and pulled his lips down to mine. His lips were soft and full, every movement of them thoughtful. He didn't push me, taking the opening to plunge his tongue into my mouth when Haru hit the ball of nerves so perfectly that I gasped. He swallowed my moan, taking it inside of him and replacing it with delicate kisses.

I wanted more, needed more. It was like all my nerves were on fire, and suddenly I couldn't stand the feel of my clothes— of their clothes. My fingers pried at Haru's shirt, sliding it off quickly before reaching back to do the same to Otto.

My shirt came next. On instinct, in front of three of the hottest men I'd ever seen, my arms wrapped around my stomach.

"Stop," Summer demanded.

It was like even time itself decided to listen. The kisses stopped, the grinding stopped, and we were a frozen statue of arms, limbs, and bated breaths that didn't dare to move.

Summer sat himself in the tall backed chair, every inch the lord of the manor. "Mari, remove your arms."

I only hesitated a moment before I did as he requested. Well, ordered.

A satisfied smile crooked his lips. *"Buena niña,"* Summer rumbled.

A small moan escaped me at the sound of those words coming from him. Being called a good girl in Spanish was a whole other level of need I didn't know I had until now. I would do just about anything to keep getting that praise from him.

A spark lit his face with devilish mischief. "You like that, Mari?"

I bit my lip, found his heated gaze, and nodded.

"Remove your bra," he ordered.

Reaching back, with Otto leaning away just enough to give me space, I unhooked my bra and slid it off.

Haru purred, fingers twitching as he stared at my bare chest.

"Good girl." Summer gave a rueful smile this time.

"In *español*," I pleaded.

A smoldering gaze seared me, turning all of my nerves raw. "*Buena niña.*"

If it wasn't for Haru and Otto, I'm pretty sure I would have actually melted to the ground. Hearing those words from him could've made me come on the spot.

"Haru," Summer said, not breaking eye contact with me. I stood bare from the waist up in Haru and Otto's arms, smoldering heat radiating from Summer's station and wafting over me, keeping me warm. His fingers curled into the armrests. "Make her come, but not until I tell you to."

Haru nodded and bent down to kiss me once more. The way his tongue danced across mine, the world felt fuzzy. He brought his hand up to cup my breast, kneading my heavyset chest. Taking a peaked nipple between his thumb and forefinger, he gave it a light pinch and I moaned.

"Now, take her pants off," Summer commanded, leaning forward.

"I think *I* will be in charge of that." Otto's delicate hands glided across my hips until they wrapped around to undo the button. Soon, the jeans were sliding over my hips and I was left in nothing but a thong.

Haru glanced down and smiled. "Fucking gorgeous," he murmured against my skin.

"Delicious," Otto added from behind.

I found Haru's eyes. "I—I want your pants off too." I turned my head to find Otto. "And yours."

I peered at Summer, worried what his reaction would be that I was giving directions instead.

Summer's sly smile slid into place. "How do you ask nicely?"

"Please," I breathed.

The two men withdrew from my body to do as they were asked, but I didn't feel cold as Summer's heat encased me. I opened my mouth to thank him, but instead I was surprised when other words came out. "You too. Please."

Summer's brow twitched with surprise. "You are a demanding little thing, aren't you?"

I flushed but didn't back down. "I did say please."

He inclined his head. "So you did." He kept his gaze locked on me as he slowly unbuttoned his shirt, parting the fabric, and smirked when I gasped at his bronze chest. He undid his belt buckle and slid off his pants, When his hard cock sprang free I bit my lip to try to hide my surprise.

Holy shit, he was massive.

Haru looked over too and a small groan escaped him. Fully naked and well-endowed himself, he walked over to Summer and ran a finger over his chiseled chest. "Well?" he asked.

Summer finally stole his eyes away from my face to find Haru's. It was like there were unspoken words between the two of them.

Otto pressed his smooth body against mine, and when I felt his hardness against the middle of my back, my panties soaked even more.

Summer finally looked to me, desire on his face. "Tell me what you want."

I blinked in surprise. I wanted them; all of them. I wanted us to find ecstasy together, but based on his darkening gaze I knew that wasn't enough. "I want Haru inside of me while . . . while he sucks you off." I had zero doubt my face turned beet red as the words left my mouth.

Summer flashed a smile and gave a single nod. "Haru." He directed him to the desk. Brushing things aside, not caring how books and papers flew to the ground, Haru substituted the items by lying on his back.

"Mari." Summer held out his hand to me.

I paused, nerves ricocheting inside my stomach.

Otto gave my hip a gentle squeeze. "We've got you," he murmured against my ear before giving my neck a soft kiss.

"W—what if the desk doesn't hold?" I took Summer's hand hesitantly, staring at the desk. If this was Ikea brand there was no way it would hold both me and Haru.

"It'll be fine," Otto assured me. "It is engineered to withstand more than just book learning."

Slowly I placed one knee on the desk, and after a deep breath I pulled myself on top. It didn't even creak.

"Haru is a great wood worker," Otto said, helping me balance as I swung my leg over to straddle Haru's waist.

Haru and I locked eyes, and I couldn't stop the smile from creeping onto my face at the innuendo. Haru matched my smirk, picking up on the same thing, and gave me a wink.

I cleared my throat. "My underwear."

Summer reached over and with a quick yank, snapped the strings holding it together leaving me fully exposed. All of them moaned in unison.

Haru sat up and found my mouth, kissing me so intensely like I was the only thing in the world. I wrapped my arms around him and a set of hands landed on me. Whose, I didn't know, but strong calloused fingers guided our movements until Haru's cock slipped inside my wet pussy. We went slow, giving myself time to adjust to his girth, and soon my hips ground against his.

I moaned into Haru's mouth. He felt so fucking good, but I needed more. Pushing at Haru's chest, he leaned away until he was on his back. I didn't need direction to know what I wanted. My hands moved along his chest, reaching between my legs, but someone grabbed my wrist and stopped me. My eyes flew open to find Otto.

"Allow me." He leaned down to kiss me as his hand replaced mine. His fingers danced around my clit, teasing me and riling me up, and when they finally landed on the perfect spot I lost myself to his touch. He kept it light and I swear this man must play piano or something with how meticulous he was to bring me so close to the edge then pull back before I could come.

Haru used his hips to move inside of me, and the combination only brought me closer to the edge.

"I'm gonna—"

"Not yet," Summer told me. He moved toward Haru and grabbed the base of his cock, tilting it in Haru's direction.

Haru happily obliged, twisting to take Summer in his mouth. Summer was huge, and despite Haru's impressive lack of gag reflex, he still needed to use his hand to work the base of Summer's cock. Methodically he sucked, pulling back until only Summer's head was inside his mouth as he swirled his tongue.

Summer's head fell back with a moan.

Haru pulled free with a pop and dipped under to caress his balls before licking a long length of Summer from the base and returning to teasing the head.

Summer growled, and his hand dipped into Haru's hair,

grasping the strands between his fingers and pushing himself further into Haru's mouth.

Haru took it, took as much as Summer wanted to give. Tears ran down his face but he smiled, his cock twitching inside of me. Otto's fingers danced across my nub again, throwing another barb of pleasure through my body. My body shook with the need for release. With one hand on Haru's chest to balance as he pumped in and out of me, I used my free hand to reach back and grasp Otto's throbbing dick.

Otto moaned, eyes fluttering, as I began to work my hand along his shaft. His fingers never stopped moving though, continuing to tease.

Wanting him to be as close as me, I reached down and played with his balls, following a similar method Haru had. Never had I done this before, but the way Otto's hardness pulsed and how his balls tightened in my palm, I knew he enjoyed it. Bringing my hand back up, I used my thumb to swirl the bead of precum around his velvet tip.

"Mari," Otto gasped. His cock was rock hard in my hand, matching how stiff Haru was inside of me.

My walls tightened with need, each wet slap as I rode Haru turning me on more and more.

Haru continued to work Summer with his mouth while I eased up and down, seeking out a deep friction, and Otto's fingers worked me harder and harder. I was so close, so fucking close. My nails dug into Haru's chest. This time Otto didn't stop, instead his swirling fingers became more frantic, matching the same desire and need as the rest of us.

Summer hastened his hips, pumping in and out of Haru's mouth, matching the pace he moved in and out of me. We were in unison, reaching our peak together, all connected.

"Come for me," Summer demanded. It took two pumps and one perfect rub of Otto's thumb and I was in freefall. I cried out as the best orgasm of my life washed over me, rolling sensations through me as Haru's cock thickened and throbbed as he released himself inside of me. Otto's cock jutted as his cum covered my arm and side. Summer moaned, coming inside Haru's mouth who eagerly sucked up every single bit.

A second orgasm blasted through me and I cried out, overwhelmed. My body was ready to give out when Otto stepped forward, wrapping his arm around my shoulders to pull me into him for support.

Between our panting breaths, the door creaking broke the dazed silence. Barely conscious, the four of us looked toward the sound.

Winter gripped the door frame, which cracked as ice overtook it. The ground frosted beneath his feet and spread, a geometric pattern of jagged crystals. A cold wind blew through the room, turning the sheen of sweat on our bodies to biting cold.

"Winter." There was a warning in Summer's voice.

"No," Winter growled. "No!"

Haru shot up, wrapping his arms around me as snow blew from Winter and across us. I leaned into Haru as he shielded me from the sudden burst of power.

When I opened my eyes, I found Summer and Otto standing side by side like a wall between us and Winter.

"Get out of here and calm down," Otto said.

Summer's heat blasted outward. "Now."

Between their bodies, Winter met my eyes. Cold fury turned his blue eyes feral, and I gasped. He turned and stalked away, flurries falling to the floor where he had been.

"Are you okay?" Haru brushed back my hair, looking over me in a state of panic I had never seen from him.

"I'm fine. What was that all about?" I mean, I knew Winter barely tolerated me, but . . . that felt personal.

"Don't worry about it," Summer said, staring at the empty doorway.

Otto rubbed my back. "As long as you're okay, that's what matters."

Haru helped me off him and grabbed a blanket from the chair to wrap around me. "Let's go get you cleaned up."

And just like that, I was left with even more questions.

Chapter Twenty-One

I didn't know what to expect after that hot, rough, and sticky session on Otto's desk, but now I was feeling twisted, stuck in a bind, and just a bit gross. I hunkered further in the blanket Haru wrapped me in, wishing I could hide my face.

I wasn't ashamed of what we had done—far from it. I was more upset that Winter had walked in on us. I'd imagined him watching, but the anger in his eyes, the blistering rage, left no doubt in my mind. He hated me, and he was dangerous.

I had a job to do: protect the Seasons, even if it was from each other. My stomach twisted, but I shoved it aside. I had to focus on my task. My orders were to lure Winter closer to door 207.

I glanced at Haru. Would he be open to helping with that? I knew they spent a lot of time together, but I was certain they all recognized how dangerous Winter was. There needed to be an intervention.

Perhaps that was why CSON was intervening now. It clicked into place. The organization was cagey with explaining their orders because, at the end of the day, I was just a grunt. A

Shield they could replace tomorrow with a reasonably fit person with the right security clearance. There was probably support waiting for him at the CSON headquarters, right? I wasn't naive enough to think that the guys wouldn't object if Winter was abducted, as they should, but there was a difference between kidnapping and an intervention.

Summer shoved his arms through his shirt and buckled up his trousers. Otto stared at the table where we had just had messy mind-blowing sex, his thoughts hidden behind a mask on his face. Even Haru was quiet, offering me a small smile but nowhere near his usual self.

"Well, this isn't awkward," I said, breaking the tension.

Summer let his arms fall to his sides. His shirt was still unbuttoned, the crisp white edges brushing against his chiseled bronze torso. I'd seen him come undone, dancing to my tune for once, and now I wanted to brush my fingers across his chest.

I wanted them all surrounding me. I could imagine it now: on the big sofa in the living room watching a movie, leaning against Summer's bare chest and the warmth there. Haru playfully sliding his hand down my panties to see if the others noticed. Otto kissing me whenever a scary scene came on, and Winter.

Winter, standing off to one side, alone, staring at the four of us with hunger and loss in his face.

God that hurt. I squeezed my eyes shut, taking a deep breath. I needed to get him help.

"Going up, Mari." Haru dipped next to me then swung me up in his arms.

"What? No! Stop! You'll break your back." I wriggled my legs.

Otto glanced up from his reverie, eyes focusing on me. "Are you ticklish, Mari, mm?"

"Oh, she just has to be," Haru chuckled.

"Don't!" I tried to kick my feet out of Otto's reach, but the blanket bound me effectively. If I properly fought back, I might end up giving Haru a sprain.

Summer touched Otto on the shoulder. "Perhaps now we can finish our conversation."

With a wistful look at me, Otto nodded. "Yes. I think I've calmed down now."

I settled as well. Ah yes, what was their conversation—or rather, argument—about? They had mentioned something happening one hundred and fifty years ago, something "he" did. Was that someone Winter?

Jeez, but immortals could hold a grudge. I had to find out what had their knickers in a twist. It related to Winter and his powers, I was sure of it.

Haru walked out with me held princess-style in his arms. "Well, that was fun," he said, smile bright. "I can tell you liked it."

"I—yes." My cheeks heated, and I buried my face in his neck.

He laughed, the sound ringing down the long corridors.

He carried me all the way to my room and into the connected bathroom. The shower stall was huge, enough for at least three of the guys and me unless it was Summer and Winter together. In which case it would just be us three. My mind wandered. What would they be like together? Fire and ice, control and passion, both vying for my attention.

My legs trembled and I groaned.

Haru turned on the shower and gave me a knowing look. "Still having lovely flashbacks, I see." He gently tugged one side of the blanket down, slowly unwrapping me like I was a present he wanted to savor. Would I ever get tired of seeing the adoration on his face?

I curled my fingers into his hair. The bathroom was steaming up, fogging my vision. Reaching behind him, Haru guided me forward, and we were both plunged into the warm stream of water.

He soaped up, rubbing his hands into a lather, then ran his hands across my chest, around my breasts, kneading my shoulders and back, playing with my nipples so they peaked. His sure touch, gentle yet firm, sent ripples of pleasure down my muscles.

"Truth or dare," he whispered.

"Truth," I returned.

He cocked his head. "What was your favorite part of our group lovemaking?"

I didn't even have to think. "Being in the center of it all, right at the heart."

"Mm. Our hub. The nexus." He pulled me to his chest, wet skin on skin, and ran his lips over my soapy shoulder.

"I could see and feel everyone," I said, but in amongst the happiness, my stomach fell. "Well, nearly everyone."

Haru's arms tightened around me, but when he pulled back, he had that false smile in place again. "Oh, don't worry about Winter, Mari. We'll take care of it."

I licked my lips, wondering how far I should push this. "Truth or dare."

"Truth," Haru said, eyes bright, no doubt waiting for me to ask what his favorite part was.

I took a deep bolstering breath. *Here goes nothing.* "Are you afraid of Winter?"

He reared back with surprise. "What? No."

He was lying to me. My gut could tell from the way his eyes avoided mine. I gripped his hands. "You can tell me, and I can help you. I can help *him.* It's clear Winter needs some professional help."

Haru waved me down. "He's fine, he's just . . . a bit hemmed in, because it's not his season, right? He just needs to chill. Haha."

Even Haru's laugh was fake and flat. It stung like water in an open wound. "Haru, I thought you trusted me. You can tell me."

"No, like, chill, you know?"

I let his hands go. When he was like this, deflecting through humor, he was childish rather than the insightful, enthusiastic Haru I preferred. "Can you please be serious for a minute? This is important."

"I know, but you don't need to worry. You aren't here to worry about us, Mari."

"Sure I am. This is my literal job now." I shook my head. "What happened one hundred and fifty years ago?"

The light and color went out not just in Haru's eyes, but across his whole face and upper body, like he had been drained of blood in seconds. I grabbed hold of him in case he fainted, and he grabbed me back, fingers digging into my arms. "How do you know about that?" he whispered, eyes searching mine.

"I overhead Summer and Otto. They mentioned something happening 150 years ago." I met his eyes steadily. It was the truth after all. I had overheard them right before Haru helped me distract them.

"Oh, yeah." Haru screwed the shower tap closed, and the warmth cut off suddenly. I shivered.

He bit his lip, looking at me. "I know it's hard, but, please, don't ask about that. We can't focus on the past, right? We have to move forward."

I frowned. "How can you all move forward if it keeps being brought up? And I'm going to keep bringing this up. Winter needs help. There are people in CSON who can help him."

"CSON?" Haru scoffed. "What do they know of wielding the powers we have?"

I tapped my foot. "So it is something to do with Winter's powers."

Haru growled at himself, running a hand through his wet hair.

I took his hand. "Look, you don't have to handle this alone. None of you do. It's important to reach out for help when you need it, and in my honest outsider's opinion, you all need it. CSON is your organization, right? You said so yourself. It's there to help you?" I waved down at myself.

Haru looked me up and down as if just seeing me anew. A stab of anxiety twisted my stomach. I was naked right now, as was he. Nothing between us except the truths we weren't telling each other.

He frowned. "I wouldn't say we exactly trust CSON. Every now and again the organization gets a bit above itself, trying to order us around and tell us what to do, like we haven't been doing our jobs for generations of operatives."

I put my hand on my chest. "I work for CSON too, though." I tried to give him an encouraging smile.

Haru took a step back. "That's right. You do." He ran a hand through his hair. "I need to . . . think. For a while. And I should get back to hopping around the world. Spring won't sprung itself." He smiled at me. "Want to come?"

I knew he was trying to extend a peace offering, but I also needed to think. How could I get through to him? How could I convince him there was a problem when he was avoiding any mention of it?

Another thing he avoided was talking about those doors. The one covered in ice or the one bound with so much foliage it looked like a gardener's greenhouse gone feral. *Where did those doors lead? What was behind them?*

I'd have to find out.

Chapter Twenty-Two

I ranged far and wide in the house over the next few days, staying the hell away from door 207. *Two weeks.* CSON had given me two weeks to lure Winter close to that damned door, and the countdown was haunting me. I couldn't focus on either the magnificent views nor my amazing new life, and every selfie with Haru in a breathtaking location—Sapporo, Singapore, Scotland, Seoul—felt fake as fuck. I couldn't keep smiling through this.

Haru was noticing, but he doubled down, determined to cheer me up but without really talking to me. He was still nursing his own secrets, and plants kept sprouting throughout the house to Otto's dismay as he was the one who needed to use his powers to help get rid of them.

I even stress-cleaned the kitchen. No one else seemed to be around and it was clearly Winter's domain, but one day I found a stack of plates leftover from breakfast. It spiraled from there. I scrubbed away at the surfaces, sinking into the rhythm the same way I would during weight training. Just me and the plates, where life was much simpler: just press on, just one more, push harder. Plus, cleaning was extremely satisfying, seeing the chrome gleaming back at me.

"What are you doing?" Winter rumbled, and I spun around. Shit, I hadn't even heard him come in.

He wore a tight black shirt which set off all his icy godness and black jeans. He set his hands on the counter, frowning down at the plates lined up on the drying rack. Then he shrugged and picked up a dish towel and set to work drying the plates. Meanwhile my mind screamed at me. I had no choice; I needed to help my family. They were always a priority, but . . . my world had grown so much. Maybe I could talk to them. But what could I say that would make it sound alright? *'Hi, I broke into your house to steal a key, which now the people I work for have access to and they want Winter. Any chance you wanna come along, buddy ol' pal?'*"

Yeah, I didn't see that going over well.

I found the gym and threw myself into it gladly. State of the art with masses of plates for every occasion, I could see now how the guys kept themselves in tip-top shape. In my mental map, it was oriented close to the east wing, so after a workout and shower, I made my way there. The vines strangling the stairway draped over the hallway, and I brushed them aside, a wistful scent of honeysuckle following me. Above, daylight barely crept through the cracks in the plants crisscrossing over the ceiling.

In the center of the room Haru knelt, head down and shoulders slumped. He turned something over in his hands, maybe a small plant from the greens and pinks I could see of it.

"Hi," I said, my voice cracking from disuse.

He startled. "Oh, hey, Buttercup!" He pushed to his feet in one smooth motion, turning to face me and slipping whatever it was in his pocket. But I was more concerned with the redness around his eyes.

I approached him, lifting my hand to his cheek. "Are you okay? Have you been crying?"

He let me soothe his cheek, leaning his head into my palm. He had a dusting of a five o'clock shadow, not the normal fresh faced Haru, and his hair was stringy with grease. "A little. Maybe."

My heart squeezed. *What was going on with us?* Maybe I should voice it out loud. I opened my mouth to do so, but nothing came out. If I challenged this now, I'd lose it, surely? If I said something didn't feel right, that I wanted to know everything and secrets stood between us, I'd be such a hypocrite. I didn't want this wonderful dream to end.

Haru's gaze studied mine as I struggled, dropping to my lips and then back up to the ceiling. "I was trying to make them listen. It came to me so easily the other day, when we . . ." He trailed off, staring at the plants. "When we made love. Maybe we need to do that again," he mused.

Made love. Whoa. My heart beat just a little faster. "I'm always up for trying," I offered with a smile, sliding my arms around his shoulders. "But maybe we should just . . . talk, actually."

He nodded, dragging a hand through his hair. "Of course." He sounded even more defeated. He scowled at his hand and picked up a tendril of hair. "Let me shower and I'll see you in the kitchen."

"Maybe we can finally make movie night a thing?" I asked hopefully.

His eyes sparked with joy, and my heart soared to see it. "What a wonderful idea! Yes, we shall." He pressed a kiss on my lips, taking my hand, then led me back toward the main area of the house, bouncing with each step. "Which movie first? Something to ease them into it."

"Eighties classics," I said immediately. "Action movies with Arnie."

"Classics?" he snorted. "Yes, I can see why they might be. What about sci-fi? Tron, or Big?"

"Big isn't sci-fi," I chided gently. "It's magic, but we can totally debate that."

"Otto would love that," he agreed. As he walked, the wood in the lintels creaked, small buds and springs poking through and yearning toward him. He was radiating happiness again, the special quality that made me want to bask in his sunlight, even if it was only reflected for a while.

"You seem happier," I noted, squeezing his hand.

"I'm more connected."

"Connected?" I glanced at the doorways. Did he mean to living things and plants?

He nodded, growing quiet again. "Yes."

I gently nudged him. "Want to tell me about that?" I tried. *Please don't pull away, Haru.*

His hand slid out of mine. "One day, Buttercup." He strode to a plant in a pot, frowning. "This needs repotting."

"Yeah? Can we do that together?"

He flashed a smile at me. "Of course! I'll make a gardener of you yet. Hang on, let's see if I can make it show for you." He closed his eyes, breathing in deeply. The tiny plant wavered on its spindly stalk toward his face, as unsteady as a newborn foal. The top bulged, tiny green points appearing and then accelerating outward.

"Haru," I said as the plant reeled, overbalanced.

"Just a little . . . More . . ." A beautiful blush pink bloom of tissue-thin petals exploded out the top of the stem. It spread wide like Haru's smile.

With a snap, the stalk suddenly bent, flower dashing itself on the kitchen counter. Haru slumped, and I grabbed his shoulders. "Haru?"

"I . . . It was too much, too soon." He rubbed his forehead ruefully. "I always rush in. Try to go too fast."

I remembered how welcoming he was, taking me out almost immediately. "Yeah, but—"

He pulled away from me. "I'll take it slow. Careful." He shook his head, shoulders slumping again.

I picked up the snapped flower. It shriveled away in my fingers, brown and ashy. "What happened?"

"I, speed things up you could say. Take all the energy inside a thing and make it come out at once." He gave the flower a sidelong look. "Don't worry about it. I'll get you a whole meadow if you want."

I gently rubbed the dust into my palm. That phrase again, *don't worry about it.* Don't think about it, don't press, don't challenge.

He planted a kiss on my forehead. "I'll be right back. Don't get into any trouble," he said with a wink.

"Sure," I replied. He gave me a little wave as he walked away, and I pulled my hand back, letting it fall. What trouble could I get into in the kitchen area? Winter wasn't there yet, so I hustled in to grab a juice and get out again, before he accused me of using the wrong glass or something.

I took my drink into the conservatory area. This place was completely overrun with plants, and Haru would need to come wrestle with them soon. I sank onto a mossed-covered couch, trying to peer through the blocked windows to the sun beyond. Little rays managed to penetrate, one spotlighting the door so covered in vines with budding flowers it was impossible to reach the handle.

I ran my finger along the vine with a waft of honeysuckle, and to my surprise it retracted a little, loosening. Now I could easily see the brass handle and more pieces of the wooden door, although it was still behind a thicket.

My heart drummed in my chest. The guys were still hiding something, despite the trust Haru spoke so much about. They had secrets, even if they were open about their powers and who they were. Yet they definitely didn't want me to see what was behind these doors.

Ask them what happened 150 years ago, the guy from CSON had told me. Haru had nearly fainted when I did. *Why?* What had happened, and why did I think the answer lay behind this door?

I stepped over a root, careful of the blooming petals. Over and under, I twisted through the branches flush with the door. Biting my lip, my hand hovered above the brass handle. I took a deep breath to calm my nerves. No going back now. This was like breaking in the first time, only I was even more underprepared. Where would this door lead me? Haru's home town, maybe? What was so bad about that?

My hand landed on the cool metal, and with a skip in my heart, I twisted it. The door creaked open, pulling away from the vines as rolls of bark fell to the ground softly. I climbed over a final branch and squeezed sideways through the space between the frame and door.

Lifting my head, I froze.

I was inside a massive room. Floor to ceiling windows were covered in billowy drapery that now sat stagnant. On the right was an open door that led to a luxurious bathroom where I could easily make out a tub that could fit six and a shower with multiple wall jets. One wall had a huge mural across it of a single tree, except across the tree the branches move from the buds of spring, to the full foliage of summer, to the colors of autumn, and finally the bare branches of winter. On another wall hung a hand carved clock that woodland creatures ran around the outside of. It read 3:15.

That wasn't right. It was eleven in the morning.

In the center of the room was a bed bigger than any bed I've ever seen, like it was made for ten people. But that wasn't what struck me, rooted me to the spot.

Off to my left was Haru, and yet it wasn't. His hair was

longer, showing some natural waves. He wore a tight fitted t-shirt and jeans, and beside him sat a woman. Her back was to me with long blonde hair, but that was all I could make out aside from the powder blue dress she wore.

I finally found my voice. "Haru?" I stepped away from the door toward them.

The woman didn't turn and Haru didn't look my way. Instead, he picked up the mysterious woman's hand and kissed it.

My stomach twisted, grief climbing up my throat. *What was this?*

"Rose, my love," Haru murmured.

Rose? Hadn't I heard that name somewhere before, and from Haru of all people? My mind wracked with so many memories—eating meals, going to Paris, racing through the streets of Japan, seeing my family—but for the life of me, I couldn't place it. Haru said something else, but in my flurry of thoughts I'd missed it.

The woman laughed. It was light, and Haru's face grew so bright, like it was the only sound he ever wanted to hear in the world.

I shouldn't be here. I turned to leave and ran smack into Winter.

I stumbled backward. His hair was the same, and he wore an all-black outfit, but there wasn't anger in his eyes. The dark, brooding man I'd come to know wasn't there. No, instead his eyes were wide, even fearful.

"Winter?" Haru's face grew stern with concern, standing and pulling the woman behind him. I still couldn't get a good look at her, but right now, I was focused on Winter.

Winter roared.

I scrambled away until my back hit the wall as frost spread from under his feet, a small circle of ice thrusting around him. Smoke that reminded me of dry ice sprayed from his arms and palms, his chest heaving with quick breaths.

"Winter!" Haru's voice was panicked, eyes widening.

"No!" Winter hollered, his skin paling to an eerie blue tinge.

"Stop! What's going on?" Haru took another step forward, but the woman behind him grabbed the back of his shirt, drawing him short.

"Be careful!" I told Haru, my fists clenched at my sides as my gaze bounced between the two of them. Puffs of air escaped my mouth as it mixed with the cold air of the room. I couldn't fight Winter at the best of times.

"I can't . . . You can't—" Winter's voice was strained, and the pain I heard in it felt like a lance through my chest.

"Winter." This time when Haru said his name, it held warning.

This time when Winter screamed, his powers burst outward. Ice, snow, sleet, and a cold so deep I felt it could flash freeze me blew in every direction. I ducked to protect myself, protect my vital organs. A similar approach that had been taught to me if a bomb ever went off.

I uncurled to find myself unharmed but Winter panted, eyes wild.

Haru stood with his hands held up, an assortment of leaves, flowers, and vines producing some kind of wall in front of him. But there were gaps like tiny windows, areas that weren't fully closed and flurries of snow glistened between the openings, landing on Haru's arm where they melted.

The woman behind him shivered, an icy texture coating her hair.

Haru turned to her, mouth opening with alarm.

"Mari?"

My head snapped to my right to the open doorway to see Haru standing there. *My* Haru. His hair was shorter, swept to the side with a single tendril falling across his forehead. Clean and still wet from his shower.

"Haru," I breathed.

Everything else in the room had frozen; Winter mid-rage, the other Haru in horror, and the unknown woman in a frigid cower. It was as though time had stopped as soon as Haru, the real Haru, had walked in.

"What are you doing here?" Haru stormed toward me. This was supposed to be my Haru, but the carefree charisma that I'd grown accustomed to was nowhere in sight as he snatched my wrist and tugged me away.

I stumbled after him, my tongue superglued to the roof of my mouth in shock. What was this room? We passed the door, and a branch whipped out behind me, pulling at the knob and slamming the door closed after us. Together we weaved back through the fray of vines, thicker now and dragging at my clothes. Once clear of the chaos, Haru dropped my hand with his back turned to me, his shoulders rising with intense inhales.

"W—what was that?" My voice was hesitant, distant. It sounded foreign to my own ears. "Was that another realm, or —I don't understand."

Haru spun around, and when his gaze landed on me I winced. His eyes were filled with so much anger they'd give Winter a run for his money. "What the hell, Mari?" The branches behind me creaked with his wrath.

I didn't know what to say because I didn't know what I just saw. Well, I understood one thing. Winter had attacked Haru and the woman, Rose. He had used his powers and tried to *hurt* them. Is that what happened 150 years ago? Was that doorway a memory?

Haru slammed his fist against the wall, causing me to jump. "You shouldn't have gone in there. That's . . . mine. Mine!"

His anger was so foreign I was struck dumb. "I just wanted answers." The sound that came from me was more air than voice.

"Answers? Answers to what?"

"I don't know what, because you won't tell me. You just tell me not to worry." I stepped forward, my hands twisting in front of me. "What I thought was I trusted you and you trusted me."

"Trust?" Haru scoffed. He shot his hand out to point at the door. "What's behind that door is horrific. It is something none of us want to remember or relive, and instead of respecting that, you went behind my back. In what world does that equate to trust?"

My mouth opened and closed as I searched for something to say, but there wasn't anything. I hadn't been able to bring it up with him, and he wasn't forthcoming. My throat tightened. "You're right." There was no trust between us, and I was a complete idiot for believing there had been or could be. I felt broken, confused. Who was I kidding? I was some girl off the street. All the while they could have any woman in the world, and I really thought I could waltz in here and make a difference. They were *immortals.*

Haru's head dropped, the vines twisting closed around the door behind me, wrapping around it so hard it creaked.

Without another word, I walked past him. There was nothing else to say.

Chapter Twenty-Three

Haru didn't follow me. That only made what happened that much more real. The carefree Haru wasn't here, and he was pissed. Secrets were driving us apart, and I hated that this secret was driving a wedge between us. I hated even more that we refused to open up. I paced the long lonely corridors as if searching for the right one to take me back somewhere where I could start fresh with no secrets between us.

I had now seen Winter in action; the dangers they talked about firsthand. I had to get him help before he hurt someone else. Part of me wanted to run to Haru and tell him everything. How CSON knew he was dangerous and could possibly help. But I was too scared that would be the final match that would completely burn down what we'd built. If he knew I had come in here to steal a key rather than protect them as they thought. I had my chance to go home, but I didn't. Was it because of my obligation to my job, or was it because I wasn't ready to be away from them? My heart tugged this way and that.

A throat cleared in front of me. Looking up from my feet, I came to a quick stop.

Winter stood there, in the center of the corridor. He wore a tank top, showing off the dark intricate tattoos circling his arms and part of his chest. Jeans hugged his hips, but with no belt they were low, showing off the top of his black boxer briefs. His hair wasn't in his usual bun. Instead it was damp and falling down to his shoulders in loose, blonde waves. It made him look younger somehow. More vulnerable.

But I'd seen how terrifying he could really be. He had attacked Haru in the memory or whatever that was. He was a danger, to himself and to the others.

And I had a job to do and my orders. I searched the ground looking for ice crystals but found none. The air didn't have its usual chill when I was around him either. He seemed rather calm, but now I knew more than ever what he was capable of. My muscles tingled as if preparing to flee or fight. What had happened in the library was a small taste of his powers. Why had he attacked Haru and the woman? Was that the secret? Haru said they were good at sharing. Hell, I had been a front row witness and recipient of it, but when Winter saw me with Haru, Summer, and Otto, he almost lost it.

I didn't move any closer, careful to keep my distance.

"I was, uh, hoping to run into you," he said. He didn't meet my eyes, looking everywhere but at my face. I think he made it as far as my chin at one point, hands opening and closing on nothing. He didn't carry anything, so he wasn't in cleaning mode.

"Okay," I said, trying to keep my voice level as if nothing was wrong. I glanced at the numbers on the doors. We happened to be in the three hundreds.

"I, um, wanted to say, uh, I was," he paused and took a deep breath, "sorry."

My brows twitched. That was the last thing I expected him to say. "What for?"

"Can we . . ." He ran his hand through his hair. "Can we maybe walk and talk a little? Standing here is making me, um, antsy."

"Sure." My mind ticked in overtime. *Be careful.* He was strong. I headed toward him, keeping more to one side of the hall, and he turned to continue down the hall with me. I led him toward the two hundreds, the numbers ticking down on either side of us.

We both kept our distance, him hugging one wall while I stayed close to the other. I folded my arms over my chest to keep the awkward ache at bay and sheltering from the cold. The silence stretched and even though dozens of questions formed on the tip of my tongue, when I opened my mouth to ask them nothing came out. I just had to get him closer to the right door . . . .

Finally, he spoke. "I shouldn't have reacted that way. I was just surprised when I came across all of you."

I flushed; we were having a foursome on a desk in the library with the door wide open. I'm pretty sure every librarian in the U.S. would've had a heart attack because we definitely weren't quiet.

"I just—my powers. They . . ." He trailed off with an annoyed huff.

"You don't need to explain if you don't want to." I didn't want to agitate him and risk another outburst.

He cleared his throat and tried again. "I get angry sometimes, and my powers react."

I tilted my head to find his sorrowful face glaring straight ahead, ice blue eyes fixed on the end of the corridor. "Are all your powers controlled by your emotions?"

He shrugged. "Yeah, or they can be when you're still learning control."

"Learning control? Is it not innate?" The questions came easier now, my curiosity getting the best of me.

A deep chuckle came from him, filled with sarcasm more than amusement. "It is definitely not innate."

Huh, interesting.

"Doesn't Otto help with emotional control? Have you ever gone to him for help?"

"That's only a temporary fix," he stated. "I need to . . . Work on it." He clearly seemed uncomfortable admitting that, but the fact that he had warmed me like a steaming mug of hot chocolate.

We fell into more silence, and my eyes dropped. We were nearly there. How did CSON think they could help? Somehow I didn't think they had an intervention over coffee and cake in mind, but they'd surely be able to help him with his control problem?

He interrupted my thoughts. "If you decide to have something with them," he swallowed hard, hands flexing, "I—I believe I can control myself now. I was just surprised, but now that I know to expect it, I think I'll be able to suppress it."

Admitting he had issues was hard. I should know, and I found myself opening my mouth. "I don't know if it'll be much more." My gut sank. "Haru and I had a bit of a fight."

"Oh?" He finally turned his head and looked at me.

Actually looked at me.

And seeing his striking ice-blue eyes so intent on mine pulled me to a stop. He truly cared.

Blinking to try to clear my head of the fuzz, I admitted, "He's usually so open, but I know he's hiding something. I think I pushed too hard. Like, broke in again too hard."

"Ah," Winter grunted before pulling his gaze away. He was usually so closed off himself but he had opened up so much just now, giving me a glimpse to someone . . . Well, not quite so frosty.

I shook myself. He was dangerous. I had to follow orders and be a good Shield to save the rest of them.

Except . . . My palm itched, still healing. He had bandaged my hand after CSON dragged me in, but I said I'd fallen in the shower and Winter had fixed it. My gut warred with what I had seen. Despite the evidence I'd just witnessed, Winter wasn't a bad guy it insisted. Perhaps there was another explanation? *What other explanation could justify attacking Haru?*

I glanced at the wall and froze when I saw three numbers.

2-0-7. It was here, and it was now or never.

I looked between Winter and the door and decided.

I tried to warn him, to get us moving and away from this area ASAP, but as my jaw opened, so did the door. Five men with guns and combat gear spread through the hall, weapons trained on both Winter and me. One man talked into what I assumed was a hidden walkie somewhere on his person. "Target found. Initiating contact."

Automatically, my stance widened and I balled my hands into fists. I stared down the men who were technically my coworkers, but my Shield training kicked in as the men shuffled toward my charge.

Leaping in front of me, Winter's hands seeped with frost and cold fog rolled. Shock as dousing as the cold he wielded flooded me. *He'd stepped in front of me?* The ground coated with ice, moving quickly across the ground and shooting out to cover one of the men's shoes.

The men shot darts, the soft 'pfft' of a silencer coupled with the fact they weren't real bullets kept the attack quiet, and a huge wall of ice sprouted in front of Winter and me, blocking the needle-like shots. Ten darts hit the ice with a quick patter, Winter grunting with each one, his forearm raised to brace against the ice. He met my eyes, the real fear in them shattering me with guilt.

I couldn't let this happen.

I rounded Winter's wall. Ducking under one man, I elbowed his side, brought my knee to his groin, and used the moment of pain and distraction to twist his wrist. The gun clattered to the ground. I kicked it behind me, further away from the men.

Another man came at me, while the other three went for Winter. Instead of shooting at me in close range, he struck the loaded tranq gun toward the side of my head. I ducked and spun, swiping my leg out to kick his ankle as I swirled behind him. But he was fast and trained too. He used his good leg to move with me while putting space between us in order to not give me an opening.

Winter shot snow and ice out of his hands, freezing the ground and trying to catch the men. One got frozen to the wall and tried to bash away at the ice with one arm.

My attacker came at me again. I wheeled backward, quick on my feet. Closer to the open doorway, I saw more men on the other side. There was an entire operation—some were on computers while others had guns trained on the door. Droves of them. They had been listening and waiting this whole time for the perfect moment, and I had provided it to them on a silver platter.

Winter roared in anger.

Yes, good. Hopefully Haru and the others would hear.

"Tranquilizer a no go," a man inside the room noted.

My stomach dropped and when Winter turned to throw an ice spear my fear was confirmed. Four tranquilizers stuck out of his back. But he still fought, his movements not yet sluggish.

"I repeat, do not use bullets. We need him alive!" A woman's voice shouted through the walkie-talkie, even though the door was open.

Someone slammed my temple so hard that I flew into the wall, and I crumpled to the ground from the sudden impact.

The world spun and my ears rang. Behind it roared Winter's furious war cry. I pushed myself up and a snowstorm burst from his hand, his blue eyes radiating with fear as they locked on mine.

This time when he sent ice out, it wasn't to lock someone in place. A spear at least a foot long flew across the room and into one of the men's necks. The other spear shattered against his bullet proof vest. It was too late though. Blood gushed from the wound, and he collapsed. Dead.

"Get out of there!" A man yelled from the doorway. "Retreat!"

"What about the target?" Another man shouted, already backing up but keeping his gun trained on Winter.

"Extract her," he shouted.

It didn't take a genius to figure out who they meant. I pushed off the ground, but collapsed from the nausea that overtook me. My shoulder throbbed and my vision refused to settle.

Arms wrapped around my waist, hauling me up. I kicked out my legs, using my weight to my advantage as I thrashed side to side as more hands grabbed me.

"Mari!" Winter called, panic clear.

"Winter!" I screamed back as I was carried closer to the door. Ice cold terror seized me, and I knew it wasn't because of him.

They hauled me through the entrance, men following behind me and the door slammed shut. I continued to fight, to cry out for Winter, for Haru, for Summer and Otto. *Someone. Anyone.*

Men filed in front of the door, covering it with some kind of weird gunk starting at the door handle. It hardened quickly, producing a barrier where even if Winter managed to pry open the door, who knew how long it would take him to burst through.

"Get off of me!" I shouted, continuing to writhe. They almost dropped me several times.

"Sir, she isn't cooperating!"

"Stick her."

There was a prick in the side of my neck. I thrashed for three more seconds until my body became sluggish and numb. The swirling lights became dim, and soon after, I blacked out.

Chapter Twenty-Four

Fighting through utter exhaustion, I knew I had to open my eyes. Was my alarm going off? Was I supposed to be at work already? Just five more minutes.

No. Something was wrong. My gut screamed at me to shake off this unnatural tiredness and wake up. Were Mom and Chris okay? Someone was in trouble!

I struggled to wake—to get out of the stranglehold of my covers. Slowly I started to remember. Haru. Haru's smiling face. Summer watching me kiss him with a sizzling smolder. Otto's sure hands massaging my breasts.

Winter stood in the doorway to the library. Winter blasting an ice spear at a Shield Operative, killing them. Winter patching up the cut on my palm, saying he had never watched a movie. Winter attacking Haru and the woman he was with, mercilessly blasting them with murderous, icy intent.

I cracked my eyes open. I was sweating profusely, strapped loosely on a gurney. Bright lights surrounded me.

I fumbled for the strips. Fortunately they were loose, only in place to stop me from accidentally rolling off the thin hospital mattress. I ripped them off, the satisfying velcro tearing sound echoing in the tiled room. A darkened mirror formed one wall, reflecting my bruised and pissed off face. The room swam around me, but planting my feet flat on the floor grounded me some.

More memory flooded back. Being ordered to lure Winter close to door 207. Haru angry I had gone behind his back and opened the door covered with plants; something his power sealed away from everyone, even him. He wasn't ready to face it, and I had forced the issue, making him come get me and confront it.

Tears pressed behind my eyes, but I couldn't let whoever had me think I was crying about my predicament. I had to stay calm and think. I'd been captured by my own organization. At least, technically I was one of them. I waited for the room to stop spinning then marched up to the mirror wall, confronting my own reflection.

"Hey there. I know you're listening. I need some water, maybe something stronger, a bagel, and a chat." I drummed my fingers against the reflective surface, staring into my own eyes.

Damn, but this felt so bad. I was in CSON hands sure, but away from the boys. What if something happened to them? What if CSON tried to secure Winter again?

I rested my pounding forehead against the cold glass. Did the guys realize I had been taken? Had Winter told them I had been "rescued" by CSON? Did they think I had betrayed them?

I swallowed hard. I had, in every sense of the word. I'd followed my orders and gone behind their backs, not telling them CSON had a key and wanted to take Winter to help him. Or at least that was the story I told myself. I didn't know for sure. Numbness stole over my skin. *Shit, was I working for the bad guys here?* I guess I'd see from how they treated me.

The door clinked open, and I spun around to face it, balling my fists in readiness. In walked three figures. Two I recognized. My colleague Julian came in first in a crisp CSON uniform, hand on his pistol. I hadn't seen him since he came into Mystique with Lilian and Bishop and the others. I searched his face, but he was resolutely not looking me in the eyes.

Next up was Mysterious Man, the guy who gave me my orders to break in in the first place. He wore his usual jacket, hands rammed firmly in the pockets. He regarded me with something like disappointment or sadness. My stomach churned. What did that look mean?

The final person was new to me. A middle aged woman with a business-like bun on the top of her head and gold wire framed glasses, smiling widely like we were meeting at happy hour. "Hello, Shield Marigold Stewart. Feeling better, I hope?"

"Sure." I rubbed the side of my neck, putting on more of a slur. It wouldn't hurt to have them underestimate me.

The woman crossed to the bed and sat on it, folding her legs. Julian stayed at the door, ramrod straight, as Mysterious Man shut it with another forbidding clank.

I tried not to flinch, turning it into a mini hop as though I was dizzy.

The woman smoothed her white coat, the color immaculate and helping her blend into the tiled walls behind her. "I am Doctor Smith. Now, it's my understanding you've been on a deep mission, haven't you, dear?" Her lips pursed with concern.

"Deep?" I asked.

"Undercover." She waved toward Mysterious Man. "Colonel Davis here has a lot to answer for, mm. Putting one of our Shields into a situation for which she had no training." The good doctor shook her head. "I'm very sorry for all the trouble we as CSON have put you through, especially with little to no support and at such short notice."

"O—kay," I said. "What is this place? Where am I?" I looked directly at Colonel Davis. "Where does door 207 lead?"

He stayed impassive.

Doctor Smith's smile broadened. "Now, dear, I know you will have . . . Seen and experienced some things, yes?"

Her weird intonation was getting on my tits. "Spit it out. What are you getting at?"

She twisted a silver bracelet around her wrist before putting her hands in her pockets. I tensed, ready for some kind of weapon, but she just produced a tiny journal from her pocket and a pink glitter pen from her breast pocket. I stared at it in disbelief. It had a dangly butterfly swinging from the end of it.

She started writing. "Now, of course you'll need the best psychological support. CSON is more than willing to foot the bill. Then there's worker's compensation, of course, which will be paid to your family." She glanced up from the notebook over the rim of her glasses. "How is that all sounding?"

"Errr," My stomach was really, really warning me about this. "I want to call my family now. And probably a lawyer. Who are you? You're not in charge."

She snapped the notebook shut. "I'm a contractor, dear, and I'm afraid none of that will be possible." Doctor Smith stood, intimidatingly tall in her heels. That pout was back, false sympathy in her gray eyes as she came toward me. "You've been under a lot of stress, Shield Marigold. I have been asked to assess your condition and, because you know some quite sensitive material, we just need to make sure you won't accidentally compromise our organization by talking to, say, an outside therapist. That's why I think it's best you stay," she patted my cheek, "right here."

I glared at her. "How long for?"

She pursed her lips, considering. "Undefined at this point. Probably a few years."

What? I didn't know whether to break her arm or bite her hand, but neither would help me with this. Head spinning for real, I breathed, "Are you pretending I'm insane or something? Assessed my case? You've literally been here all of two minutes." I glared behind her at Colonel Smith and Julian.

Colonel Smith cleared his throat. "We cannot have sensitive information leaving these walls."

My heart thudded in my chest. "What?" I felt like the air had been sucked from the room. They were just throwing me away. I'd been useful to them to get the key and then to lure Winter, and now I was no good to them.

I looked to Julian, full on pleading. "Julian, help."

He shifted his weight. "You're in the right place, Marigold. I don't know what horrors you saw or what you were subjected to, but it's best for you to rest here."

I almost growled. I wouldn't find help from him. Whether he believed what he was spouting or not, it was clear he was the perfect Shield, just here to follow orders.

I pulled away from Doctor Smith. "I understand you would want to tie up loose ends, but this is my life we are talking about!"

"Balanced against national security." Doctor Smith shrugged. "No contest, I'm afraid. Of course, we are also protecting our interests. You might have been compromised. We can't have someone like you, who knows both sides, walk about freely, now can we?"

She sounded so damned reasonable, like she expected me to agree. I whirled around to Colonel Limp Dick. "I haven't been compromised. I followed every order you gave me!"

He smirked, the first sign of life in his cold face. "Unwillingly, I might add. In fact, I wonder if you even meant to lure your target to the predefined location. You seemed to regret it and attacked CSON agents."

Doctor Smith tutted, shaking her head causing her bun to bob. "And there we have it. Either you have been manipulated into betraying us, or your personal views have been compromised." Doctor Smith smiled again, sucking on the end of the butterfly pen. "Of course, a demonstration that your loyalties are indeed where they should be would be welcome, and added as evidence into your file that you are a good Shield agent in recovery from a very intense mission."

I ran my hands through my hair, trying to pull out the meaning in her convoluted words. My breathing was uneven and too fast. No. *No.* I'd thought my life was small before, but this tiny room was even smaller and closing in.

Doctor Smith patted my shoulder. I flinched away from her, but she carried on with her horrific smile. "We can have some one on one therapy sessions together, just us girls, where you can detail your experiences on the mission. Everything. Leave no stone unturned, daily accounts, assessments, and even inventories. You are a good Shield, Marigold, so I'm sure you will be very good at reporting every single detail." She licked her lips, waiting for my answer.

Now the air was supercharged and hot. This was it. Describe the boys in detail, their powers and weaknesses.

"Why?" I asked. "Don't we work for them?"

Doctor Smith cocked her head. "They should work for us. Suffice to say that there are layers within CSON, but that's above your security level, my dear."

I closed my eyes, trying to fight back the waves of nausea. I'd been pitched out to sea, and this time I was drowning.

"Come on, Mari," Julian said. "We all work for the same organization."

Did we? Did CSON really have the boy's best interests at heart? I didn't know, but I didn't like their methods at all.

I curled my hands into fists. "Fuck you," I said, slowly and deliberately.

Doctor Smith's face barely even trembled. "Oh, dear. Well." She noted that in her stupid little notebook. "Uncooperative. What a shame."

Colonel Davis narrowed his eyes. "Is this some kind of misplaced loyalty?"

I glared at him. "I am protecting my charges," I growled.

Doctor Smith looked sharply at me as if she was really looking at me for the first time. "Hm. Interesting." She looked over my head at the colonel. "Do we have a blood sample from her?"

He frowned. "Blood sample? No."

"Pity. I'd like one," she said, snapping her fingers at Julian.

He startled but then came toward me. "Marigold, hang tight. It's all going to be okay."

I backed away, narrowing my eyes. "No, it isn't. They're lying, Julian!"

"More raving," Doctor Smith said, and that blasted pen came out again to make more notes in that tiny little notebook that would determine my fate forever.

I slapped the pen out of her hand. She shrieked, and I darted to the other side of the room toward the door.

"Marigold, stop!" Julian bellowed, and I heard a click behind me. A terribly familiar click.

I raised my arms and turned to face him, confronting the end of his pistol. Julian was breathing hard, but so was I. He kept his eyes firmly on me as he said, "You're not well."

"I am," I said softly. "No matter what they've told you, no matter what orders—"

"This is the best place for you."

"Julian, no," I whispered.

He shook his head, but the doubt in his eyes haunted me.

"You've been compromised. Now, stand still so the doctor can get a blood sample and start treating you."

"Treating me with interrogation framed as therapy sessions, locking me away from my family and friends." My lips trembled. I bit down hard. "Julian, this isn't right."

He met my gaze squarely. "Right or not, these are orders."

I closed my eyes, my soul bleeding. *Orders were orders, after all.*

Chapter Twenty-Five

The lights turned on, the only indication I had that it was morning. Well, that and the breakfast tray that soon slid through a small opening at the bottom of the door.

"I'm not hungry!" I hollered, ignoring the rumble in my stomach. I pulled at the hospital gown I was now in. Thankfully it was more like a dress, not open in the back, but it was made of the same thin material. Despite my desire to stick it to the man, I did eventually go over and guzzle down the bottle of water it came with. Food I could live without for a time, but not water. I wanted to protest, not die.

How many breakfast meal trays had this been by now? Four? How were Mom and Chris? Curling myself up tightly, I knew they wouldn't be worried about me yet. They thought I was guarding Haru in a top secret assignment. My throat closed thinking of Haru dismissing me.

A knock sounded on the door.

"Go away!" I yelled.

The door opened and a new Shield operative with a gun in hand walked in, soon followed by some orderly with a mask and a tray of medical supplies. I moved until my back hit the far wall.

"Stay the hell away from me," I barked.

The orderly set the tray down on a table, ignoring me.

The guard's hands tightened around his AK-47. "We can do this the easy way or the hard way."

"What?" I scoffed. "You're gonna shoot me?"

He shrugged, and the pit in my stomach grew tenfold.

First they made me their captive and now they're sending in gun happy pricks that wouldn't mind shooting an innocent and unarmed woman. *What the actual hell?*

The orderly turned to me. "Arm," he commanded.

I didn't move.

The guard took a step forward, his grip tightening. "He said arm."

I narrowed my eyes. "No."

"No?" The guard raised one bushy eyebrow. "They told me you might not be obliging, but I didn't realize you'd be obstinate. Guess it's my lucky day." He looked at the orderly. "Shall I?"

The orderly's brown eyes, the only characteristic I could make out due to the mask, scrub cap, and scrubs, found mine. "May I see your arm, Marigold? It's for the best. Dr. Smith is very adamant about acquiring more samples."

"Samples," I emphasized, "as in plural?"

The orderly nodded. "Saliva, blood, discharge," he listed off.

Discharge? My eyes widened with what exactly he planned to do to me, but I tried to stay levelheaded. "What for? What are you looking for?"

"That's not for me to know. I have my orders," he said, but that struck a terrible chord in me. There wasn't any leeway here and appealing wouldn't help. Just like me, he was going to do his job.

"Stay back! You are not coming anywhere near me!" I searched the room for something, anything, and aside from a metal bed that was bolted to the floor, I had a mattress, a pillow, and an empty plastic water bottle.

The orderly sighed. "We believe you may have had relations with one of the men."

My heart jumped. *How would they know that? Had they talked to them?* "Haru," I whispered, hope swirling inside of my chest.

"So it's true." The guard grimaced.

"Screw you," I spat, talking clearly done with.

"No thanks," he said. "I don't sleep with traitors."

"I'm not a traitor!" I burst. "They were my charges! I was doing my job! I was tasked with protecting them! I want to talk to my boss!"

The agent gave one hearty, "Ha!" before adding, "I highly doubt your boss ordered you to spread your legs. You're a disgrace. No wonder they haven't come looking for you."

My mouth snapped shut from the outburst I was ready to have. They hadn't come for me? Like at all? I couldn't believe it. Had I really pushed Haru too far? Did I mean so little to the others as well? I mean, I know I had made mistakes but . . . That was cold, even for Winter.

My throat tightened with unshed tears. I was all alone. No one knew where I was, and my only chance of escape just evaporated.

"Shall we?" The orderly interrupted my spiraling thoughts.

I shook my head. I didn't care if I was alone. I didn't care if I was stuck here. There was no way I was giving them what they wanted. "I said it before and I'll happily say it again," I gave them a huge grin and put as much sass as I could into my next words. "Fuck. You."

The orderly turned his head to the guard and nodded.

He came at me, but he didn't try to use his gun, which gave me an opportunity. It meant he underestimated me. When he reached for me, I brought the heel of my hand up and slammed it into his nose.

"Mother*fucker*!" he cried as blood gushed from his nostrils.

I ran around him and straight to the door, but the handle didn't budge as I yanked at it. I banged against the door. "Help!" I screamed. "Someone help me! Let me out! Dr. Smith! I'll tell you what you want to know! Just get me out!" The last part was a lie, but part of my training for this shit job was knowing when to lie and how to do it well.

It seemed it wasn't good enough because no one came, and arms banded around me, dragging me backward.

"No!" I flailed, kicking my legs out, heels bouncing on the ground. Every time my heel hit the cold marble it hurt, but I didn't care. I wiggled and writhed, trying to break the guard's hold, but he had me good, throwing me to the side. I landed on the bed and my hands went to the mattress to push myself up. The guard jumped on top of me and pinned my arms down. No matter how much I bucked, I couldn't loosen his hold on me.

"Hold her steady," the orderly instructed, striding to my arm with a needle.

"No! Help!" I cried as tears freely fell down my cheeks. This was so messed up. This couldn't be my life. This couldn't be happening. "Help!"

The orderly bent down, the sharp tip headed straight for the middle of my arm. They weren't even trying to find a vein. They were going to mindlessly stab until they got what they wanted. I readied myself for the stab, my stomach tightening at the thought of all the 'samples' they would take after this.

There was a loud boom, and the door burst open.

The three of us flinched away. Cold spread across my

body, and I blinked through the dots appearing in my vision. No, it wasn't dots.

It was snow.

Heat came next, melting all the ice in sight and causing sweat to instantly bead over my body like I was suddenly thrown in a broiler.

"Get the fuck away from her." Haru stepped forward, with Summer, Otto, and Winter at his back.

They had come! They were here! They had come for me. This time the tears that fell were ones of relief.

The guard jumped up, swinging his gun around to train it on the guys.

My breath caught. There was no way they'd survive bullets.

The metal of the gun heated, turning an ember red. The guard screamed and dropped it, staring at his hands in horror as bubbling blisters ignited over his palms.

Suddenly, there was a sharp pain in my arm. I yelped and looked over as the orderly pulled at the syringe. Dark red blood oozed into the tube.

Roots shot from the ground, wrapping around the man and pulling him against the wall. They crawled up his legs, around his torso and neck. The one around his arm squeezed until the man dropped the syringe. The glass shattered on the ground, spreading my blood across the floor.

Otto came over and scooped me into his arms like I weighed nothing, cradling me to his chest. My stomach swooped like the first dive of a rollercoaster.

Summer stepped forward, staring down the guard who now rocked on the floor with his hands on his lap and the orderly still attached to the wall with slithering branches. "Leave her alone. She's ours now." The heat in his voice was menacing, and it brokered no other choice but to obey.

I was theirs now. My heart quickened. I liked the sound of that.

Haru raced to me, finding my hand and giving it a squeeze. "Mari? Are you alright?" His voice shook, eyes rimmed red and awash with tears.

I nodded once. I was, now that they were here.

He kissed the back of my hand reverently. "Let's go home."

They flanked me like some kind of honor guard, Otto marching with determination out of the facility. Haru trotted next to me holding my trembling hand. Any staff who poked their heads out of their offices got a face full of vegetation.

"Is that poison ivy?" Summer asked, nonchalant.

"No. I saved that for the prick holding her down." Haru's hand vibrated in mine.

"Oh. Shame," Summer said, glaring around him. Anger wafted off him in hot, simmering waves.

Winter brought up the rear, blistering cold following in his wake. The floor iced over, lightbulbs burst in their sockets, and doorways cracked as an all-consuming cold flooded the halls like death.

Doctor Smith came running from up ahead, four Shields around her. She pasted on her fake smile. "Boys, boys, welcome!"

Otto clutched me close before placing me on my feet and pulling me around to his back. "Summer, I can take them out if they get close enough."

"Me too," Haru said between gritted teeth.

"Save your power," Summer said. He drew up in front of our team. "We are leaving right now, with or without causing major structural damage to this facility and wreaking havoc with the local weather systems. Which do you prefer?"

Doctor Smith tapped a manicured finger to her lips. "How about a chat? We were just extracting our operative."

My gut clenched. Doctor Smith smirked at me. Damn it, if she told the guys I'd snuck in under orders and compromised their security, would they be angry enough to leave me here?

Summer cut the air with his hand. "She's a Shield Operative, which means she's ours. End of story."

His possessive tone lit a fire deep in my core. I clung to Otto's shoulders, fighting the urge to bury my head in his chest and wish this all away.

Haru snorted and said, "She has a choice. Mari?"

I looked up quickly at them all. Summer with one eye on me, Otto holding me tight, Haru looking heartbroken with concern, and, behind Otto's shoulder, Winter, his ice blue eyes fixed on me. "Of course I want to come with you," I said simply.

Winter snarled, pushing through our throng to get in front and face the soldiers. "It's settled. Get out of our way."

Summer studied his nails and raised an eyebrow. "Don't make me set Winter on you."

Doctor Smith held up her hands and backed away, cool as a cucumber. "You'll be back, gentlemen. I can't wait for us all to sit down and realize we are on the same side."

Winter said something in a stream of guttural, aggressive sounding syllables. At the end, Otto said, "Here here."

"Twice over," I added, putting up my middle finger.

"Good girl," Summer murmured before raising his voice again. "Well, then. Dr Smith, your nameplate says? I'll be using that information. I'd say it was a pleasure to see you, but it really wasn't. If I ever see you again it will be too soon."

Doctor Smith said nothing, but her eyes followed me as the guys walked right past her. She especially ran her eyes over Winter, lingering on his thick shoulders. I shifted to put myself in front of him and get him away from her, and her eyes sparkled with mirth.

I flipped her the bird.

Winter breathed heavily like he'd run up a hill, shoulders shaking. I touched his shoulder to reassure him, and he was warm, not cold as I expected. "It's okay," I murmured, even though I wasn't even sure of that myself. I just had to say something to calm him, and damn it, I would make it all okay if I could.

We tramped back up the corridor, and up ahead I could see the carnage. A wall had been blasted in, plants covered the rubble, and water dripped from the ceiling. A bunch of big buff soldiers were sobbing in the corner, and melted metal puddled on the floor.

"Whoa. Okay," I said.

"Quite." Otto stepped over one of the crumpled soldiers. "Don't worry, they'll recover. I gave them just a little taste of our worry," he said.

I eyed the Shield operatives. "Oh." Curling my hand into Otto's jacket, I let myself close my eyes. I wanted to be home, right now. Home, with them, I realized. *When had that happened?*

Outside a pickup truck idled. It wasn't anything flashy, and in fact looked rather beat up; when Winter got in the back, the rear dipped alarmingly.

Summer opened the back door for me, and I grinned at him. "This doesn't seem your style."

"It's what we could get on short notice. Believe me, the Belarusian farmer was delighted with his end of the deal."

"Yeah, shoving a million dollars at a man to take his old truck really made his day," Haru quipped.

A million dollars? What? "I have so many questions, but I want to get home, please. I need to see my family."

The guys nodded, in sync, and Otto said in a soothing voice, "Let's get you inside."

I looked up at him drowsily as he strapped me in, taking his hand. "Are you using that empathy stuff on me?"

He smiled down at me, squeezing my hand. "Just a touch to keep you calm and reassure you." His brown eyes held my gaze. "You are safe. We won't let anything bad happen to you."

Relief washed over me. Even though I knew it was his power, it was also an effect of being in their midst once again.

"Never, ever again," Haru added, swinging in from the other side and scooting next to me. Otto went around the back and next to Summer, who got in the driver's seat.

Winter rapped the roof, making me jump. "Hit the gas!" he bellowed.

"Already on it!" Summer hollered back.

I giggled, relaxing into Haru's arms. He kissed the top of my head and held me as if I might be snatched away at any second.

A rattle on the windows startled me upright. Huge globs of hail pounded the ground. The trees around us whipped in the wind, and sunlight broke through the cloud cover with a glaring intensity.

"Well, this place is screwed," Otto said lightly.

"Don't give a crap," Summer muttered, hands flexing on the steering wheel.

"It's not the local population's fault I was here," I pointed out. "Where is here, anyway?"

"Belarus. Door 207 led to Minsk, the capital city, but they sealed it off and killed that door." Haru closed his eyes, leaning into me. "You were gone, and we couldn't get to you." His voice shook and he swallowed.

Otto took over the tale. "We had other doors into smaller towns. Mogilev, Lepiel, Lida, Grodno." The syllables leaping from his tongue were all in a perfect Russian-sounding accent. He shook his head. "You could have been put on a plane and taken anywhere. You—"

"Enough," Summer barked. "We don't need to relive that terrifying shit."

I looked at them all anew. They were all drawn and haggard. Summer unshaven, Otto's shirt dirty, and Haru's eyes tired. Behind me, through the small grimy window, Winter stood sentinel in the flatbed of the pickup truck, still on edge and so tense his muscles were standing out like rocks.

"You were worried?" I asked.

"Worried?" Haru's jaw dropped. "We were devastated."

"None of us rested, not for a second," Otto said. "I'm sorry it still took us so long to find you."

"I'm putting a tracker chip in your neck," Summer growled, his knuckles turning white.

I blinked tears away and my voice was raw as I said, "Thanks. Except no chips. How did you find me?"

"Trial and error. Lots of errors." Otto glanced up at the sky. Heavy storm clouds lay gray and low above us like they were about to drop, but Summer had the AC on all the way up.

"We are in Gomel," Haru explained. "Summer and I broke into Shield's head office and got all the locations, but we had to check every single one."

"And then we would have started going wider." Summer's hands slammed at the stick shift, shoving it into a higher gear. The engine squealed with protest, and I settled back into Haru's arms.

Safe at last. My head went dizzy with an afterthought.
Until they realized what I'd done.

Chapter Twenty-Six

We drove for twenty minutes at high speed before pulling into a town. When Summer stopped, Winter jumped down off the back of the truck, scattering snow and glaring at some passersby. He thumped toward a warehouse, looking back at me then scanning the street. Summer opened the door for me, holding out his arm, and Otto and Haru came round from the other side.

Summer tossed the keys at a young man, saying something in a flood of lyrical syllables. *All the languages they knew were so sexy.*

The young man seemed to think so too, babbling in response with a red face and then scrabbling for the door of the truck.

"You made his day," Otto noted as the guy accelerated off.

"Christmas has come early," Summer said, glancing at the snow on the ground.

I walked toward Winter, but my legs were weak and I tried not to lean on Haru heavily. Both Summer and Otto started forward, but I said, "I can do this. Leave me be."

Haru looked at me sadly. "We want to help, Mari. You don't have to struggle alone."

His words unleashed a torrent of feeling in me, and suddenly I was sobbing. "I'm sorry, I don't mean to cause a scene."

"It's okay." Otto rubbed my back, and I felt a flood of calm wash over me.

Summer glowered behind us as though he could see all the way back to the facility. "They are gonna pay."

"First things first," Haru said. "Home, bath, and food. Everything you need in whatever order you need it."

I didn't even know where to start. "Thank you."

We walked through a door and immediately the familiar smell of the house hit me. "I didn't even realize it had a familiar smell," I said out loud.

Winter sniffed and grunted. "Eau de four unwashed men going out of their minds."

My stomach clenched. "I'm so sorry—"

"Enough, Mari," Summer said, grabbing my shoulders. "You have done nothing to be sorry about, so stop saying that."

But I had. My spirits fell as low as they had in that damned facility.

Summer cupped my cheek in his hand, his eyes softening as he looked deep into mine. Then he shook himself. He really did look great with stubble, shirt collar undone, and loose slacks. *Delish.*

He bent slightly and reached around my waist, then full on swept me off my feet and into his arms for what seemed to be a reassuring hug before placing me back on my feet.

"Jeez, guys, stop! You're gonna break your backs!" I put my hands over my face.

Summer laughed. "You question my strength? I know my limits, little . . . hmm." A considering expression lit his face, eyes brighter despite how tired he must be. A small smirk tipped up one side of his lips, revealing a flash of white teeth. "*Mariposa*, hm? Do you like it?"

"What does that mean?" I asked. It was part of my name, sure, but what was the rest? Poser?

My gut twisted painfully. I was a poser. Posing as someone helping them when I slid the key card under the door in the first place.

But as Summer grinned, satisfied and not answering my question, Haru laughed, Otto chuckled, and Winter grunted with a shake of his head. I pushed it out of my mind. I scowled, annoyed that it was one more thing I'd have to figure out. That was a problem for tomorrow's Mari. Right now, I could regroup and make the most of all of them before something changed on us again.

We walked upstairs, still in a close herd, their footsteps echoing around the stairwell. Summer's firm steps, Haru's taking two at a time, Otto's measured, and—

I startled to a stop. "Where's Winter?"

The others looked around as though they had only just noticed he was gone.

He stood at the entrance of the corridor, hanging back from the stairwell. He backed away when I faced him.

"What's wrong?" I asked.

He looked from me to each of the guys. "I—I'll stay here. I can send up food later."

"No!" I said it with force. The idea of him standing alone in this huge house while we were all together hurt me deeply, as if I was seeing him again standing in the corridor when they took me. "Get over here right now," I ordered him.

His eyes widened slightly, but then he jerked forward as if I might change my mind. He pounded up the stairs like they'd insulted his mother and drew to a stop behind Otto. "Carry on," he said, back to grumpy mode, but I could read his moods a little better now. He was more relaxed than I'd seen him, well ever, with only a mild frown like he was concentrating in place of the normal scowl.

As Summer continued, I put my hand out to trail it on the dragon. "I wanted to ask you something," I said, voice drowsy. "Can we finish this? All of us?"

"All of us?" Haru beamed. "Sure! I'm up for artistic interpretation."

"As long as it's shades of blue," I said dreamily. I closed my eyes, yawning.

"What the—" Otto's exclamation had me startling. *What was wrong now?*

They had stopped in front of a corridor I was sure wasn't there before. Haru's bedroom door was here, closer to the stairs than before, and next to it was a light blue door, the same shade as the sky after rain clouds had passed over.

"Whoa. House shift," Haru said.

I remembered they said it did that. "Why is it shifting things around?"

Haru grinned at me. "Making room for someone special." He opened the door with a flourish, bowing as I passed him. I playfully nudged his arm, but my jaw dropped as I took in the space.

We walked into a huge room with floor to ceiling windows on the far side and a green door half way down. The walls were painted a blue ombre starting as a deep sea green at the floor and moving to pale ice blue on the ceiling. The floors were wooden, and the drapes sumptuous. Best of all was the walk in wardrobe and bathroom attached to the space.

"This is amazing!" I said.

"Thank you, house!" Haru said happily, doing a little dance. "And, hey, we're next door neighbors. I even have my own way in here." He opened the green door into his own room, then shut it. "That'll be handy."

"Hmm." Summer's grumble reached me through the thin shirt on his chest. I was leaning against him. I stood straighter, my back cold without him next to me, and dug my toes into the thick pile. "We can leave you in privacy, if you want. We will be right outside," he explained, his throat bobbing.

I touched his wrist. "No. I want you all to stay." I didn't want to let them out of my sight.

A satisfied smile crossed his face. "Very well."

I looked longingly at the open shower, but before I could say anything, Haru took my hand. "Let's get you freshened up."

"I suspect we could all do with some freshening up," Otto said.

He was right. The guys were in disarray, sexy stubble everywhere. They grimed up well, but it was proof they tore the world and themselves apart looking for me. And I sure as hell wanted to wash that place off me.

Haru reached up, cupping my face as though I might break or disappear before him. "We thought we lost you," he whispered.

"Lost me?" My heart wrenched at the forlorn look in his eyes. Even as my stomach twisted at the exposure, I slowly slipped out of the hospital robe, leaving nothing to the imagination. "I'm yours for as long as you'll have me."

And I meant it. I didn't know how long this would last. How long I would keep their attention riveted on me. But I would take what I could get while I still had it.

Haru's lips parted as he drank me in. "Until the end of time." A shiver traveled down my spine and I preened under their gazes.

Turning on the water, he stripped off his clothes and held my hand to guide me into the perfectly warm water. The quadruple shower would be big enough for all of us, and little benches lined the inside at different levels. I could well imagine using one to rest my raised leg, or using another to brace my hands while bent over . . .

"I love this house. It thinks of everything," I said happily.

Haru ducked under the water, shaking out his hair. Water beaded and ran down the planes of his body. I frowned. He was leaner than before.

"Have you been eating?" I asked.

He scrunched his nose, thinking. "Probably not. We didn't have any time to waste." He ran his fingers down my arm, leaving a tingling warmth in his wake. He brought me closer under the rushing roar of the water. His hands slide over my body as if memorizing every dip, curve, and line. He gasped at each bruise as if it cut his heart, touching them gently. The pain seemed to ease, probably from the water and the sheer relief of being home.

"We were so worried about you." Haru glanced over my shoulder. "We all were."

I turned my head over my shoulder to see through the steamy haze. Summer, Otto, and Winter all stood in the bedroom looking in, a pane of clear glass etched with branches separating us. Otto stood with his hands loose, but Summer and Winter had their arms folded, and they were all focused on us. Me.

I turned around to face them, and all three reacted in their own way. Otto blinked slowly, his chest rising and falling more rapidly. Summer's eyes grew darker, more heated. Winter's glare turned sharper, angrily glaring at the bruises on my arms and legs.

I set my sights on Otto. Backing up, I put my arms over my head and draped them over Haru's shoulders.

Haru took the invitation immediately, long fingers caressing up the sides of my ribcage. I shivered in the warm water as my skin seemed to up its sensitivity, and his hands meandered to my breasts. He circled each nipple, and I arched back, pressing my backside against his hardened shaft.

I kept my eyes on Otto and smiled when his tongue darted out, licking his dry lips.

"You saucy thing." Haru chuckled. "You're doing that on purpose. When he gets heated, everyone does."

"And?" I questioned innocently, even though we both knew that was far from the truth. I had been away from the guys for days, fearful I had upset Haru too much and that they didn't care for me. Yet they came for me. I wanted to show them my gratitude and show them how much I missed them.

Haru turned my chin toward him and finally latched his lips to mine.

His kiss was teasing, playful, the culmination of our truth or dare together. His body spoke a truth; he was attracted to me, and he'd been out of his mind with worry when I was captured. As I kissed him, lips easing over his, I thought of all of them. They had all been afraid, all working so hard to make sure I was okay and I came home safe. Their bodies couldn't hide the truth either; they wanted me just as much as I wanted them.

It made me feel so incredibly powerful and, yes, turned on. Flaunting myself in front of these men, kissing one of them as a dare to see who would take the bait.

Otto broke first, striding over and dropping his jacket to the floor. He could hardly get his shirt unbuttoned, his fingers were shaking so much. He kept his eyes locked on me, and I reached for him as if to help. When he came into range, I grabbed just below his collar and ripped his shirt wide open.

"Good grief," he said, open mouthed but clearly turned on by it from the bulge leaping in his trousers. I laughed as I pulled him into the stream of water with a kiss. Haru massaged my breasts and ground against my backside from behind. Otto held my cheek and slid his hand between us, gliding toward my sex and humming in my mouth with appreciation.

With Otto in front and Haru behind, I felt cocooned, safe enough to let my inhibitions go, to grow and transform. I tugged Otto's belt open, ravenous and wanting more. I looked over his shoulder to see who might break next.

Summer spread his stance, of course. Winter kept his legs firm, so they ended up pressing their knees against one another, neither willing to budge. Summer had his hand down his pants, mouth slightly open as he stared.

I crooked a finger at him, beckoning.

He smirked at me then sauntered toward us, undressing smoothly as he came. Otto's fingers found my folds, already slippery for him, and I moaned into his mouth. Water cascaded everywhere, drumming down on my head and shoulders. Haru nibbled at my neck and flicked each of my nipples. Otto dipped into my center as he darted his tongue between the lips of my mouth.

Haru's hands slid from my breasts to my shoulders, gently squeezing my biceps and holding my wrists. He moved my arms behind my back, and I bucked on Otto's fingers. Otto sank slowly onto one knee then the other, and I panted as he kissed all down my stomach, sensation shooting from my g-spot as he gently pressed and stroked me. *How did he know where that spot was?* I looked down at him, and he winked back. Maybe he was feeling some kind of feedback loop.

Summer had rounded the clear glass, fully naked. I eyed him with appreciation, knowing he'd get a kick out of it. He ran a hand through his hair as he gave me the same treatment, gaze drinking me in, His eyes darted to my throat, my breasts, my hips where Otto knelt, and my arms held by Haru.

Haru kissed the back of my neck. "Is this okay?"

"Okay?" I breathed. "This is hot as fuck." I wanted each

and every one of them, greedy as I was, and I was thrilled they felt the same way.

"Mmm." Summer's throaty consideration sent reverberations through my chest. He loomed closer, dick standing proud, each step deliberate. His eyes burned into me, and here I was, standing with my arms held, albeit gently, while Haru kissed my shoulders and neck and Otto tried to get me to cum standing up. Summer drank it all in with hungry eyes.

Summer leaned toward me, but he had to do so over Otto, who swiped at Summer's cock with a scowl. "Get that out of my face," he grumbled.

"I don't mind," Haru said with a wide smile. "Switch?"

Otto looked up at me, eyebrow raised. "Do you mind?"

I stroked his face, fingers catching on his five o'clock shadow. "I'd like a kiss and a cuddle, please."

He took my hand and kissed it like a courtly knight, if both knight and princess were naked. And surrounded by other naked dudes. I smiled as he said, "Of course," and watched with awe as he got to his feet smoothly.

"Hurry up," Summer growled. "I want in."

Otto rolled his eyes so only I could see, and I giggled. They quickly turned to gasps as Otto kissed his way from my wrist and up the inside of my elbow. Each press of his lips sent a zing across my skin, my nipples tightening as he got closer and closer to my neck.

Summer confronted me, suddenly right in my reach, pressing his body against mine. He was dry and hot, so very hot, mouth claiming mine and kissing me deeply. His thumbs found my nipples, fingers pressing in grabbing handfuls, right on the edge of pleasure and pain. He was urgent, hungry, and demanding.

A touch at my calf made me glance down. Haru was stroking up my leg, grinning as he tickled the inside of my thigh. I wriggled, and Summer growled. I couldn't help it!

I broke off the kiss with Summer, pulling my head back. "Work together, guys." I looked over, a stab of worry for Winter worming through me.

He had come close, pressed against the glass and still fully clothed. His eyes were cuttingly cold and intense, almost too much to bear, and locked on me. He had a hand raised, resting his forehead on his forearm, and the other deep in his open zipper, grasping the long length jutting down his tight pants.

He jerked back when our eyes met, his widening slightly. I smiled reassuringly, and he settled, his breath fogging the glass on his side. I'd imagined this, and God, it was hot having him see everything. See me and the water dripping down my curves. How each man handled me. How I reacted to each stroke and lick and kiss . . .

Summer reached down and curled his hand in Haru's hair. "*Levantarse.*"

Haru gasped as he stood, water running into his open mouth. Summer fumbled with Haru's nipples, grinding against his back, all the time watching me and my reaction. Haru's eyes were half open and he watched me too, like my reaction was the only one that mattered, his hand holding mine.

"Hot," I moaned, because it was.

Summer licked Haru's ear. "You want him to make you cum, *Mariposa*?" Summer asked sweetly.

"Oh, please," Haru said, pulling my hips closer. He was so hard, had been since I first initiated this. They were all waiting on my answer, hands moving, lips parted, wanting and hanging on my every word.

"Fuck me," I said, halfway between begging and ordering. Otto slid behind me to hold me from behind, hands cupping my breasts as if preparing them for Haru. Haru's eyes brightened.

"Oh ho." Summer let Haru's hair go with a smirk. "You heard the lady. Better give her what she demands."

Haru surged forward, head between my breasts in moments. He pushed me back but Otto was there, a strong backstop. I reached behind me and wrapped my hand around Otto's long shaft. His contained gasp thrilled me, and I ran my thumb over the top of his pulsing cock. As he slowly unraveled, so did we all.

Haru angled his body, bending down a little and guiding the head of his cock into my folds. Winter was slack-jawed, blistering gaze on me as Haru's cock slid into my soaked pussy like his dick glided on silk. He was exactly what I needed, pressure opening me up and radiating all through me.

"Well? How is it?" Summer asked us, demanded of us.

"So tight," Haru breathed, smiling at me.

"So good," I gasped, moving my hand up and down Otto's cock.

"*Bien*," Summer purred, coming around the side and kissing me as Haru moved slowly in and out of me, Summer's hard length jutting into my hip. I grabbed hold of him too and immediately owned him. Owned all these powerful men.

I tipped my head back as Otto's kissed one side and Summer's the other, someone's hands roving over what seemed like every part of my body. Haru's rough and ragged strokes pounded against me, each slap sending splashes of water. I was surrounded by passion as if I were the eye of a hurricane, the center of everything.

Haru opened me further and further. Summer's fingers slid down my stomach to my perfectly presented clit. His finger teased me, and I shot him an exasperated look.

His lips twitched upward, satisfied, his hair plastered to his head and water cascading over his wide shoulders along the ridges of his muscles. Haru pressed against me, trapping Summer's arm, but Summer seemed content. Behind me,

Otto's strong arms encircled me, supporting me and massaging my breasts, and his fingers flicked over my nipples, teasing and twisting. I flew, each of their hands and lips and thrusts setting off sparks in me, flames of safety, home, happiness, and aching needs met and overfilled. Otto grunted as his hot seed spurted on my lower back. Cries left his lips as Summer released against my stomach, and Haru met my eyes, thrusting, thrusting, and daring me to keep pace with him.

I came with a spasm just before Haru, our groans intermingling. I'd never orgasmed standing in a shower before. My legs buckled, but Haru's and Otto's arms wrapped across my bare body to catch me. Summer turned my chin toward him, concern drawing his brows closer together. I was so touched tears trickled down my cheeks, mingling with the water, and pulled them all closer to me.

Well, not all of them. "Winter?" I asked, looking over Summer's shoulder.

The water had frozen into crystals against the glass Winter stood behind. Frost patterns spiraled all over the glass, obscuring his lowered face. His pants had fallen down his thick thighs, and he trembled with the glistening of his own release covering his hand.

Haru reached past me and turned off the faucet. Heat washed over me from Summer, keeping me warm, and Otto lifted me into his arms, kissing me on the forehead.

I nuzzled into his chest, exhausted, yet so content and satisfied.

Chapter Twenty-Seven

Stretching, the world around me came to. I was warm, tucked under a blanket and still in the nude, and my body felt relaxed if not a bit sore from the tussle with the guard and clinician the day before.

Despite that, a smile spread across my face as I thought of last night, coming together with all the men—no pun intended.

I chuckled to myself.

They made me feel wanted, safe, and for the first time in my life I felt I had a little bit of a say with my own wants and needs. Boy did they happily oblige. Winter's icy stare, Summer's heated gaze, Otto's calculating fingers, and Haru's dreamy presence were each a gift in their own way. Although, the fact that Winter had his powers spreading across the glass after his orgasm . . .

A shiver ran through my body. He was so powerful, but he lacked control. *What was going on there?*

The lightness in my chest dashed away as my heart sank. Trying to get to the bottom of this was exactly what had gotten me into this mess. And I had to sort it out now. The fact that no one had stayed with me through the night spoke volumes. They didn't feel close to me yet, but I wanted them to get closer.

Gritting my teeth, I threw the covers off the bed and hastily threw on some clothes. Annoyance radiated through my body, making each movement rigid. I caught sight of myself in the mirror, cataloging the minor bruises. *And man, was I hungry.*

I glared at myself. It wasn't what they were hiding that got me into this mess. It was *my* secret that got me into it. *I* was the one who broke in for the key. *I* was the one who stayed behind to watch them. *I* was the one who knew CSON's plan for Winter and said nothing.

I was filthy and if I had any hope of moving forward with them, I needed to fess up. And if they didn't want me, if they kicked me back to the curb or dropped me back on CSON's doorstep, then so be it. I was tired of this secret. Haru wanted trust, and so did I, but it needed to start with me. They were all essentially immortal. I wouldn't unveil all of the skeletons in their closet in a single night, and wasn't that part of the beauty of a relationship or, in this case, relationships? Learning things over time about someone, getting to know them—all versions of them—and letting them reveal parts of themselves when they were ready.

That settled it. I had to come clean.

On the way to the door I stopped at my dresser and pulled open the top drawer to snag a paper from it. I clutched it against my chest, heart hammering. So much was at stake, and even if my honesty couldn't be forgiven, I wanted them to understand the impact they'd had on me.

I headed straight for the kitchen, taking the stairs two at a time. And just like I knew they would be, they were all there. But instead of sitting at the table or on the stools bickering away while Winter cooked, they all circled something that Haru held.

"It's perfect," Summer beamed.

"I'm quite impressed by the attention to detail," Otto added.

"I like the blue," Winter grunted.

Haru was bouncing. "You must see it, right?" He looked up expectantly at Summer, and I noticed a blotch of something brightly colored streaked across his cheek.

"The resemblance is uncanny, I'll give you that." Summer gave his shoulder a squeeze.

"I know, right?" Haru nodded his head with so much enthusiasm his already messy hair seemed to become messier. "I couldn't stop! As soon as we left her to sleep, I couldn't get the image out of my head. I spent all night on it!"

"On what?" I finally piped in as I fully entered the room, and all four of them turned in unison at my voice, mild surprise splashed across all their faces. My stomach warmed seeing them, but dread caused my skin to heat more than their welcoming gazes.

"Mari!" Haru recovered the quickest, hands squeezing the sides of some kind of canvas. A painting. Now that I could see the rest of him, splashes of paint covered what should be clean clothes. "How'd you sleep?"

"Fine," I said with a bit of unease as I eyed what he held. "Are you all okay?"

"I—yes." Haru flushed, unsure.

Summer rolled his eyes. "Just show her already."

Haru chewed on his lip, and after a deep breath flipped it around.

Across the cream canvas was a splash of blues, pinks, and yellows. Some colors morphed and blended to create variations of purples, greens, and oranges. It looked like Haru hadn't used a paintbrush at all but spread the paint with his bare hands, and all it took was a quick glance of his paint-coated fingers and palms to confirm that theory. But it wasn't the fact it was a full painting done by Haru that had me frozen before them, but what the painting was of.

It was me. And not me sitting and reading or swimming or even doing combat. It was a painting that very few had seen, and now it was memorialized. It was a painting of my head tilted back, eyes shut with a slightly crinkled forehead and my mouth wide open as I orgasmed.

"You didn't," I said in disbelief.

"Oh, he did," Otto said with a chortle.

"Definitely did," Winter added with a satisfied grunt.

"And it captured you perfectly," Summer surmised.

"No. No, no, nonononono." The word came out faster and faster as I marched forward and made a grab at it, but Haru held it high above his head so even when I jumped I couldn't reach. "You. Will. Burn. This." I heaved as I ran out of breath. Finally, I gave up and stood in front of them with folded arms and a glare like a petulant child surrounded by a bunch of bullies.

"Burn it?" Summer scoffed. Winter let out an annoyed huff, and Haru pouted like I'd kicked a puppy.

"I think it should go in the library above the fire," Otto added.

"Yes!" Haru's eyes sparked, as I cried reflexively, "No!"

"No," Winter said. He pointed at a blank wall in the kitchen. "Right here. Heart of the home."

"Absolutely!" Summer grabbed the painting and handed it to Otto.

I came around the kitchen unit to intercept him, but halfway down the breakfast bar he handed the painting to Winter, who lifted it way out of my reach. Haru and Summer stepped in my way, one with a huge smile and the other with a warning gaze, so I couldn't go chasing off after him. Winter put the painting up right opposite the goddamn fridge. And the house created a hook for him to do it, popping out with a little "ping."

"Not fair," I grumbled.

"We never destroy works of art," Summer said.

Haru's eyes widened up at Summer. "Do you really think it's a work of art?"

"Absolutely." The soft smile Summer gave Haru, and the way he looked so proud, melted my resolve.

Anyway, there was a good chance that in a moment they were going to burn it anyway out of anger toward me.

Haru's attention landed on the piece of paper in my hand, a corner of color exposed to him. "What's that?" His eyes sparked, the corner of his lips curving up.

"Uh, I . . ." My resolve melted as nerves jittered through my body making it difficult to speak.

Summer stepped up beside Haru, his intense gaze staring at what I held so intensely I thought it would burst into flames.

My hand shook as I held it out. "For you."

Haru took it, his finger grazing against the back of my hand with silent encouragement. He flipped it for them all to see, and his eyes widened. "Buttercup," he breathed.

"*Magnifico.*" Summer's voice held an awe I wasn't expecting, especially when a true master of the arts stood beside him.

Otto took the piece of paper, holding it at an angle for Winter to see too. A smile grazed his soft face, while Winter sucked in a small breath.

My brain stuttered while my mouth came to the rescue, trying to fill the silence that had my heart ricocheting through my chest. "I know it's nothing like what Haru can produce, but I was inspired and found some art supplies lying around and—"

"It's perfect." Haru beamed as he reached forward and drew

me into his firm chest. He nuzzled into my hair as he wrapped his arms around me. "I love it." His breath was hot against my ear and my body relaxed against his as I released a sigh of relief.

Winter grabbed it and walked over to the fridge, putting the painting I had made on it with a magnet. It felt like I was a child who had brought home an art project from kinder-garten, but the fact Winter decided to display it in his domain had a thrill electrifying my pulse.

Summer *tsked*. "We can find a better place."

"I was thinking the library," Otto added with a smile.

Summer frowned. "I was thinking the garage with the best of my cars."

Haru shook his head. "The arboretum. It is intrinsically meant for there given what's on it."

They all expectantly stared at me for an answer. I swallowed and looked at the piece of art I had created for them. It was a vine, twisting across the page but quartered off. In the top left flower buds of spring were readying to bloom. As it moved to the top right the vine was filled with the rich green leaves of summer. Moving down into the bottom left the leaves turned orange to signify the start of autumn before traversing across the page to the bottom right where it was barren with the ice of winter. At its center was a gray shield, protecting and connecting each of the four seasons.

I met Winter's icy stare with a smile. "I think the fridge is the perfect place." I patted Haru's chest when he groaned. "That is until I get some lessons and paint something special for the library, arboretum, and garage."

Everyone smiled, nodding their approval.

Well, I would if I even got lessons after they heard what else I had to say.

"Hungry?" Haru inclined his head at the breakfast buffet spread across the kitchen counter.

My stomach was already in knots. "Yes, but also no," I mumbled, pulling myself from his embrace.

Summer's brows drew together. "What is it? Everything alright?"

"Actually . . ." I picked at my nails as I wondered how to broach the topic. There didn't seem to be an easy way to do this. Trying to make myself sound innocent or list the excuses of doing it in the first place or why I hadn't said anything sooner seemed like a cop-out. It was just being here before them, realizing what I was probably seconds away from losing, made it a thousand times harder to actually form the words that would potentially end everything.

Tears pricked the corner of my eyes and Haru stepped forward, reaching out to take my arm in support.

"What is it?" He urged, playfulness stripped away. Serious Haru ready to leap to my defense. The sincere concern in his voice made it difficult not to burst into tears.

I pulled out of his grasp. If I were to get through this, I couldn't have them supporting me. I didn't want to feel them pull away first, so I needed distance. I took two more steps back, closer to the door, closer to my exit.

I took a steadying breath. "I have something to admit," I finally said.

"We're listening." Summer watched me with a calculating stare.

"I," I swallowed before trying again, "I stole a key."

"Oh?" Summer raised an eyebrow. Meanwhile, Haru looked confused and Winter was completely unreadable.

"When I first snuck in, I stole a key and gave it to CSON underneath a door. Then, later, like way later, they contacted me again and told me to lead Winter near it." I peeked up at Winter, my breath rushing in and out of me, scared that he would freeze me on the spot.

He didn't move, not an inch. I didn't even think he was breathing.

"I had orders, and CSON said they wanted to help Winter." I released a low breath. "They also offered me money, and you saw how my family was, how close we were to the edge. One hundred thousand is a lot for us, and . . . I took it." I raised my hands, desperation leaking into my voice. "But I promise you what happened with Winter I didn't plan." I screwed up my fists, bracing myself, and lifted my head to meet Winter's icy stare. "I swear I didn't lead you there on purpose."

Still, no response from Winter. He just stood in front of that damned painting with his brows furrowed, gaze locked on mine.

Haru stared at me. "Was . . . Was any of the stuff with us a ploy?" His voice scratched with pain.

"No, not at all!" I interjected quickly. To hell with no excuses. I wanted to save this, needed to try to save what I had with them. "It seemed so innocent at first: get a key, and the compensation would help my family. Then I got caught and was ordered to stick around. When the operative found me and told me to get Winter close to the door, I—"

"Did you intend to do it?" Summer cut in.

"What?" I blinked in surprise.

"Did you intend to give Winter to them, if not in that moment, then at some point?"

"I—I . . . I don't know," I admitted, completely ashamed. My head dropped and this time the tears ran freely. "I don't think I would have, but even though I . . . thought he could be a danger, I knew he needed help." Still did. I mulled it over before lifting my head to meet Summer's penetrating stare. "No," I said finally. "No, I wouldn't have if I knew what CSON had in store."

"Then why hide it from us?" Haru's voice was sad, and it broke my heart into pieces.

"I was scared." Those words, this truth, came easily. "Scared like I am right now. Scared I'd lose all of you and lose what we have."

"Winter?" Summer cocked his head at his friend. "What do you think?"

"I think she's telling the truth," he said, and I released my tight breath. "But that doesn't excuse what she did," he grumbled, folding his arms.

"I agree." Summer pressed his lips together. "Seems someone needs to be punished for their betrayal."

Words stuck in my throat. What would they do? Kick me out? Give me over to CSON? Let Winter freeze me?

Summer side-eyed Haru. "We did it your way. Now it's my turn to be in charge."

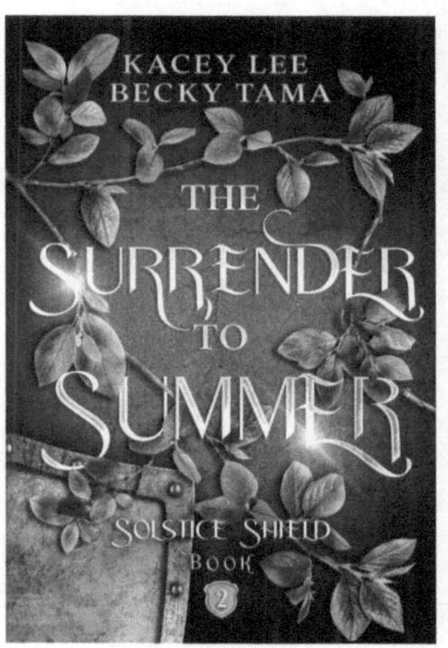

Is it hot in here or is it just my four new boyfriends? Can I even call them that?

The seasons are changing, and I find myself completely caught in the thrall of dating the four magical god-like men. And, yes, it is as delicious as anyone would expect. Minus the fact I'm still hiding secrets, my family is on the run, and I have to face my old employers who held me captive in their weird experiments.

But Summer keeps trying to take charge of everything, and it's boiling up between us. He's hiding something behind that smooth facade, I know it, but in order to strip Summer back to his true self, I will need to lay secrets bare myself.

So maybe things could be better, but I'm finally learning to live my life a little... At least when it's not being risked.

Grab your copy of The Surrender to Summer, Solstice Shield Book 2 now!

Follow Us For Updates

KACEY LEE

The best way to stay updated on news, releases, and giveaways is by following my facebook reader group!

Kacey Lee's Thirsty Readers (https://www.facebook.com/groups/393866872107819/)
        or
        Follow me on Instagram (@authorkaceylee)

The second best way is by joining my newsletter:

Join Newsletter Here

BECKY TAMA

Stay up to date with new releases, giveaways, and freebies by joining my reading group!

https://www.facebook.com/groups/tamabooks

Thank you so much for joining Mari on her journey of self discovery with four delectable men. Their story definitely isn't over, you could say we are about to get into the 'heat' of things. Hehe. We cannot wait to continue to share with you what's in store for these five! It's always a risk to pick up a new series, and we greatly appreciate you taking a chance with The Sutra of Spring. We hope you enjoyed reading it as much as we enjoyed writing it! We wouldn't be able to do what we do without your support.

Kacey & Becky

Acknowledgments

FROM KACEY:

First, a huge, huge thank you to Becky! You are without a doubt my author bestie, and going from beta reader to friend to coauthor has been a dream come true. You really know how to pull at the heart strings of characters and readers, and I love that you were able to bring the amazing 'Becky flair' to this series. The plot would be 'pleh' and the tension would be tens-none without you. Also, for pushing so hard before the arrival of my first child and taking the brunt of the work the first few months after he was born as I figured out how to be a mom, or 'mum' as you would say.

Also, thank you to my husband, who never has once scoffed at me for pursuing my dreams. Your support has always been at 100% and you have never made me feel like I couldn't accomplish something. Because of you this author journey is possible, and continues to be possible.

To my son...Eek! This is the first time I'm ever writing a dedication to you! So weird and sorry it's in a WC/RH series but there's a reason for it. It's because of you, or rather the idea of you, years ago that I decided to pursue indie authoring. Child care isn't cheap, nor is having a kid in general, and I started this journey with the goal of whatever I made going towards you, and somehow, it has worked out. Without the possibility of you, this career of mine wouldn't have started, and now you're here! So thank you for inspiring me to pursue my dreams.

Thank you to the amazing beta readers, Kendra, Danielle, Jessica, and Raven and fabulous editor, Sarah Kammer. This story would be nothing but "good bones" without you all. Also, all our ARC readers who signed up and dedicated their time to read and review, we thank you!

Finally, thank YOU, the readers, who are here. As you read before, I started this journey to help fund having a family in this crazy world we live in. A crazy world we often use books to escape from. It's because of you my son will have a better life, and it's because of you that my dreams were made a reality. I truly wouldn't be anywhere without the readers willing to give my books a shot and who stick with me through my career. You are the best of the best.

As always, happy reading!
Kacey

FROM BECKY:

Firstly, a huge thank you to our awesome beta readers, Sierra, Jessica and Danielle! You gals are the best, and Mari wouldn't be as kick ass without you.

I'm never sure what to say for these things, so a PSA: while writing this series I was / am dealing with severe depression and anxiety. It's no joke, but there is support out there for you when you need it. I want to thank the NHS for getting on top of things pretty darn quick. It's a long road but it helps to be open (yeah, Mari!) Really, people aren't judging you as badly as you think they are, and that's your distorted viewpoint cropping up and getting in the way anyways. People are generally understanding as long as you give them an opportunity to be; they can't help with what they don't know! For those who know how it feels to carry everything, every task, chore, physical and emotional burdens... It's okay. Breathe. Keep your energy for the china plates and leaves the ones that can drop to spin down, and let it go, as Elsa would say. Smile, because you are so worthy, my friend.

Finally, thanks to Kacey. We knew we wanted to work together, but the right idea never popped up until you mentioned seasons and I threw together an outline. (Which changed hugely, by the way!) We have had to learn how to cooperate across time zones, understand idioms, different author processes and more. It's been some of the hardest writing (especially when the digital equivalent of your red pen comes out on my first draft!) and some of the most fun writing. Who knew wet noises came in all sorts of shapes and sizes!

IF YOU ENJOYED THIS NOVEL, PLEASE CHECK OUT OUR OTHER WORKS!

When the humans and angels left, they forgot one thing… me.

A supernatural's touch is like a stun gun for me. I avoid it at all costs.

Doing what I do best, spying and getting information, a supernatural dies at my feet. Lo and behold, I'm the one blamed by none other than the Demon Lord himself.

He gave me two choices: die or help solve the murder. I'm not an idiot, so I made a pact with him to clear my name. Wait… maybe I am an idiot because I just made a deal with the son of Lucifer.

There's one caveat, when I shook his hand it felt good, really freaking good, and now I can't stop thinking about him. Working with the

Demon Lord is the last place I should be because if he finds out what I truly am, I'm as good as dead.

Perfect for fans of Jaymin Eve, Kelly St. Clare, Leia Stone, Linsey Hall, and other PNR Indie Author Goddesses. If you enjoy sexy, dominant men and a headstrong heroine, with humor, steam, and action, this is for you! Recommended for 18+ due to explicit scenes and language.

Grab Deal With The Demon Lord <u>HERE</u>

Fae fantasy romance, with rare Scottish fae struggling to save their dying world. Co-authored with USA Today Bestselling Author Becky James!

The world is ending. Rory can't wait.

Stealing souls from under the noses of the guardians of the underworld is hard work, but for immortal Cat Sidhe Rory, it's all he has ever known. Hiding behind humour, he masks the dark waters closing overhead, but the longer he puts a smile on his face, the more real the threat becomes.

The world is beginning. Darla can't wait.

Darla is an explorer, endlessly fascinated by the land above. As a selkie, she remains trapped under the waves except for once every seven years. But, as luck would have it, now is her time to escape the waves. Desperate to sate her hunger for adventure, she finds her way to the surface, ready to experience all of the wonders of existence, including love, for the very first time.

But the fae world is ending. What will they risk to save it... and each other?

GET IT HERE